Dazai at his home in Mitaka, 1947.

SELF PORTRAITS

Osamu Dazai

Translated and introduced by
Ralph F. McCarthy

KODANSHA INTERNATIONAL
Tokyo • New York • London

The original publication dates of the stories are, in chronological order: "Train," February 1933; "Female," May 1936; "A Promise Fulfilled," September 1938; "I Can Speak," February 1939; "One Hundred Views of Mount Fuji," February/March 1939; "Seascape with Figures in Gold," April 1939; "A Little Beauty," August 1939; "Canis familiaris," August 1939; "My Elder Brothers," January 1940; "No Kidding," January 1940; "Thinking of Zenzō," April 1940; "Eight Scenes from Tokyo," January 1941; "Garden," January 1946; "Two Little Words," January 1946; "Early Light," December 1946; "Merry Christmas," January 1947; "Handsome Devils and Cigarettes," March 1948; "Cherries," May 1948.

Photo Credits: The photograph on p. 222 is © 1948 by Tamura Shigeru. All other photographs in this book have been provided by courtesy of the Museum of Modern Japanese Literature, Kobiki-sha, Mainichi Newspapers, and the Photo Library of Kodansha Ltd.

Distributed in the United States by Kodansha America, Inc., 114 Fifth Avenue, New York, N.Y. 10011, and in the United Kingdom and continental Europe by Kodansha Europe Ltd., Gillingham House, 38-44 Gillingham Street, London SW1V 1HU. Published by Kodansha International, Ltd., 17-14 Otowa 1-chome, Bunkyo-ku, Tokyo 112, and Kodansha America, Inc. Copyright © 1991 by Kodansha International Ltd. All rights reserved. Printed in Japan.
First edition, 1991
First paperback edition, 1992
92 93 94 10 9 8 7 6 5 4 3 2 1
ISBN 4-7700-1689-1

CONTENTS

Acknowledgments

I want to thank Tsushima Michiko for permission to translate these stories, Kita Morio for his inspiration, Jules Young for getting me started, Stephen Shaw for championing the book and offering advice and solace, Leslie Pockell for being a dynamo of an editor, Kuramochi Tetsuo for helping obtain all the photos, Nakatani Takao for sharing with me his reminiscences about Dazai, Moriyasu Machiko for patiently answering my questions, Professor Suga Atsuko for her guidance, and Satomi for showing me heaven and hell.

R.F.M.

NOTES ON THE TRANSLATION

All Japanese names in the text are given in the Japanese order: family name first.

When someone's age is referred to in the stories, it is usually according to the antiquated "year-count" system, whereby a person was "one" at birth and "two" on New Year's Day of the following year. Dazai is less than meticulously consistent about dates and ages, however.

Dazai mentions money a lot. Before World War II, one yen (100 sen) was generally worth about fifty American cents. Rampant inflation after the war drove the value down until it was pegged by the Occupation forces at 360 yen to a dollar.

"Higher school" is so called here because it corresponds neither to "high school" nor "college." In Japan's prewar educational system, those relatively few students who entered higher school did so when they were at least seventeen or eighteen. After three years of higher school, a still smaller percentage went on to university.

Where the use of Japanese words seemed inevitable, every attempt was made to render them more or less self-explanatory. The reader will find some of the photos helpful for identifying certain articles of clothing (*geta* clogs, *tabi* socks, *hakama* trousers, *haori* coats, *obi* sashes, *yukata*).

Tatami are the woven straw mats (about six feet by three) used for flooring in Japanese-style rooms, and serve as units of measurement for living space. Rooms are "three mats," "four-and-a-half mats," "six mats," and so on. A *tsubo* is a unit of land measurement that corresponds to two tatami mats.

INTRODUCTION

Though he died in 1948, Dazai Osamu still has an almost cult-like following in Japan. An outcast and rebel in a rigidly conformist society, he is a perennial favorite of young people, and his reputation is based as much on his own life story as it is on his extraordinary work. Dazai was many things in his thirty-nine years: the rich boy who got himself expelled from his ruling class family by associating with communists, running off with a lowly geisha, allowing a young woman he scarcely knew to die in the first of three "love suicides," and, what was worse, writing about it all; the heavy-drinking, whoremongering, self-absorbed, weeping, whining *enfant terrible* who was at odds with a staid and pompous literary establishment from the moment he appeared on the scene; the deranged drug fiend with a severe persecution complex who was both a tireless self-promoter and his own harshest critic; the one Japanese author who consistently turned out entertaining and worthwhile literature during the late thirties and early forties, when the entire nation was toeing the ideological line of militarism and fanatic patriotism; the immensely popular writer of the postwar era who ended his life at the height of his popularity by jumping into a river with a neurotic, death-obsessed mistress, leaving behind an im-

poverished wife with three young children and another
mistress with a child he'd never even seen. It's not a pretty
story, but it's a fascinating one, and no one tells it better than
Dazai himself.

Dazai was primarily a short story writer. Though he
employed an astounding variety of techniques, styles, and
voices throughout his career, a good one-third of his fairly prodigious output took the form of what might be called, for lack
of a better term, "autobiographical fiction"—first-person
stories fashioned out of the raw material of his life. The purpose of this collection is simply to present some of the best of
these works as a roughly chronological series of self portraits,
with all the artistic leeway that implies. Some of the stories
are more clearly fictional than others, but all of them are informed by the realities of the author's life—realities with
which Japanese Dazai fans are well acquainted—and famil-
iarity with the basic events of that life can only serve to
increase the reader's enjoyment.

Dazai Osamu was the pen name of Tsushima Shūji. Born on
June 19, 1909 in Kanagi Village, Northern Tsugaru District,
Aomori Prefecture (the northernmost prefecture of Honshu,
the main island of Japan), Shūji was the eighth surviving child
of Tsushima Gen'emon and his wife Tane. Tsugaru was an
impoverished farming district, but the Tsushimas were
among the wealthiest landowners in Aomori Prefecture, and
Gen'emon wielded considerable political influence, serving
in both the Lower House and the House of Peers.

In his earliest years, Shūji scarcely knew his parents. He
was suckled by a nursemaid, handed over to his aunt, then
left in the care of a nanny, all of whom were to disappear
from his life before he entered elementary school.
Throughout elementary school he was at the top of his class.
In 1923, the year he was to enter middle school, his father

Tsushima Shūji (second from left) in the garden of his family home in Kanagi, c. 1920.

died and his eldest brother, Bunji, took over as head of the household.

Shūji did well in middle school and excelled particularly in composition. In March of 1925 he published his first story in a school magazine. He was to continue publishing works in school publications and little literary journals throughout his middle and higher school days. He entered Hirosaki Higher School in 1927, lodging at the home of a distant relative. In July of that year, Akutagawa Ryūnosuke committed suicide, and this is said to have had a tremendous affect on Shūji, who idolized the great writer and whose behavior subsequently underwent radical changes. He began to neglect his studies, devoting himself instead to writing and making use of his princely allowance to dress foppishly and to hire the services of geisha at expensive restaurants in Aomori and Asamushi Hot Springs. In the fall of 1927 he met Oyama Hatsuyo, an apprentice geisha whom he was later to marry.

In contradiction to these dandified, mildly decadent tendencies and his status as a member of the ruling class was Shūji's growing concern with Marxist thought, which in spite of government suppression took firm root in Japan during the economically troubled 1920s. In late 1929 he began a novella entitled *One Generation of Landowners*, an indictment of the cruel treatment of tenant farmers by a wealthy family who not coincidentally bore a strong resemblance to the Tsushimas.

It was on the night of December 10, 1929—the night before year-end exams—that the author's celebrated history of suicide attempts began. He took an overdose of Calmotin (a sleeping medicine he used regularly and with which he was to try to do himself in on at least three separate occasions) and remained unconscious until late the following afternoon. He described the incident years later, in a 1946 essay entitled "An Almanac of Agony":

> Dictatorship of the proletariat.
>
> Here, to be sure, was a new sensibility. It wasn't conciliation. It was dictatorship. The enemy were to be destroyed without exception. All rich people were bad. All aristocrats were bad. Righteousness belonged only to the poor, humble masses. I was in favor of armed rebellion. A revolution without the guillotine was meaningless.
>
> I, however, was not one of the proletariat. My role in all this would be to submit to the guillotine. I was a nineteen-year-old higher school student. In my class at school, I alone stood out for my gorgeous attire. There was really nothing for it, I thought, but to die.

I swallowed a large quantity of Calmotin, but I didn't die.

He spent the winter vacation recuperating at a hot springs resort with his mother, during which time several members of the school's leftist-oriented newspaper and magazine club, to which Shūji belonged, were arrested and expelled from school.

Shūji graduated in March 1930, and in April he enrolled in the French Literature Department at Tokyo Imperial University. He took a room in a boardinghouse near the residence of the youngest of his elder brothers, Keiji, who was studying sculpture at a fine arts college. In May he met Ibuse Masuji, then an up-and-coming young writer whom he admired immensely (and who agreed to the meeting only after Shūji wrote a letter threatening to kill himself if he wasn't granted an audience). Ibuse became Shūji's mentor and was to be the younger writer's friend, confidant, and greatest supporter throughout the rest of his life. It was also in May that, at the request of a former upperclassman from Hirosaki, Shūji began to contribute money to and involve himself in the illegal Communist Party.

In June Keiji died of tuberculosis [**My Elder Brothers**]. After Keiji's death, Shūji rarely attended classes. In October Oyama Hatsuyo ran away from her geisha house in Aomori and joined him in Tokyo, and the following month, Bunji, who had been informed by the geisha house of Hatsuyo's disappearance, came to Tokyo to confront his younger brother, finally agreeing to permit him to marry Hatsuyo on the condition that he set up a separate branch of the family, thereby freeing the Tsushimas of financial responsibility for him. Bunji took Hatsuyo back to Aomori to pay off her redemption fee and smooth things over with the geisha house. On November 19 Shūji was formally expelled from the family, and nine days later he and Tanabe Shimeko, a nineteen-year-old married woman who worked as a waitress at the Ginza bar Hollywood and whom he had met only a few days before, attempted a double suicide in Kamakura [**Female**]. They took overdoses of Calmotin and were discovered lying on the rocks beside the sea the following morning. Shimeko was dead; Shūji survived. He was interrogated by the police on suspicion of aiding a suicide, but charges were dropped after intervention by the Tsushima family. In December Shūji and Hatsuyo were wed at a hot springs resort in Southern Tsugaru.

In January 1931 Bunji and Shūji signed an agreement whereby Shūji was to receive living expenses of one hundred twenty yen per month for the next two years, provided he refrained from dropping out of school, getting himself arrested, squandering money, becoming involved with socialist movements, or just generally exhibiting scandalous behavior. Hatsuyo joined him in Tokyo in February. Despite his promise, Shūji's involvement with the Communist Party continued; he was still contributing money, and his house was used as a sort of liaison office for party members. He wasn't writing much, although for a time he composed haiku (a typical example: "Outside, sleet is falling/What are you smiling for/Statue of Lenin?"). In late October or early November he spent a night in jail and was interrogated about his political activities. After this arrest (his second or third), he began to distance himself from the party and ceased contributing money to the cause [**Train**].

In early June of 1932 Bunji learned from the police in Kanagi of his brother's arrest the previous year and promptly cut off the allowance. In late June, the police were once again searching for Shūji. He went into hiding, renting an apartment under an assumed name, and it was at this apartment that he learned that Hatsuyo had not been the unsullied flower he'd imagined her to be when he married her. By his own account, this was a tremendous shock. Meanwhile, Bunji managed to get word to him that his allowance would be reinstated and continued until his graduation from university if he surrendered to the police in Aomori and vowed to cease all involvement with the party. In mid-July he did exactly that. He was held and interrogated for two or three days and then released, but was to be called back to Aomori to reiterate his pledge in December.

Back in Tokyo with the allowance reinstated (although reduced to ninety yen), Shūji and Hatsuyo moved into a cottage on an abandoned estate, where he began to write seriously again. Tobishima Sadashiro, a reporter for a Tokyo newspaper and an old friend of Keiji's, lived in two rooms of the main house with his wife and son. **Train**, the first story to bear the pen name Dazai Osamu and his first experiment with first-person autobiographical fiction, was published in February 1933.

Throughout that year and the next, Dazai continued to write feverishly, churning out the stories that were to make up his first volume of collected works, *The Final Years*. He spent August of 1934 in the resort town of Mishima on the Izu Peninsula, staying at a friend's house [**A Promise Fulfilled**]. The story he wrote in Mishima, "Romanesque," was published in the first and only edition of *The Blue Flower*, a literary journal Dazai put together with several acquaintances, including Yamagishi Gaishi and Dan Kazuo, who were to become his closest friends.

By March of 1935 it was clear that Dazai's chances of graduating were nil. This would mean the end of money from home. He applied for a position at a Tokyo newspaper but failed the examination. *The Final Years*, his farewell to the world, was finished, and he decided to end it all. On March 15 he took his entire monthly allowance from the bank and went

Seated, from left: Dan Kazuo, Dazai, Yamagishi Gaishi, Kodate Zenshirō.
At Yugawara Hot Springs, September 1935.

out for a wild night of drinking with Kodate Zenshirō, a student at the Imperial Arts College and the younger brother of
Dazai's elder sister's husband. (Dazai had befriended and
looked after Kodate, five years his junior, ever since Kodate's
arrival in Tokyo three years before.) They parted in
Yokohama, where Dazai spent the night, and the following
day Dazai went to the mountains outside Kamakura and tried
to hang himself. Either the rope broke or he simply lost his
nerve—at any rate he returned to Tokyo that night with red
welts on his neck to find Hatsuyo, Ibuse, Dan, Tobishima,
and other friends waiting at his house, frantic with worry.
Bunji, too, was there, having been notified by telegram that
Dazai was missing and the worst was feared. Ibuse later convinced Bunji to continue sending Dazai an allowance for one
more year.

Less than three weeks after this suicide attempt Dazai developed acute appendicitis and was hospitalized. His condition was complicated by a bad case of peritonitis, and he nearly died. He was in the hospital for three months, during which time he became addicted to Pabinal, a morphine-based painkiller. After his release, Bunji rented a house for him in Funabashi, Chiba, where he was to live for a year and a half, recuperating. His addiction only worsened, however, and soon he was borrowing money from practically everyone he knew in order to support his habit [**Seascape with Figures in Gold**].

In July 1935, at about the time he moved to Funabashi, Dazai was nominated for the first Akutagawa Ryūnosuke Prize (a semiannual award which ever since its inception has been the most prestigious for Japanese writers) on the basis of two stories entitled "Against the Current" and "Flowers of Buffoonery." Dazai sorely needed the five hundred yen prize money and yearned for the prestige and recognition that winning would give him. He didn't win, however. Shortly after the results were announced in August, Yamagishi Gaishi introduced him to the great poet Satō Haruo, one of the judges for the Akutagawa Prize and a member of "The Japan Romantics" (a coterie which five of the contributors to the defunct *Blue Flower*, including Dazai, Yamagishi, and Dan, had joined). Satō agreed to be Dazai's mentor.

In September Kawabata Yasunari, another of the judges, published an account of the selection process in which he wrote that "personally, I feel that the odious clouds hanging over [Dazai's] private life prevent the direct expression of his genius." Dazai was furious when he read this, and replied the following month by publishing an open letter entitled "To Kawabata Yasunari," which read in part: "I'll stab him. I actually thought that. I thought you a great villain." Kawabata responded with "To Dazai Osamu, Concerning the

Akutagawa Prize," in which he apologized for his words but took Dazai to task for his "groundless delusions and suspicions."

In December Dazai received a postcard from Satō Haruo regarding the second (Spring 1936) Akutagawa Prize, in which Satō said, "This time the five hundred yen should be yours," and in February 1936 Dazai sent a letter to Satō saying "If I receive the Akutagawa Prize, I shall surely weep with gratitude for the compassion of others. I shall be able to overcome any sort of suffering and live on. . . . Please help me." Satō responded immediately, but only to order Dazai to enter a hospital to cure his addiction. Two days later Dazai entered a hospital, where he was to stay for ten days, but sneaked out with friends on at least two consecutive nights to drink and shoot morphine. He left the hospital uncured. Neither Dazai nor anyone else was awarded the second Akutagawa Prize.

The Final Years was published June 25, 1936. In August Dazai learned from Satō that *The Final Years* was being considered for the *third* (Fall 1936) Akutagawa Prize. Dazai was certain he was going to win this time. Hoping to cure himself of his addiction, he went to Minakami Hot Springs in Gunma Prefecture, and while there he learned that he'd been disqualified from the competition because of having been a previous candidate. Enraged, he wrote a piece accusing Satō of deceiving him and appended it to a story entitled "Genesis," which was published in October. A month later Satō published a story called "The Akutagawa Prize" in which he portrayed Dazai as something of a paranoid, drug-crazed maniac (albeit an "incomparably talented" one). Dazai was not to meet Satō again until 1940, having been "excommunicated" for his scandalous behavior, and he was never to win his coveted prize. But the notoriety he'd achieved as a result of all this had made a name for him anyway.

On October 7, 1936 Hatsuyo visited Ibuse Masuji to inform him of Dazai's increasingly severe addiction to Pabinal and to ask for his help in seeing to Dazai's hospitalization. Ibuse visited Dazai in Funabashi on October 12 and the following day convinced him to enter a hospital. That night he was taken to a mental institution in Itabashi, where he was kept in a locked room. For about a week he underwent extreme withdrawal symptoms, tearing his clothes, breaking windows, writing on the walls, and screaming at the doctors and nurses. He was allowed no visitors during his stay. Hatsuyo, denied permission to see her husband, began paying daily visits to Kodate Zenshirō, who since October 10 had been in a different hospital after attempting suicide by slitting his wrists. Eventually she and Kodate engaged in a bit of adultery. They agreed to keep their affair a secret, and when Kodate was released from the hospital he went back to his family's second home in Tsugaru.

Dazai was released November 12. Bunji had come to Tokyo for the occasion, and once again Ibuse and others had convinced him to continue providing Dazai with a monthly allowance—this time for three more years. (In fact, the allowance was to continue until after the end of World War II, when Dazai finally declared he didn't need it any longer.) Immediately after being released and moving into an apartment in Amanuma, Dazai began writing "HUMAN LOST" (the title is in English), and in late November he wrote Kodate Zenshirō a postcard with a quote from this work: "I think of the silence in the heart of that great defeated general, standing beneath the smoke of his burning flags on some peak in the Alps./A tooth for a tooth. A glass of milk for a glass of milk. (It's no one's fault)." Reading this cryptic message, Kodate mistakenly interpreted it to mean that Hatsuyo had revealed their secret, and when he returned to Tokyo in March of 1937, he went straight to Dazai's apartment and confessed all. This, of course, was the first Dazai had heard of Hatsuyo's infidelity, and he was devastated.

In late March, Dazai and Hatsuyo went to Minakami Hot Springs, spending a night at the inn they had stayed at the previous year, and the next day they attempted a double suicide in the mountains there by swallowing Calmotin. Both survived. They returned to Tokyo separately, Dazai to the apartment and Hatsuyo to Ibuse's house, and it's unlikely that the two of them ever met again. They were legally separated in June, after which Dazai moved to a cheap boardinghouse. (It's said that Hatsuyo returned to Aomori, then later moved on to Hokkaido and finally to China, working as a barmaid, and that she died in Tsingtao in 1944 at the age of thirty-three.)

For the next year, Dazai published little except for the occasional essay. Then, in August 1938, he produced **A Promise Fulfilled**, and suddenly he was writing again. That same month he wrote "Old Folks," which was, he tells us, "an honest account of the time H[atsuyo] and I went to Minakami Hot Springs to die." In mid-September he traveled, at Ibuse Masuji's bidding, to Misaka Pass in Kōshū (Yamanashi Prefecture), a secluded spot in the mountains with a spectacular view of Mount Fuji [**One Hundred Views of Mount Fuji**]. He was to spend the next sixty days there writing.

Ibuse, determined to find a proper bride for Dazai, introduced him to Ishihara Michiko, a woman living in Kōfu, and it was quickly decided that they would wed. Dazai came down the mountain in mid-November to stay at an inn in Kōfu [**I Can Speak**], and on January 8, 1939 he and Michiko were married at Ibuse's house in Tokyo. They returned to Kōfu the same day and settled down in a little house they had rented on the outskirts of town. The next eight months were a productive time for Dazai, and provided him with the greatest stability and repose of his entire career. The first story he wrote in the house in Kōfu was **Seascape with**

Figures in Gold. No Kidding, A Little Beauty, and *Canis familiaris* were also written there.

Dazai and Michiko moved to a little three-room house in Mitaka, just outside the Tokyo city limits, in September 1939. On September 20 Dazai attended an event called "Hometown Autumn," a gathering of artists from Aomori Prefecture who lived in Tokyo. He got stupendously drunk and apparently made quite a spectacle of himself [**Thinking of Zenzō**].

On New Year's Day of 1940 Dazai paid a visit to his old mentor Satō Haruo for the first time in four years. He mentions this meeting in **Eight Scenes from Tokyo,** which he wrote in July of that year during a ten-day stay at the Fukudaya Inn in Yugano, Izu.

Dazai's first daughter, Sonoko, was born in June 1941. In August, Dazai returned to his family home in Kanagi for the first time in ten years to see his mother, who was critically ill. (He was to return with his wife and daughter in late October 1942, and again in December of that year, when his mother died.) In November 1941 he was called up for the "writer's draft" but was excused because of his chronic chest problems. On December 8 (Japan time), the country entered a state of war with England and the United States.

During the years of the Pacific War, the censors kept a wary eye on Dazai and publishers became more reluctant to ask him for manuscripts. He nevertheless remained quite prolific and managed to publish more than twenty short stories and several longer works, including *Tsugaru* (a travelogue/novel that recounts a journey through the land of his birth), *New Tales of the Provinces* (retellings of stories by the great seventeenth-century writer Ihara Saikaku), *Regretful Parting* (a novel about the Chinese revolutionary writer Lu Xun's days as a medical student in Japan), and *Bedtime Stories* (parodic retellings of Japanese folktales).

Dazai's son, Masaki, was born in August 1944. In November of that year B29s bombed Tokyo for the first time, and in March of 1945 Dazai escorted his wife and children to her family home in Kōfu to escape the bombings. He returned to Mitaka alone, but shortly afterward his house was damaged by a bomb and he decided to join his family in Kōfu. When Kōfu was firebombed during the early morning hours of July 7 [**Early Light**], the Ishihara house was destroyed, and three weeks later Dazai, Michiko, and their two children left for Kanagi, to stay at Dazai's family home. The trip took some four days. A week after their arrival the atomic bomb was dropped on Hiroshima, and on August 15 Emperor Hirohito came on the radio to announce Japan's unconditional surrender.

Dazai settled down in a guest house on the Tsushima estate. Aside from writing a great deal, he visited with old friends and did a bit of lecturing. He was to stay in Tsugaru for fifteen months [**Garden; Two Little Words**].

Dazai and his family returned to Mitaka in November 1946, and in December he rented a workroom near the Mitaka Post Office. The first piece he wrote on his return was **Merry Christmas**.

In January 1947 a woman named Ōta Shizuko visited Dazai's workroom. Dazai had first met Shizuko in late 1941 when she and two friends, all fans of his, called at his house. He and Shizuko had met several times since then, and while Dazai was in Tsugaru they had carried on an increasingly passionate correspondence. She was hoping to become a writer, and Dazai had been encouraging her to keep a diary. In late February Dazai went to Shizuko's house in Shimo Soga, Kanagawa Prefecture, and stayed for five days. He borrowed her diary, which he was to use as a partial inspiration for his novel *The Setting Sun*.

On March 27 Dazai was introduced to a young widow

Movie actress Seki Chieko interviews Dazai for a popular magazine.
Spring 1947.

named Yamazaki Tomie. Tomie was a beautician who had lost
her husband in the war after they'd spent only ten days of
married life together. She was already contemplating suicide.
On March 30 Dazai's second daughter, Satoko (who grew up
to be the great contemporary writer Tsushima Yūko) was
born. It was also at about this time that Ōta Shizuko informed Dazai that she was pregnant with his child.

Dazai finished *The Setting Sun* in July 1947. His health was
deteriorating rapidly. He was coughing up blood, suffering
from insomnia, and drinking more than ever. At some point
that fall, Yamazaki Tomie's apartment became his
"workroom." She was to be his nurse, secretary, and virtually
constant companion until the end. In November Ōta
Shizuko gave birth to a daughter, and at Shizuko's brother's
request, Dazai wrote and signed a statement recognizing the
child as his own.

The publication of *The Setting Sun*, which became a bestseller, turned the already popular writer into something of a celebrity, although many influential literary figures continued to regard him as frivolous and insignificant. **Handsome Devils and Cigarettes** was published in March 1948, as was the first installment of "Thus Have I Heard," a bitter, rancorous attack on Shiga Naoya, who sat at the head of the Japanese literary establishment. It was also in March that Dazai went with Yamazaki Tomie to the seaside resort of Atami to begin writing *No Longer Human*. They stayed in Atami some three weeks.

In May **Cherries** was published, *No Longer Human* was completed, and Dazai began work on his final novel, *Goodbye*, a story about a man who rids himself of a number of entangling relationships with women (the first being that with a beautician and war widow). *Good-bye* was to remain unfinished. Late on the night of June 13, 1948 Dazai and Tomie drowned themselves in the Tamagawa Canal. Their bodies were not discovered until June 19, exactly thirty-nine years after the day Tsushima Shūji was born.

My Elder Brothers

兄たち

Anitachi

When Shūji was born in 1909, the enormous Tsushima home
housed some seventeen members of the extended family
and about the same number of servants. His eldest brother,
Bunji, took over as head of the household in the spring of
1923, when their father died in Tokyo shortly after being
appointed to the House of Peers. Shūji was to enter middle
school that year in Aomori.

In November 1925 Shūji, his younger brother Reiji, and
several schoolmates put out the first issue of Mirage. Shūji was
to edit and contribute stories, sketches, and essays to this
little literary journal for each of the twelve months of its
existence. It's said that Keiji, the youngest of Shūji's three
elder brothers, described Mirage as infantile and suggested they
put together a magazine that was a little more grown up.
The title he chose, Aonbo (Green Boy), was a play on the
Japanese word for infant, akanbo, which means, literally, "red
boy." The first of the two issues of Green Boy was published
in September 1926.

Reiji, who does not appear in "My Elder Brothers," died of
septicemia in January 1929, at the age of seventeen. Keiji
died of tuberculosis on June 21, 1930.

The Tsushima brothers, 1923. Seated, from left to right: Keiji, Bunji,
Eiji (Dazai's third, first, and second elder brothers, respectively). Standing:
younger brother Reiji, Shūji (Dazai).

Wthen my father died, my eldest brother was twenty-five
and had just graduated from university, my second
brother was twenty-three, the third twenty, and I was
fourteen. My elder brothers were all so kind to me and so grown up
and sophisticated that I scarcely felt the loss of my father. The
eldest was exactly like a father to me, and the second eldest like a
long-suffering uncle, and I let myself be thoroughly pampered by
them. However stubbornly selfish my demands, they would always
smile and let me have my way. They told me nothing of what was
going on and allowed me to do as I pleased, but they could hardly
have been having an easy time of it themselves, looking after the
millions my father left behind and trying to keep a grip on the
political influence he'd accumulated. With no uncles or anyone of
that sort to rely on, my two eldest brothers had no choice but to
join forces and struggle along as best they could. At only twenty-
five, the eldest became town mayor, and at the age of thirty-one,
after gaining a bit of experience in the political world, he was
elected to the prefectural assembly. He was said to be the youngest
prefectural assemblyman in the nation, and such was his popularity that the newspapers called him the Prince Konoe of Aomori
Prefecture and even featured him in cartoons.

In spite of this acclaim, however, my eldest brother always
seemed rather gloomy. His heart wasn't in politics. His bookshelves
were crammed with the complete works of Oscar Wilde and Ibsen
and volumes by various Japanese playwrights. He himself wrote
plays and when, from time to time, he assembled all the brothers
and sisters in one room and read a new work to us, his face would
light up with genuine pleasure. I was too young to understand very
well, but it seemed to me that most of his plays shared as a common theme the sorrows of fortune. I can still clearly recall, down to
the expressions on their faces, the characters in one of his plays, a
long one called *The Struggle*.

When my eldest brother was thirty, our family published a little
literary magazine with the peculiar title *Green Boy*. My third elder

brother, who was then in the sculpture department at a fine arts college, acted as editor. He had come up with the title himself and seemed quite proud of it, and he also designed the cover, an incomprehensible, surrealistic mess coated with a liberal sprinkling of silver dust. My eldest brother contributed an essay to the first issue. He entitled it "Rice" and, rather than write it down himself, he dictated it to me. I still remember it well. We were in the Western-style room on the second floor. My brother clasped his hands behind his back and peered up at the ceiling as he paced about and said, "Ready? I'm going to start. Are you ready?"

"Yes."

"I'll be thirty this year. Confucius says that at thirty he stood firm, but I, for one, far from standing, feel as if I'm about to collapse. I no longer have a tangible sense that my life is worth living. One might even say that, except for the moments I'm eating rice, I'm not really alive. I use the term 'rice' here not as an abstraction or symbol for life or the will to live, but as exactly what the word signifies. A heaping bowl of rice. I'm referring to the sensation I have when I chew a mouthful of those fluffy white grains. It's an animal sort of satisfaction. There's nothing lofty about this. . . ."

I was only a middle school student, but as I scrawled down this effusion of my eldest brother's feelings, I felt so sorry for him I could hardly stand it. For all the mindless flattery, calling him the Konoe of Aomori and what not, no one really knew the loneliness inside him.

Though my second brother didn't write anything for the premiere issue of *Green Boy*, he was not without a literary bent of his own. He had been a fan of Tanizaki Junichirō from the beginning, and also admired the poet Yoshii Isamu. This brother had a great capacity for liquor and the generous spirit of a born leader, but was at the same time a self-effacing, modest man who never let alcohol get the better of him, was always prepared to advise my eldest brother, and applied himself singlemindedly to solving any problems that arose. "He who goes off/to the red-light district/and never returns/Can it be that this/is the real me?" I wonder if it wasn't the pent-up fire in Yoshii, who wrote these lines, that my brother loved so well. He once published an essay about pigeons in a local newspaper, and when it appeared, along with a photo of himself, he displayed it to us all and jokingly boasted, "Feast your eyes on this. Quite the man of letters, eh? I look like Yoshii Isamu here, don't I?" He did have a splendid face, rather like that of the kabuki actor Sadanji. My eldest brother's features, on the other hand, were more on the delicate side, and the consensus in our house was that he resembled the actor Shōchō. Both of my brothers were well aware of these comparisons, and occasionally, when they were in their cups, they would act out scenes from *Love Suicides at Mount Toribe* or *The Ghost of the Plates* in rhythmic, stentorian kabuki diction.

Stretched out on a sofa in the Western-style room on the second floor would be my third elder brother, snickering derisively as he listened to these histrionics. Though enrolled in the fine arts college, this brother, who was frail of constitution, put little energy or effort into his sculpture, being instead engrossed in the literary arts. He also had a lot of friends with literary aspirations, and together they put out a little magazine called *Crossroads*. My brother drew cover illustrations and sometimes contributed light stories—one I remember was entitled "It All Ends with a Rueful Smile." His pen name was Yumekawa Riichi. Yumekawa, written with the characters for "dream" and "river," struck the elder brothers and sisters as appallingly mawkish and provoked a good deal of laughter among them. He once had calling cards printed up with the name spelled out in Roman letters, and when he handed me one with a rather affected flourish, I was startled to see that it read RIICHI UMEKAWA. I asked him if he'd changed his pen name to "Plum River," in reference, perhaps, to the play about the geisha Umegawa and her lover Chūbei.

"My God, you're right!" he cried, his face turning crimson. "It says 'Umekawa.' That's not me!" He'd already given the card to friends and mentors and left them at tea shops he frequented. It hadn't been the printer's mistake, either; it seems my brother had specified that the name be spelled this way. Since the letter *u* is pronounced "yu" in English, it's a mistake anyone might make, but this incident only served to increase the general hilarity in regard to his *nom de plume*. We began referring to him as Professor Plum River, Doctor Chūbei, and so on.

As I've mentioned, this brother of mine had a frail constitution, and ten years ago, when he was twenty-eight, he died. He had an incredibly lovely face. My sisters were readers of a monthly girls' magazine that always featured a frontispiece drawn by a man named, if memory serves, Fukiya Kōji. These were invariably pictures of slender young girls with enormous eyes whose features bore such a striking resemblance to those of my brother that I would sometimes look up from them and gaze at him dreamily, experiencing, not envy, but an oddly ticklish sort of pleasure.

He was by nature a serious sort—one might even say austere— but his personal tastes led him to emulate *les précieux*, the literary dandies who are said to have once flourished in France. He also adhered to the spirit of burlesque and was forever mocking others, even as he himself maintained an air of aloof indifference. No one was spared his barbs. My eldest brother had married and his first daughter was born shortly before summer vacation, when all her young uncles and aunts returned home from our various schools in Tokyo, Aomori, and Hirosaki. We'd gather in one room and contend boisterously for a chance to hold the baby, saying "Come see your uncle from Tokyo," "Come to your aunt from Aomori," and so on, and at such times my third elder brother would be standing apart from everyone else, disparaging his newborn niece with comments like, "Hell, her skin's still red. It's disgusting." Finally, however, with a sigh of resignation, he'd stretch out his arms and say, "Come on. Come to your uncle from France."

At dinnertime, we would all take our designated seats, with my grandmother, mother, eldest brother, second brother, third brother, and myself on one side of the room and the family clerk, my sister-in-law, and my elder sisters sitting across from us. Even on the hottest days of summer, my two eldest brothers would stick to their warmed saké and kept large towels beside them to wipe the sweat that dripped from their foreheads as they drank. Both of them could hold their liquor, and though they put away nearly half a gallon between them each night, not once was there any sort of drunken unpleasantness. My third brother never joined these drinking bouts, but would sit at his own tray with an air of disdain, pour wine into an elegant glass, drain it, bolt down his dinner, excuse himself with a solemn bow, and vanish. A truly splendid performance.

As the editor of *Green Boy*, this brother ordered me to collect manuscripts from the other members of the household, and when I brought them for him to read, he would invariably cackle with scorn. After I'd finally gotten my eldest brother to dictate his essay "Rice" to me, I presented it to the editor rather triumphantly, but as he read it he guffawed as usual and began to ridicule it mercilessly, saying, "What the hell's this? The princely proclamation. 'Confucius says . . .' Can you believe it? What dreadful bilge!" Though perfectly aware of the sadness permeating our eldest brother's soul, he was forever deriding him in this way, if only for the sake of maintaining his own pose. But what, you might ask, is to be said for the literary efforts of this editor who was so quick to abuse the works of others? Well, if you must know, I'm afraid they weren't much. Though he prudently refrained from publishing any of his prose in the first issue of our strangely titled magazine, he did include a pair of lyric poems. Looking back at them now, however, it's difficult to imagine any criteria by which they might be considered outstanding. Why would a man like my brother see fit to publish such things? That he did so strikes me now as simply regrettable. This won't be easy for me, but allow me to give you some idea of what these poems were like. One was called "Red Canna."

> It was a red canna
> It resembled my heart ...

Et cetera, et cetera. Believe me, copying down these lines is far from a pleasant task. The second poem was entitled "Bachelor's Buttons" and went like this:

> Dear little bachelor's buttons
> One, two, three
> I slip them into my sleeve ...

And so on. What is one to think of poems like these? I now wonder if, for his own sake, it wouldn't have been better for our dapper *précieux* to keep these little treasures of his locked away forever. At the time, though, I had great respect for my brother's absolute dedication to burlesque, and since he was a member of the rather well known literary coterie in Tokyo that put out the magazine *Crossroads*, and since, furthermore, he seemed particularly proud of these two poems and when going over the proofs at the local printer's had read them aloud with a peculiar, lilting rhythm ("It *was* a red *can*na. It re*sem*bled my *heart*"), even I began to think they were masterpieces of some sort.

I have a lot of memories concerning *Green Boy*, some poignant and some laughable, but today I just don't have it in me to go on relating them. Instead, I think I'll leave you with an account of the events surrounding the death of this brother of mine.

For two or three years preceding his death, as the tubercle bacilli began to eat away at him, my brother was in and out of his sickbed. In spite of this, however, he remained animated and cheerful and neither entered the hospital nor displayed a desire to return to the country. He rented a house in Totsuka, Tokyo and led a leisurely existence, letting one room to a married couple from our home town and keeping the remaining rooms for himself. Once I'd entered higher school, I rarely went home for vacations but went instead to Totsuka to stay with my brother, and together we would wander about Tokyo. He was quite a fibber. Once, as we were walking on the Ginza, he suddenly gave a small cry, pointing at a portly old gentleman and saying, "Ah! There's Kikuchi Kan!" with such a perfectly straight face that I could scarcely doubt he was telling the truth. Another time, when we were drinking tea at the Fujiya in Ginza, he nudged me with his elbow and whispered, "Sasaki Mosaku. Look. Sitting at the table behind you." It wasn't until years later, when I had occasion to meet both of these famous writers in person, that I realized my brother had been lying to me. I also recall that among his books was a collection of short stories by Kawabata Yasunari, and on the title page was the brushed ink inscription, "To Yumekawa Riichi, from the author." My brother told me that Mr. Kawabata had given him the book after they'd become acquainted at a hot springs resort in Izu or someplace, but now I can't help but wonder about this as well. I'll have to ask Mr. Kawabata next time we meet. It would be nice if it turned out to be true, but it seems to me that the handwriting of that inscription, as I remember it, was somewhat different from the handwriting in letters I've received from him. My brother was always playing harmless tricks of this sort on people. You couldn't let down your guard for a moment. "Mystification," I understand, was one of the favorite forms of amusement among *les précieux*, and I suppose my brother was simply unable to suppress his own attachment to this vice.

He passed away the summer after I'd entered university. At New Year's that year he'd hung a scroll in the alcove of his sitting room adorned with a sample of his own calligraphy that read "At one this spring with the Buddha Mind, I take delight neither in bread nor wine." All his visitors laughed heartily when they saw this, and he himself would wear an ironic grin. Though this was probably not mystification but words that came straight from my brother's heart, his friends were all so accustomed to having their legs pulled that no one thought to fear for his life. Before long he took to wearing a small string of prayer beads around his wrist and to referring to himself as "the witless monk." He would do so in such a deadly serious tone of voice that his friends quickly picked up on it and for a while it was quite the rage among them to refer to themselves in the same way. For my brother, however, it was not merely a joke, but something he took to saying because, though he quietly sensed that the end was near, his taste for burlesque prevented him from displaying his sorrow naturally. Instead, he did his utmost to make sport of the situation, fingering his prayer beads like a Buddhist priest to provoke our laughter. He would invite us out to Takadanobaba and lead us totteringly to a certain tearoom there, saying things like, "The witless monk confesses that the lady has moved his heart. It's a shameful thing, but proof that there's life in him yet." This witless monk of ours was quite the dandy, however, and if he happened to realize on the way to the tearoom that he'd forgotten to put on his ring, he would unhesitatingly spin on his heels, walk back to the house, fetch the ring, and rejoin us with a cool and offhand "Sorry to keep you waiting."

When I first entered university, though I stayed in a boarding-house in Totsuka only a stone's throw from my brother's place, we refrained from meeting more than once or twice a week in order to keep from interfering with each other's studies. When we did meet, we would inevitably go out on the town to listen to performances by *rakugo* storytellers or make the rounds of tearooms, and it was during this period that my brother came down with a mild case of love. Unfortunately, however, as a result of his taste for dandified elegance, he was so frightfully affected that women weren't interested in him at all, and his chances didn't look very good. The girl he was secretly in love with worked in the Takadanobaba tearoom. We went there often, but my brother's pride would absolutely not permit him to give her lascivious looks or engage her in vulgar banter; he would merely slip quietly in, drink a cup of coffee, and slip out again.

One night we went to the tearoom together and, as usual, he was making no headway. We drank a cup of coffee and left, but on the way home my brother stopped at a florist's, where he bought a huge bouquet of carnations and roses that set him back nearly ten yen. When he came out with the bouquet in his arms, he hesitated and merely stood there fidgeting until I, who understood his feelings completely, leaped into action, grabbing the bouquet out of his arms and tearing back down the street to the tearoom, where I stood in the shadow of the doorway and called to the girl.

"You remember my brother, don't you? You mustn't forget him. Here, he bought these for you." I said this all in one breath and handed her the flowers, but she just stood there with a blank, vapid look on her face. I could have punched her. I shambled despondently back to my brother's house and found him already in bed, buried under the covers and in an ugly mood. He was twenty-eight at the time, and I was twenty-two.

From about April of that year, my brother began sculpting with an extraordinary passion. He had a model come to his house and started work on a large torso. I didn't visit him much during this period because I didn't want to disturb his work, but one night when I did drop by, I found him lying in bed. "I've decided to give up the name Yumekawa Riichi," he told me, his cheeks slightly flushed. "From now on it's Tsushima Keiji all the way." (Tsushima Keiji, of course, was his real name.) He made this pronouncement with such gravity, so unlike his habitual spoofing manner, that I nearly burst into tears.

Two months later, before my brother could complete his sculpture, he died. The couple lodging at his house had told me that something seemed seriously wrong with him, and I had to agree, so we consulted his physician, who calmly said that it was now only a matter of four or five days. I was devastated. I dashed off a telegram to my eldest brother back home, and for the next two nights, while I waited for him to get to Tokyo, I slept at my sick brother's side, clearing away with my fingers the phlegm that accumulated in his throat. When my eldest brother arrived he immediately hired a nurse, and friends began to gather. This lifted my spirits considerably, but those two nights I'd spent waiting seemed like sheer hell to me at the time, and in fact they still do. Beneath the dim electric light, my brother had made me go through the drawers in his room and dispose of various letters and notebooks he'd kept, gazing at me in a bemused sort of way as I ripped the papers to shreds and sobbed uncontrollably. I felt as if he and I were the only two people on earth.

As he was breathing his last, surrounded by his friends, our eldest brother, and myself, I frantically called out his name. He responded in a clear voice, saying, "I have a diamond tiepin and a platinum chain. They're yours." This was a lie. To the very end, my brother, unable to abandon his pose as a true *précieux*, was trying to trick me with this dandified pretense. His famous mystification had become such a part of him that he was, perhaps, scarcely even conscious of it. Knowing he didn't have any diamond tiepins or platinum chains only made his foppishness seem all the sadder to me, and I broke down and cried like a baby. My brother, who, though he left no works behind, was an artist of the highest order. My brother, who, though he had the most beautiful face in the world, was completely ignored by the ladies.

I was of a mind to write about him shortly after his death, but when I thought it over and realized that I was not alone in having experienced this sorrow, that everyone goes through the same sort of thing when someone close to them dies, and that it would be an insult to my readers to display these feelings as if only I had a right to them, I found myself shrinking before the task. KEIJI DIED FOUR A.M. THIS MORNING. As my eldest brother, thirty-three years old at the time, wrote these words on the telegram form to send back home, he suddenly began to sob and unleashed a torrent of tears, and even now, remembering the sight of him weeping like that is enough to make my skinny, withered breast swell with emotion. However much money they may have, brothers who lose their father at an early age are to be pitied, it seems to me.

Train

列車

Ressha

"Train" was the first story to be published bearing the pen name Dazai Osamu. The rather coy references to "a certain radical organization" and to Japan being "at war with another country" are perhaps more central to the story than the contemporary reader might suspect, and a little background may be helpful.

Japan's Communist Party was driven underground almost as soon as it was formed, in 1922. "Proletarian" parties nonetheless won eight seats in the Diet in the February 1928 elections, the first to be held after the establishment of universal manhood suffrage. In response to this, the government arrested more than 1600 leftists on March 15. Arrests of "thought criminals" were to increase annually until they reached a peak of some 14,000 in 1933. Dazai began contributing money to the outlawed Communist Party and providing food and shelter for "comrades" in May 1930, but ceased all involvement with the party following his arrest in November 1931.

Japan's military activities in China, meanwhile, were growing more and more aggressive. In September 1931, leaders of the Japanese troops stationed in Manchuria blew up a small section of the Japanese-owned Manchurian Railway. They labeled the incident sabotage and used it as an excuse to overrun all of Manchuria. In February 1932 the army declared Manchuria an independent nation, renamed it Manchukuo,

Oyama Hatsuyo in her geisha days. Hatsuyo is, of course, the model for the "thickheaded wife" in "Train."

and set up a puppet state headed by the last Manchu emperor.
Dazai had apparently written "Train" by June 1932.

B uilt in 1925 at a place called the Umehachi Works, that C51
locomotive, along with three third-class coaches, a dining
car, a second-class coach, a second-class sleeper, and three
freight cars for mail and cargo, all made at the same factory during
the same period—a total of nine boxes bearing upwards of two
hundred passengers and a hundred thousand pieces of correspondence, not to mention the countless heartrending tales con-
tained therein—that locomotive would leave Ueno Station, pistons
pumping, at two-thirty each afternoon, rain or shine, and head for
Aomori. If at times it was sent on its way with triumphant shouts
of *Banzai*, at other times its departure was marked by handkerchiefs waving reluctant farewells, or bewailed by the inauspicious
parting gift of sobs and tears. Engine one-oh-three.

Even the number is unpleasant. Eight years have passed since
1925; how many tens of thousands of hearts has this locomotive
torn apart in that time? I myself, in fact, was dealt a bitter experience by this train.

It happened just last winter, when Shiota sent his girlfriend,
Tetsu, back home.

Tetsu and Shiota had grown up in the same village in the country and had been close since childhood. I shared a room with
Shiota in the dormitory at our higher school and had occasion to
hear from him the ongoing saga of their romance. Because Tetsu
was from a poor family, Shiota's parents, who were rather well off,
would not agree to their marriage, and as a result Shiota and his
father had any number of fierce arguments. During their first confrontation, Shiota had worked himself into such a passion that he'd
nearly passed out and ended up with a dripping nosebleed. Hearing of even such innocent little episodes as this was enough to set
my young heart pounding.

In time Shiota and I graduated from higher school and entered university in Tokyo together. Three more years had now passed. They'd been years of hardship for me, but not, apparently, for Shiota—he seemed to be leading a free and easy life. The first room I'd rented in Tokyo was near the university, and Shiota had visited me there two or three times, but what with the growing, glaring disparity in our circumstances and ways of thinking, it would have been futile to hope for our friendship to remain what it had been. Perhaps it was only my jaundiced view of people's intentions, but it seemed to me that if Tetsu had not shown up in Tokyo that time, Shiota would have been content to let our paths diverge forever.

It was during the winter of the third year since Shiota and I had ceased to be close that he suddenly visited me at my house on the outskirts of town and reported that Tetsu had come to Tokyo. She'd come alone and unbidden, unable to wait for his graduation.

I myself was by then married to a certain uneducated country girl and was no longer the callow youth who might have been thrilled by this news, and though at first I was somewhat startled by Shiota's unexpected visit, I did not forget to look for the ulterior motive behind it. It was obvious that relating the details of how Tetsu had chased after him served to inflate his pride. I found his rapture annoying, and even doubted the sincerity of his feelings for Tetsu. This suspicion of mine was, sadly enough, to prove correct. After a brief display of excitement and exultation, Shiota furrowed his brow and lowered his voice to say, "What do you think I should do?" No longer capable of sympathizing with idle frivolity of this sort, I lost no time in telling him just what he wanted to hear. "So you've come to your senses, eh? If you don't love Tetsu the way you used to, you don't have much choice but to break it off." The corners of his mouth lifted in a clearly discernible smile as he pondered this, saying, "Yes, but . . ."

A few days later I received a special delivery postcard from Shiota. It bore a short and simple note to the effect that, on the advice of friends and for the sake of both their futures, he was sending Tetsu back to the country, and that she'd be leaving the following day on the two-thirty train. Though no one was asking me to, I resolved then and there to see Tetsu off. I am sadly prone to reckless decisions of this sort.

The next day it rained from morning on.

Hurrying my reluctant wife along, I set out for Ueno Station.

Engine one-oh-three was belching black smoke in the cold rain as it awaited departure time. We walked the length of the train, carefully checking each window, and found Tetsu sitting in the third-class coach just behind the locomotive. Shiota had introduced me to her once three or four years before. Her complexion was considerably paler now, and she'd grown plump about the jawline. She remembered me, and when I called to her she immediately got up and leaned out the window, smiling brightly as we exchanged greetings. I introduced my wife. I'd brought my wife along because I was convinced that she, having been raised, like Tetsu, in poverty, would be far more effective than I at finding the right words and attitude with which to console the girl. She thoroughly betrayed me, however. She and Tetsu merely bowed to each other in silence, like a pair of society ladies. I keenly felt the awkwardness of the moment and stood there tapping the handle of my umbrella against the side of the train, where some sort of serial number was painted in white: SU-HA-FU 134273.

Tetsu and my wife exchanged a few remarks about the weather, but once this dialogue ended we were all left with nothing to say. Tetsu had placed her hands demurely on the windowsill, and she was now clenching and unclenching her round fingers, her eyes fixed on nothing. Unable to bear watching this scene any longer, I edged away and began wandering down the platform. The steam expelled from beneath the train, transformed into a cold, white mist, crawled and swirled about my feet.

I came to a halt in front of the electric clock and looked the train over. Thoroughly wet from the rain, it glistened with a dull, hard sheen.

An ashen-faced fellow was leaning out a window of the third third-class coach, bidding a faltering farewell to five or six people who'd come to see him off. Japan at that time was at war with another country, and this fellow, no doubt, was a soldier being mobilized. I felt as if I'd seen something I had no right to see, and an oppressive weight bore down on my breast.

A few years before, I'd become marginally involved with a certain radical organization, withdrawing shortly afterwards with an excuse that failed to save my face; but now, fixing my eyes in turn on this soldier and on Tetsu, who was returning home humiliated and sullied, it occurred to me that whether that excuse of mine had been face-saving or not was hardly the point.

I looked up at the electric clock above me. Three minutes or so still remained before departure time. I couldn't stand it. I suppose it's the same for anyone seeing someone off—nothing is more confounding than those last three minutes. You've said all you have to say and can do nothing but gaze helplessly at each other. And in this case it was even worse, because I hadn't been able to come up with a single thing to say in the first place. If my wife had been a bit more competent, it wouldn't have been so bad, but look at her: standing there with her mouth clamped shut and a sullen look on her face. I walked resolutely back to Tetsu's window.

The train would leave any moment now. The locomotive, with a journey of four hundred fifty miles before it, huffed and puffed angrily, and an agitated flurry of activity swept over the platform. At this point there was no room in my heart for concern for anyone else's troubles, and in my attempt to comfort Tetsu I rashly used words like "this castastrophe." My thickheaded wife, meanwhile, was peering at the blue metal plate attached to the side of the train, muttering aloud to herself as she used her recently acquired knowledge to decipher the circles and lines of the Roman letters imprinted there: FOR A-O-MO-RI.

Female

雌に就いて

Mesu ni tsuite

———◆———

*"This is where we sprinkle in the atmosphere of the times,"
says the narrator of "Female" as he and his visitor dream up
the story within the story. "A fire at the zoo. Nearly a hundred
monkeys fried to a crisp in their cages."*

As for the story proper, however, the "atmosphere of the
times" is established by Dazai's seemingly offhand reference to
the February 26 Incident. In the early morning hours of that
day in 1936, some 1400 troops, led by young officers who
belonged to the "Imperial Way" faction of the army, occupied
the central buildings of the government in an attempted coup
d'état and set out to assassinate a number of high-ranking
officials. Four men were brutally murdered in their own homes,
and several others narrowly escaped death. The rebels then
created an occupied zone in central Tokyo and issued a
manifesto that blamed Japan's domestic and international
troubles on the political parties, the bureaucracy, the elder
statesmen, and big business. They were inspired by the dream
of a "Shōwa Restoration" whereby the Shōwa emperor,
Hirohito, would be freed from his "traitorous" advisors and
lead his family-nation (and eventually the whole world) in the
creation of a glorious new order. They saw themselves as
following in the footsteps of the heroic leaders of the Meiji
Restoration, but in fact they had no clear plan as to what was
to be done once they'd destroyed the old order and martyred
themselves.

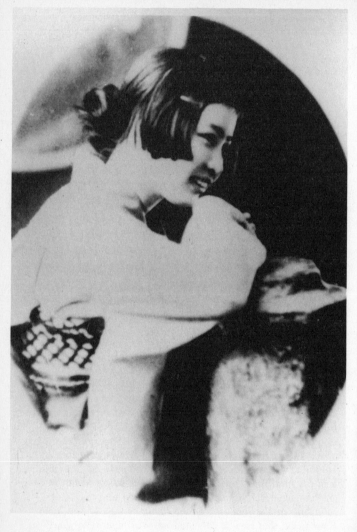

Tanabe Shimeko (a.k.a. Tanabe Atsumi), who died in Dazai's first "love suicide."

*The rebels held out for four days, but, having been
denounced by the emperor himself, their cause was doomed.
Two of the leaders committed suicide and fifteen more were
court-martialed and executed.*

*The famous author and fanatic nationalist Mishima Yukio
idolized the rebels and contributed to the continuing popular
fascination with the incident by writing about it a number of
times and finally emulating the "spirit" of the revolt with his
spectacular suicide in 1970.*

*Dazai's attitude toward the whole thing was revealed in his
1946 essay "An Almanac of Agony":*

An extraordinarily heavy snowfall covered the entire
Kantō region. On that day, the thing called the 2-26
Incident occurred. I was indignant. What did they want?
What were we supposed to do?

It was truly repulsive. I thought they were damned fools.
My reaction was something like rage.

You have a plan? You have an organization? Nothing.

Unorganized terrorism is the most abominable of
crimes. "Folly" wasn't the word for it; there were no words
for it. The stench of this vainglorious farce hung in the air
until the end of the so-called Greater East Asia War.

*Dazai was heavily addicted to drugs when he wrote
"Female."*

---

*It is said that once a native of Fiji has tired of a wife, even one whom he has
loved deeply, he will not hesitate to kill her and eat her flesh. It is also said
that when the wife of a Tasmanian dies, he calmly buries her children along
with her. And certain aborigines of Australia reportedly take the remains of
their dead wives into the wild, strip the fat from the bones, and use this as bait
for fishing.*

P ublishing a decrepit, world-weary story like this in a
magazine that calls itself "Young Leaves" is neither a bid to
be thought eccentric nor evidence of a disregard for the

reader. I am doing so, rather, because I believe that this sort of story, too, can be appreciated by the young. I happen to know that the youth of today are more elderly than most people think. They'll have no problem at all accepting something like this. This is a story for those who've lost hope.

On February 26 of this year, in Tokyo, the young officers caused quite a commotion. I was sitting at my hibachi that day opposite a friend. Not having heard anything of the incident, we were discussing a woman's robe.

"I just don't see it. Can't you be a little more concrete? Put some realism into your technique. What kind of robe? An under-kimono?"

The type of woman who, were she to exist, would save one from having to die—we were probing the deep recesses of each other's hearts where our respective images of this ideal woman were enshrined. My visitor was conjuring up a frail, delicate mistress of twenty-seven or twenty-eight. She rents the second floor of a house in Mukōjima and lives there with her five-year-old, fatherless child. He has gone to visit her on the night of the river festival fireworks, and is drawing a picture for the little girl. He draws a circle, colors it in neatly with a yellow crayon, and tells her, "That's the moon." The woman, it turns out, is wearing a pale blue terrycloth robe and a sash with a wisteria-flower pattern. Once my friend had got that far, he said it was my turn, and I began, responding to his comments and questions as they arose.

"Not crepe, that's for sure. There's something unsanitary, and dowdy, about crepe. I guess we're just not very chic, you and I."

"Pajamas, then?"

"Absolutely not. She might as well not be wearing anything. If it were only the top, it'd be something out of a comic strip."

"All right, then, what? Terrycloth?"

"No. A freshly laundered man's *yukata*, with rough, uneven stripes. And a thin sash of the same material. Tied in the front, like a judo belt. Like the *yukata* they give you at an inn, that's the kind

I mean. The woman should have a sort of boyish air about her, I think."

"I see. For someone who's always saying how worn out he is, you're awfully flashy, aren't you? It's like what they say about funerals being the gaudiest of all rituals. You're really going for the erotic touch. What about her hair?"

"Not done up in the Japanese style. I hate that. Too oily and unwieldy. And the shape is so grotesque."

"I knew it. A simple Western-style cut, right? She's an actress. One of the house actresses at the old Imperial Theater."

"No. Actresses are too worried about their precious little reputations."

"Don't make light of this. It's serious business."

"I know that. It's not just a game for me either. To love someone is to put your life on the line. I don't take it lightly."

"Well, I'm not getting the picture. Let's have some of that realism. Why don't you take her somewhere, on a trip or something? You might be surprised how moving a woman around like that can bring her into focus."

"The thing is, she's not a woman who moves a lot. She's like . . . It's as if she's asleep."

"You're too self-conscious, that's the problem. All right, we're just going to have to plod ahead with it, then. First of all, let's put her in that *yukata* you're so fond of."

"Why not start from the beginning, at Tokyo Station?"

"Fine. So, you've promised to meet her at the station."

"The night before. All I said was 'Let's take a trip,' and she nodded. That's all there was to the promise."

"Wait, wait. What is she? A writer?"

"No. Women writers don't have a very high opinion of me, somehow. An artist, a painter who's grown a bit weary of life. There seem to be some wealthy women artists out there, you know."

"Artist, writer—it's the same thing."

"You think so? Well then, what? A geisha? Anyway, as long as it's a woman who's had some experience, who's no longer overwhelmed by the presence of a male."

"Have you had relations with her before this?"

"Maybe, maybe not. Even if I have, the memory of it is hazy, like a dream. We see each other no more than three times a year."

"Where are you going on your trip?"

"Two or three hours out of Tokyo. A hot springs resort in the mountains would be nice."

"Don't get carried away. The woman isn't even at Tokyo Station yet."

"The promise of the night before seemed so unreal that now I'm sure she won't come, but, well, you never know. It's like that. I go to the station without really expecting her to be there. She's not there. So I think, all right, I'll take a trip alone. But still I decide to wait until the last five minutes before the hour."

"You have luggage, of course."

"One small suitcase. Just at the last moment, at five minutes to two, I glance around behind me."

"The woman's standing there, smiling."

"No, she's not smiling. Very sober expression. She says, in a quiet voice, 'I'm sorry I'm late.' "

"She tries to take your suitcase."

"I tell her no, I'll carry it."

"Second-class tickets?"

"Either first-class or third. Well, third, I guess."

"You get on the train."

"I take the woman to the dining car. White tablecloth, flowers on the table, the scenery flowing by outside . . . It's all very pleasant. I sip dreamily at my beer."

"You offer her a glass of beer, too."

"No, I suggest cider for her."

"Is it summer?"

"Fall."

"So you're just sitting there daydreaming?"

"I look at her and say, 'Thank you.' It sounds honest and natural, even to me. It's very touching—to me, anyway."

"You arrive at the inn. It's evening by now, right?"

"When the time comes to enter the baths, it gets critical."

"You don't bathe together, do you? Or do you?"

"I just can't see myself doing that. I go first. I keep it short and simple and go back to the room. The woman has put on a padded kimono."

"All right, let me take it from there. If I get it wrong, just say so. I think I've pretty much got the picture. You sit in the rattan chair on the veranda and smoke a cigarette. You're treating yourself— the cigarettes are Camels. The light of sunset plays on the autumn leaves in the mountains before you. After a while, the woman comes back from the baths. She unfolds her hand towel and hangs it on the veranda railing. Then she stands behind you and quietly gazes at the same spot you're gazing at. She's empathizing with you, trying to see the beauty of the scenery as you see it. This goes on for, at most, five minutes."

"No, one minute's plenty. Five minutes of that and we'd both go under."

"Dinner comes. There's a bottle of saké on the tray. You going to drink it?"

"Wait a minute. The woman hasn't said anything since back at Tokyo Station, when she apologized for being late. It wouldn't hurt to have her say a word or two here."

"No, not now. Saying something stupid here could ruin the whole thing."

"I wonder. Oh, well, all right, we don't say anything, just sit down before the trays of food, and . . . I don't know, it's strange."

"Nothing strange about it at all. You can exchange a few words with the maid. That'll do, won't it?"

"No, wait, here's what happens: The woman sends the maid away. Abruptly, in a quiet voice, but pronouncing the words distinctly, she says, 'I'll take care of it, thank you.' "

"I see. She's that sort of woman, is she?"

"Then she pours me some saké. Clumsily, like a young boy. She's demure, composed. The evening newspaper is on the floor beside her cushion. Still holding the little saké bottle in her left hand, she opens the paper and begins to read, with her right hand on the tatami mat."

"There's a story about the Kamo River flood."

"No. This is where we sprinkle in the atmosphere of the times. A fire at the zoo. Nearly a hundred monkeys fried to a crisp in their cages."

"Too gruesome. Anyway, wouldn't it be more natural for her to turn to the horoscope column?"

"I put the saké aside and say, 'Let's eat.' We start eating. Omelets—that's one of the dishes. It's unbearably dismal. I throw down my chopsticks suddenly, as if I've just remembered something, and move to the desk. I take some paper out of my suitcase and begin writing like mad."

"What's the meaning of that?"

"It just shows how weak I am. I can't retreat without putting on airs. It's my karma or something. Anyway, I'm in a terrible mood."

"Come on. You're just floundering now."

"I've got nothing to write. So I copy out the forty-seven characters of the *iroha* alphabet. Again and again, over and over. I tell the woman as I'm writing that I've just remembered some work that can't wait, and I want to get it out of the way before I forget. I tell her to go out and see the town while I'm doing this. It's a nice, quiet little town, I tell her."

"This is getting to be a real mess. All right, then what? The woman changes her clothes and leaves the room."

"I collapse on the floor and lie there staring at the ceiling and walls."

"You read your horoscope in the paper. It says 'Avoid travel.' "

"I smoke one of my three-sen-apiece Camels. I feel slightly

extravagant, and grateful. And I feel affection for myself."

"The maid will come in soon and ask how you want the bedding laid out."

"I sit up and tell her breezily, 'Two futon.' Suddenly I want to drink more saké, but I suppress the urge."

"The woman will be coming back about now."

"Not yet. Once the maid has left the room, I begin to do something very strange."

"Don't tell me you're going to run off and leave the woman there?"

"I count my money. Three ten-yen bills. Two or three yen in change."

"No problem. So, when the woman returns, you've started your bogus writing again. She timidly asks if she should have stayed out longer."

"I don't answer. Or, I tell her not to mind me, to go ahead and get into bed while I finish my work. It sounds rather like a command. I keep writing: *i-ro-ha-ni-ho-e-to* . . ."

"From behind you, the woman says, 'Goodnight.' "

"I write: *chi-ri-nu-ru-wo-wa-ka.* Then: *we-hi-mo-se-su.* Then I rip up the paper."

"This is getting crazier and crazier."

"Can't be helped."

"Now you go to bed?"

"To the baths."

"It's getting cold out, right?"

"That's not why. I'm becoming a bit disoriented. I stay in the bath for about an hour, just sitting there like an idiot. When I finally climb out, I'm just a blur, a ghost. I get back to the room, and the woman's in bed. The electric lampstand by the pillow is on."

"She's already asleep?"

"No. Her eyes are open. Her face is pale. She's looking up at the ceiling with her lips pressed tightly together. I take some sleeping tablets and get in the futon."

"The woman's?"

"No. After about five minutes I get up quietly. Or, no—I leap to my feet."

"You're weeping."

"No, I'm angry. I glance at the woman. She stiffens beneath the covers. Seeing that, I feel perfectly satisfied. I take the book *Cold Smile* by Kafū out of my suitcase and get back in the futon. I turn my back to the woman and read, utterly absorbed."

"Isn't Kafū a little corny?"

"All right, then—the Bible."

"I know what you mean, but . . ."

"One of those old picture books, maybe?"

"Listen. That book is an important point. Let's take our time and get it right. A book of ghost stories wouldn't be too bad. I don't know. There must be something. *Pensée* is too heavy. . . . A collection of Haruo's poems? No, too close to home. There must be something just right."

"I've got it. My own book. My first and only collection of stories."

"This is getting awfully bleak."

"I start right at the first page and plow ahead, gradually getting more absorbed. Fervently hoping for some sort of salvation."

"Is the woman married?"

"I heard a sound like water flowing behind me. It was only a faint sound, but a chill ran down my spine. The woman had quietly turned over in bed."

"What happened?"

" 'Let's die,' I said. She, too—"

"Stop right there. You're not just making this up."

He was right. The following afternoon the woman and I attempted suicide. She was neither a geisha nor a painter. She was a girl from a poor background who'd been a maid in my home.

She was killed simply because she turned over in bed. I didn't die. Seven years have passed and I'm still alive.

Seascape with Figures in Gold

黄金風景
Ōgon Fūkei

———◆———

Dazai wrote "Female" when he was living in Funabashi, recuperating from appendicitis, peritonitis, and lung problems, addicted to morphine, deep in debt, and lusting after the Akutagawa Prize. "Seascape with Figures in Gold," written three years later, presents a portrait of the artist during those harrowing days.

———◆———

*Near the seashore stands a green oak tree
And tied to that tree is a fine golden chain.*

—Pushkin

I was not a very pleasant child. I used to give our maids a hard time. Slow-wittedness was something I could not abide, and I was especially hard on the more obtuse maids. Okei was one of them. Two or three times in the course of peeling a single apple she would stop, knife in one hand and apple in the other, and stare into space, daydreaming about heaven knew what, and would continue to do so indefinitely until one called out to her in a stern voice. I wondered if she was all there. Often I would see her in the kitchen doing nothing whatsoever, just standing there, and, child though I was, I found it terribly irritating, almost scandalous, and even now it sends a chill of self-disgust down my spine to recall

53

Dazai in Funabashi in 1936, at the height of his drug addiction.

how I used to affect a grownup air and shout at her—"Okei! The day is short!" I once summoned Okei, handed her a picture book that portrayed hundreds of soldiers on parade—some on horses, some bearing flags, some carrying rifles—and ordered her to clip them all out with scissors. Anything but dextrous, Okei took from morning till evening, skipping lunch, to cut out some thirty figures, and these were such a mess—the general with only half a beard, infantrymen with hands the size of bears' paws, all of them wet with perspiration, for it was summer and Okei tended to sweat—that after yelling at her for each infraction I finally lost my temper completely and kicked her. She was sitting on the floor, and though I was sure I'd kicked her on the shoulder, Okei put her hand to her right cheek and collapsed in tears. Between sobs, in a broken groan, she said that not even her parents had ever "stepped on" her face, and that she would remember this all her life. That's one time, I must admit, that I felt quite awful in spite of myself. It didn't stop me from continuing to torment Okei, however; it was almost as if I thought it my mission in life to do so. I simply had no patience with doltish people, and that's a trait that to some extent remains with me to this day.

The year before last I was expelled from my family and, reduced to poverty overnight, was left to wander the streets, begging help from various quarters, barely managing to stay alive from one day to the next, and, just when I'd begun to think I might be able to support myself with my writing, I came down with a serious illness. Thanks to the compassion of others, I was able to rent a small house in Funabashi, Chiba, next to the muddy sea, and spend the summer there alone, convalescing. Though battling an illness that each and every night left my robe literally drenched with sweat, I had no choice but to press ahead with my work. The cold half pint of milk I drank each morning was the only thing that gave me a certain peculiar sense of the joy of life; my mental anguish and exhaustion were such that the oleanders blooming in one corner of the garden appeared to me merely as flickering tongues of flame.

It was during this time that a small, skinny policeman of about forty showed up at my door on his census-taking rounds. Looking closely at my name in his register and then peering up at my unshaven face, he said, with a strong northern accent, "Why, you're Mr. Tsushima's boy, aren't you?"

"I am," I said impudently. "And you?"

The policeman's thin countenance creased with a smile so big it looked painful.

"Well, you don't say. You probably don't remember me—it's been some twenty years now—but I used to keep a livery stable back in Kanagi."

Kanagi is the name of the village I was born in.

"Well, as you can see," I said gravely, "I've sunk pretty low."

"Nothing of the sort!" he said, still beaming. "A writer—now, that's what I call making something of yourself."

I gave him a wry smile.

"By the way," he said, lowering his voice a bit, "Okei's forever talking about you."

"Okei?" It didn't sink in at first.

"Okei. I suppose you've forgotten her. She used to work as a maid for your family. . . ."

I remembered. A groan escaped my lips. Still crouching on the front step before him, I hung my head, my mind going back to twenty years before and all the wicked things I'd done to that dullwitted maid. I could scarcely bear to face the man.

"Is she happy?" Raising my head, I asked this absurd question with the craven smile of a criminal accused.

"Oh, sure, everything's fine now, I guess," he replied in a carefree, expansive way, wiping the sweat from his forehead with a handkerchief. "Say, if you don't mind, I'd like to bring her along some time so we can pay our respects properly."

This gave me such a start that I nearly leaped into the air. "No, no, really, that won't be necessary," I stammered, shuddering with an indescribable sense of mortification.

"My son's working in the station here now, you know," the policeman continued cheerfully. "He's the oldest. Then there's another boy and two girls. The youngest is eight, and she entered primary school this year, so now we can finally take a bit of a breather. It hasn't been easy for either of us. But let me tell you, there's something different about a woman who's learned how to comport herself working for a family like yours." He blushed slightly and smiled. "We're indebted to you, really. And, as I said, Okei's forever talking about you. I'll bring her by on my next day off." His expression suddenly grew serious. "Well, then, I won't trouble you any longer. Do take care of yourself."

Three days later, preoccupied more with my financial straits than with my work, I found myself unable to sit still and picked up my bamboo stick with the intention of taking a walk down to the seashore. When I slid open the front door, however, I was confronted with three figures primly lined up as if for a family portrait, the mother and father clad in *yukata* and a little girl in a red dress. The mother, of course, was Okei.

I addressed them in a voice so loud and so like an angry shout that it startled even me.

"So you've come. I'm terribly sorry, but I'll have to ask you to make it another day. I've got some business to attend to, and I was just on my way out."

Okei as a middle-aged housewife had acquired an air of refinement. Her eight-year-old daughter, whose face looked a lot like Okei's had when she was our maid, was gazing vacantly up at me with rather dull, cloudy eyes. Gripped with sorrow, I fled toward the seashore before Okei had a chance to speak. Mowing down the weeds with my bamboo stick and not once turning to look back, I stormed off, stamping my foot with every step, and followed the shoreline toward town. And what did I do in town? Gazing up at the posters on movie theater marquees, peering at the window displays of kimono shops, clucking my tongue and shuddering to shake off the voice that, somewhere inside me, kept whispering

"*You lose*," I walked about aimlessly for what must have been half an hour or so before turning back and heading for home.

I reached the seashore and came to an abrupt halt. There before me was a picture of peace and harmony. Okei and her husband and daughter were tranquilly tossing stones into the sea and laughing together. I could hear their voices from where I stood.

"I'll tell you," said the policeman, grunting as he heaved a stone, "that's one intelligent young gentleman. He's going to be somebody, mark my words."

"Of course he is," said Okei, her voice clear and proud. "Even as a child there was something different about him. Always so kind and attentive, even to the servants."

I was weeping now as I stood there. My fierce agitation melted soothingly away with the tears.

You lose, I told myself, and I was glad of it. I wouldn't have had it any other way. That victory of theirs illuminated the road I must walk tomorrow.

No Kidding

座興に非ず

Zakyō ni arazu

It's difficult to place this story in any specific time frame—
Dazai never had an apartment in Hongō, as far as we know—
but we might imagine that it describes his state of mind in,
say, the fall of 1937, when he was living alone in a
boardinghouse after his divorce from Hatsuyo. In July of that
year, the Marco Polo Bridge Incident had signaled the
beginning of a fullblown war with China and the prelude to
World War II.

Even today one can see shady characters loitering around
Ueno Station, waiting for runaways from the country to
victimize.

What was to become of me? Just to think about that was enough to leave me shuddering and too distraught to sit still, so I left my Hongō apartment dragging a walking stick and headed for Ueno Park. It was an evening in mid-September. My white *yukata* was already out of season, and I felt horribly conspicuous, as if I glowed in the dark, and so full of sorrow I no longer wanted to live. A stagnant wind, reeking of sewage, raked the surface of Shinobazu Pond. The lotuses growing there had begun to decay, their grisly carcasses entrapped between bent, elongated stalks, and the idiot faces of people streaming by in the evening cool were etched with such total exhaustion that one

The statue of Saigō Takamori in Ueno Park. Saigō was one of the leaders of the Meiji Restoration and is revered as representing the epitome of the samurai spirit. Once the Restoration was an accomplished fact, he fell out with government leaders and led another rebellion but was defeated, whereupon he committed suicide by having one of his lieutenants behead him.

might have thought the end of the world was at hand.

I walked all the way to Ueno Station. Through the portals of this "Wonder of the Orient" swarmed a dark, writhing, numberless throng. Vanquished souls, one and all. I couldn't help seeing them that way. For the farming villages in the northeast, these are the Gates of Hell. You pass through them to enter the big city, and again to return home, broken and defeated, with nothing but the rags that cling to your ravaged body. *What did you expect?* I sat down on a bench in the waiting room, smirking. *Don't think they won't say they told you so. How many times did they tell you that going to Tokyo would get you nowhere?* Daughters, fathers, sons on the benches around me, bereft of their wits, squinting through cloudy eyes. What did they see? Phantom flowers that dance in the air, their own life histories unfolding before them like scrolls or revolving lanterns decorated with faces and failures of every description.

I stood up and fled the waiting room, then walked toward the gate. The seven-oh-five express had just arrived at the platform, and a swarm of black ants pushed and shoved and fell over one another in the crush to file out. Suitcases and baskets here and there. Ah, and one of those old cloth hold-alls—who'd have thought they still existed? Don't tell me—they ran you out of town on a rail.

The young men were dressed to kill and, without exception, tense and excited. The poor bastards. Nitwits. A fight with the old man and off they go. Morons.

One young fellow in particular caught my eye. He had a magnificently affected way of smoking his cigarette—something he'd learned from a movie, no doubt. Imitating some foreign actor. He came out through the gate carrying a single small suitcase, lifted one eyebrow, and surveyed his surroundings. Still acting. He wore a suit with a startlingly gaudy checked pattern, and the trousers were, if nothing else, long—they seemed to begin just south of his neck. White sports cap. Red leather shoes. He pulled back the corners of his mouth and breezed out toward the street, so elegant it was comical. I felt like teasing him. I was bored to distraction in those days.

"Hey, you. Takiya." I could see the nametag on his suitcase. "C'mere a minute."

Without looking at his face, I walked briskly ahead, and the kid followed as if being sucked into the whirlwind of destiny. I had some confidence in my grasp of human psychology. When people are in a distracted state of mind, the most effective way to handle them is to be overwhelmingly commanding. They're like putty in your hands. Trying to put your victim at ease by acting natural and reasoning him into a sense of security can actually have the opposite effect.

I walked up Ueno Hill. Slowly climbing the stone steps, I said, "I think you ought to put yourself in your old man's shoes."

"Yes, sir," he said stiffly.

I came to a stop at the base of the statue of Saigō Takamori. No one else was around. I took a pack of cigarettes from my sleeve and lit one, glancing at the kid's face by the light of the match. He was standing there pouting with all the ingenuousness of a child. I began to feel sorry for him and guessed I'd teased him enough.

"How old are you?"

"Twenty-three." He had a strong country accent.

"That young, eh?" I sighed inadvertently. "All right. You can go." I was going to add that I'd only meant to give him a little scare, but then I was suddenly seized with the temptation, not unlike the thrill of cheating on one's wife, to tease him just a little bit more.

"You have any cash?"

He fidgeted and said, "Yes."

"Give me twenty yen." This was hilarious.

He actually took the money out.

"May I leave now?"

Here, of course, was my cue to burst out laughing and say, "I was only teasing you. It's a joke, you idiot. Now you see what a scary place Tokyo is. Go on back home and set your father's heart at ease." But I hadn't begun this routine merely for the fun of it. The rent was due on my apartment.

"Thanks. I won't forget you, pal."

My suicide was postponed for another month.

Dazai and Hatsuyo (seated) at the home of one Sakabe Keijirō in Numazu in 1932, two years before Dazai's stay in Mishima with Sakabe Takerō, Keijirō's younger brother and the "acquaintance" mentioned in the second sentence of "A Promise Fulfilled." The two young men standing behind them are unidentified, but it seems fair to assume that they are the Sakabe brothers.

A Promise Fulfilled

満願
Mangan

———◆———

*This story, published in September 1938, marked a turning
point in Dazai's life and career. After writing very little for a
year or so while living a dissipated and rather solitary existence
at the boardinghouse in Ogikubo, Dazai suddenly bounced
back with a renewed determination to live on and to continue
writing. This vignette, a lyrical, humorous, epiphanic
affirmation of life, seems to symbolize that determination.*

———◆———

This is something that happened four years ago. I was spending the summer at Mishima in Izu, staying in a room on the second floor of an acquaintance's house, writing a story called "Romanesque." One night, in the course of riding a bicycle through the streets of the town, drunk, I suffered an injury. The skin above my right ankle was split open. The wound wasn't deep, but, because I'd been drinking, the bleeding was frightful, and I made a frantic dash to the doctor's. The town doctor was a portly man of thirty-two who resembled Saigō Takamori. He was very drunk. When he wobbled into the consultation room in a condition that clearly rivaled mine, it struck me as terribly funny, and as he treated my wound I began to giggle. The doctor soon joined in, and before long we were both laughing uncontrollably.

We were good friends from that night on. The doctor preferred

65

philosophy to literature, and since I, too, felt more at ease with that subject, our discussions were always lively. The doctor's view of the world was one that might best be described as a primitive sort of dualism. He saw in all worldly matters manifestations of the struggle between Good and Evil, and this allowed him to explain everything in admirably clear and concise terms. Even as I inwardly strove to maintain my monotheistic belief in the deity we call Love, the doctor's expositions of his theory were like breaths of cool, fresh air briefly dispelling the gloom in my heart. One of his illustrations, for example—that he himself, who immediately called to his wife to bring beer whenever I visited them at night, was Good, whereas his wife, who would smilingly suggest that tonight, instead of drinking beer, we play bridge, was a true representative of Evil—struck me as flawless, and I had to concur. The doctor's wife, though small and plain, had very white skin and an air of elegant refinement. They had no children, but the wife's younger brother, a quiet, serious youth who attended a commercial school in Numazu, lived upstairs.

Five different newspapers were delivered to the doctor's house, and in order to read these I would drop by for thirty minutes or an hour almost every day during my morning walk. I would come in through the back gate and circle around to the veranda, where I'd sip the cold barley tea the wife brought me and read, holding the newspaper down firmly with my free hand as it flapped noisily in the breeze. Not more than ten or twelve feet from the veranda, an ample little stream flowed lazily through the edge of a green meadow, and along the narrow lane that bordered the stream, a boy who delivered milk would pass on his bicycle and invariably call out "Good morning!" to me, the stranger from out of town. At about the same hour, a young woman would sometimes come to the doctor's house for medicine. There was always something refreshingly clean and healthy about her, in her light summer dress and *geta* clogs, and I would often hear her and the doctor talking and laughing together in the consultation room. Occasionally, however, the doctor would accompany her to the door as she left and call out after her in a scolding tone of voice, "It's only a question of persevering a little bit longer, young lady!"

The doctor's wife explained it all to me one day. The woman was married to a primary school teacher who'd developed a lung problem some three years before and whose condition had just recently begun to show marked improvement. The doctor had spared no effort in making it clear to the young wife, however, that certain things were still strictly forbidden, reminding her that now was a crucial time in her husband's convalescence. She faithfully obeyed his commands, but there were, nonetheless, times when one look at her would be enough to move anyone to pity. It was then that the doctor would steel his heart and scold her, saying it was only a question of a little more perseverance, the implicit meaning of which was obvious to them both.

One morning near the end of August, I witnessed something beautiful. I was sitting on the veranda, reading the newspaper, when the doctor's wife, who sat nearby with her feet tucked up beside her, whispered, "Ah! She looks happy, doesn't she?"

I glanced up and saw a radiant figure in a light summer dress walking briskly along the narrow lane before us, her clogs scarcely seeming to touch the earth, her white parasol spinning round and round.

"The ban was lifted this morning," the doctor's wife whispered again.

Three years, I thought, and a wave of emotion swept through me. As time goes by, the image of that young woman at that moment seems ever more beautiful to me. And that, for all I know, may be just as the doctor's wife intended.

Mount Fuji from above Misaka Pass.

Tenka Chaya.

One Hundred Views of Mount Fuji

富嶽百景

Fugaku Hyakkei

———◆———

This is also, of course, the title of the famous collection of
ukiyoe *prints by Hokusai. Dazai described this story, one of his*
most famous and best-loved works, as "a series of sketches." It
was published in two parts, in February and March 1939, and
the fact that Ibuse Masuji is mentioned by name in the first
part and only as "a certain mentor" in the second is due to
Ibuse's objection to seeing his name in print.

Ibuse later wrote that this story was quite close to the truth,
but that there was one passage on which he

> *would like to set the record straight. That's the description*
> *of me sitting in the fog atop Mitsu Pass looking out of*
> *sorts and breaking wind. I did climb to Mitsu Pass with*
> *Dazai, but I don't remember breaking wind. Later, when*
> *Dazai came to my house, I voiced my protest, but he*
> *merely burst out laughing and said, "Oh, no, you did*
> *condescend to break wind," trying to lend credence to his*
> *story by using polite language. "Twice you condescended*
> *to break wind," he said.*

The novel Dazai was working on at Misaka Pass was The
Phoenix, *described by some as yet another attempt to resurrect*
Tanabe Shimeko, who died in Dazai's double suicide of 1930.
It was to remain unfinished.

Dazai makes reference in this story to a number of folktales,
plays, songs, poets, and other "things Japanese" which may
require some explanation.

"Fujiyama": The correct name for Mount Fuji in Japanese is Fujisan, "san'" being another reading for the character "yama" (mountain). Why Westerners began calling it Fujiyama is hard to say, but it is a mistake that the Japanese delight in and seem to encourage.

Sensei: A term of respect accorded teachers, doctors, and anyone who is recognized as a master of some art or craft.

Saigyō and Nōin: Great tanka poets of the Heian period.

The Asagao Diary: An old kabuki play about a girl who falls in love with a man, is separated from him, leaves home, goes blind, meets up with the man again only to have him leave her behind, chases him as far as the Ōi River, which she cannot cross, and loses her mind.

Lady Kiyo: A girl in a popular legend who falls in love with the monk Anchin but is later rejected by him. She transforms into a serpent as she swims across the Hidaka River in hot pursuit of her unfaithful monk.

Kuzu-no-ha: The heroine of another play. She is in reality a white fox who transforms herself into a beautiful woman to marry a man who saved her life. Foxes are known in Japanese folklore for casting spells on people and changing their shapes.

Kurama Tengu: A fictional character from a popular novel who was depicted fighting on the side of Saigō Takamori and the other royalists in the Meiji Revolution.

Eulalia: An obscure word for susuki (Miscanthus sinensis), more commonly translated as "pampas grass," which it resembles.

Chinese lantern plant: A popular potted plant with orange flowers that look like paper lanterns.

The slopes of Hiroshige's Mount Fuji converge at an angle of eighty-five degrees, and those in Bunchō's paintings at about eighty-four, but if you study survey maps drawn by the army, you'll find that the angle formed by the eastern and western slopes is one hundred twenty-four degrees, and that formed by the northern and southern slopes is one hundred seventeen. And it's not only Hiroshige and Bunchō—most paintings of

Fuji, in fact, depict the slopes meeting at an acute angle, the summit slender, lofty, delicate. Some of Hokusai's renditions fairly
resemble the Eiffel Tower, peaking at nearly thirty degrees. But
the real Fuji is unmistakably obtuse, with long, leisurely slopes; by
no means do one hundred twenty-four degrees east–west and one
hundred seventeen north–south make for a very steep peak. If I
were living in India, for example, and were suddenly snatched up
and carried off by an eagle and dropped on the beach at Numazu
in Japan, I doubt if I'd be very much impressed at the sight of this
mountain. Japan's "Fujiyama" is "wonderful" to Westerners simply because they've heard so much about it and yearned so long to
see it; but how much appeal would Fuji hold for one who's never
been exposed to such popular propaganda, for one whose heart is
simple and pure and free of preconceptions? It would, perhaps,
strike that person as almost pathetic, as mountains go. It's short. In
relation to the width of its base, quite short. Any mountain with a
base that size should be at least half again as tall.

The only time Fuji looked really tall to me was when I saw it
from Jukkoku Pass. That was good. At first, because it was cloudy, I
couldn't see the top, but I judged from the angle of the lower
slopes and picked out a spot amid the clouds where I thought the
peak probably was, only to find, when the sky began to clear, that I
was way off. The bluish summit loomed up twice as high as I'd expected. I was not so much surprised as strangely tickled, and I
cackled with laughter. I had to hand it to Fuji that time. When
you come face to face with absolute reliability, you tend, first of all,
to burst into silly laughter. You just come all undone. It's like—this
is a funny way to put it, I know, but it's like chuckling with relief
after loosening your belt. Young men, if ever the one you love
bursts out laughing the moment she sees you, you are to be con-
gratulated. By no means must you reproach her. She has merely
been overwhelmed by the absolute reliability she senses in you.

Fuji from the window of an apartment in Tokyo is a painful
sight. In winter it's quite clear and distinct. That small white

triangle poking up over the horizon: that's Fuji. It's nothing; it's a Christmas candy. What's more, it lists pathetically to the left, like a battleship slowly beginning to founder. It was during the winter three years ago that a certain person caught me off guard with a shocking confession. I was at my wit's end. That night I sat alone in one room of my apartment, guzzling saké. I drank all night, without sleeping a wink. At dawn I went to relieve myself, and through the wire mesh screen covering the square window in the toilet I could see Fuji. Small, pure white, leaning slightly to the left: that's one Fuji I'll never forget. On the asphalt street below the window, a fishmonger sped by on his bicycle, muttering to himself ("You can sure see Fuji good this morning . . . Damn, it's cold . . ."), and I stood in the dark little room, stroking the mesh screen and weeping with despair. That's an experience the like of which I hope never to go through again.

In the early autumn of 1938, determined to rethink my life, I packed a single small valise and set out on a journey.

Kōshū. What distinguishes the mountains here is their gentle and strangely aimless rise and fall. A man named Kojima Usui once wrote, in *The Landscape of Japan*, that "to these mountains come many cross-grained, self-willed sorts to disport themselves like wizard monks." As mountains go, these are, perhaps, freaks. I boarded a bus in Kōfu City and arrived, after a bone-shaking, hour-long ride, at Misaka Pass.

Misaka Pass: one thousand three hundred meters above sea level. At the top of the pass is Tenka Chaya, a small teahouse, in a room on the second floor of which my mentor Ibuse Masuji had been holed up writing since early summer. I'd come with the knowledge that I'd find him here. Provided it wouldn't be a hindrance to his work, I, too, intended to rent a room in the teahouse and do a bit of disporting amid those mountains.

Mr. Ibuse was hard at work. I received his permission and settled in, and spent each day from then on, like it or not, face to face with Fuji. This pass, once a strategic point on the road to Kamakura that connected Kōfu with the Tōkaidō Highway, offers a prospect of the northern slope that has been counted as one of the Three Great Views of Mount Fuji since ancient times. Far from being pleased with the view, however, I found myself holding it in contempt. It's too perfect. You have Fuji right before you and, lying at its feet, the cold, white expanse of Lake Kawaguchi cradled by hushed, huddling mountains on either side. One look threw me into blushing confusion. It was a wall painting in a public bath. Scenery on a stage. So precisely made to order it was mortifying to behold.

On a sunny afternoon two or three days after I'd arrived, when Mr. Ibuse had caught up on his work somewhat, we hiked up to Mitsu Pass together. Mitsu Pass: one thousand seven hundred meters above sea level. A bit higher than Misaka Pass. You reach the top after climbing a steep slope, more or less on all fours, for about an hour. Parting the ivies and vines as I half crawled toward the summit, I presented a spectacle that was far from lovely. Mr. Ibuse was in proper hiking clothes and cut a jaunty figure, but I, having no such gear, was clad in a *dotera*—a square-cut, padded cotton kimono—that the teahouse had provided me with. It was too short and left a stretch of hairy shin exposed on either leg. I was also wearing a pair of thick, rubber-soled workshoes lent me by an old man at the teahouse, and was acutely aware of how shabby I looked. I'd made a few adjustments, securing the dotera with a narrow, manly sash and donning a straw hat I'd found hanging on the wall, but the only result was that I looked even more bizarre. I'll never forget how Mr. Ibuse, a person who would never stoop to belittling someone's appearance, eyed me with a compassionate air and tried to console me by muttering something about it not becoming a man, after all, to concern himself very much with fashion.

At any rate, we eventually reached the top, but no sooner had we done so than a thick fog rolled over us, and even standing on the observation platform at the edge of the cliff provided us with no view whatsoever. We couldn't see a thing. Enveloped in that dense fog, Mr. Ibuse sat down on a rock, puffed slowly at a cigarette, and broke wind. He looked decidedly out of sorts. On the observation platform were three somber little teahouses. We chose one that was run by an elderly couple and had a cup of hot green tea. The old woman felt sorry for us and said what a stroke of bad luck the fog was, that it would surely clear before long, that normally you could see Fuji right there, looming up before you, plain as day. She then retrieved a large photograph of the mountain from the interior of the teahouse and carried it to the edge of the cliff, held it high in both hands, and earnestly explained that you could generally see Fuji just here, just like this, this big and this clear. We sipped at the coarse tea, admiring the photo and laughing. That was a fine Fuji indeed. We ended up not even regretting the impenetrable fog.

It was, I believe, two days later that Mr. Ibuse left Misaka Pass, and I accompanied him as far as Kōfu. In Kōfu I was to be introduced to a certain young lady whom Mr. Ibuse had suggested I marry. Mr. Ibuse was dressed casually, in his hiking clothes. I wore a kimono and a thin summer coat secured with my narrow sash. He led me to the young lady's house on the outskirts of the city. A profusion of roses grew in the garden. The young lady's mother showed us into the parlor, where we exchanged greetings, and after a while the young lady came in. I didn't look at her face. Mr. Ibuse and the mother were carrying on a desultory, grown-up conversation when, suddenly, he fixed his eye on the wall above and behind me and muttered, "Ah, Fuji." I twisted around and looked up at the wall. Hanging there was a framed aerial photograph of the great crater atop the mountain. It resembled a pure white waterlily. After studying the photo, I slowly twisted back to my original position and glanced fleetingly at the girl. That did it. I made up my mind then and there that, though it might entail a certain amount of difficulty, I wanted to marry this person. That was a Fuji I was grateful for.

Mr. Ibuse returned to Tokyo that day, and I went back to Misaka Pass. Throughout September, October, and the first fifteen days of November I stayed on the second floor of the teahouse, pushing ahead with my work a little at a time and trying to come to terms with that Great View of Fuji until it all but did me in.

I had a good laugh one day. A friend of mine, a member of "The Japan Romantics" who was then lecturing at a university or something, dropped by the teahouse during a hiking excursion, and the two of us stepped into the corridor on the second floor to smoke and poke fun at the view of Fuji we had through the windows there.

"Awfully, crass, isn't it? It's like, 'Ah, Honorable Mount Fuji.' "

"I know. It's embarrassing to look at."

"Say, what's that?" my friend said suddenly, gesturing with his chin. "That fellow dressed up like a monk."

A small man of about fifty, wearing a ragged black robe and dragging a long staff, was climbing toward the pass, turning time and again to gaze up at Fuji.

"It reminds you of that painting, *Priest Saigyō Admiring Mount Fuji*, doesn't it?" I said. "The fellow has a lot of style." To me the monk seemed a poignant evocation of the past. "He might be some great saint or something."

"Don't be absurd," my friend said with cold detachment. "He's a common beggar."

"No, no. There's something special about him. Look how he walks—he's got style, I tell you. You know, they say the priest Nōin used to write poems praising Fuji right here on this pass, and—"

I was interrupted by my friend's laughter. "Ha! Look at that. You call that 'having style'?"

Hachi, my hosts' pet dog, had begun to bark at Nōin, throwing him into a panic. The scene that ensued was painfully ludicrous.

"I guess you're right," I said, crestfallen.

The beggar's panic increased until he began to flounder disgracefully about, threw away his staff, and finally ran for dear

life. It was true, he had no style at all. Our priest was as crass as his
Fuji, we decided, and even now, thinking back on that scene, it
strikes me as laughably absurd.

A courteous and affable young man of twenty-five named Nitta
came to visit me at the teahouse. He worked in the post office in
Yoshida, a long, narrow town that lies at the base of the mountains
below the pass, and said he'd learned where I was by seeing mail addressed to me. After we'd talked in my room for a while and had
begun to feel at ease with each other, he smiled and said, "Actually, I was going to come with two or three of my friends, but at
the last moment they all pulled out, and, well, I read something by
Satō Haruo-*sensei* that said you were terribly decadent, and mental-
ly disturbed to boot, so I could hardly force them to come. I had no
idea you'd be such a serious and personable gentleman. Next time
I'll bring them. If it's all right with you, of course."

"It's all right, sure." I forced a smile. "But let me get this
straight. You came here on a sort of reconnaissance mission on
behalf of your friends, summoning up every ounce of courage you
could muster, is that it?"

"A one-man suicide corps," Nitta candidly replied. "I read Satō-
sensei's piece again last night and resigned myself to various possible fates."

I was looking at Fuji through the window. Fuji stood there impassive and silent. I was impressed.

"Not bad, eh? There's something to be said for Fuji after all. It
knows what it's doing." It occurred to me that I was no match for
Fuji. I was ashamed of my own fickle, constantly shifting feelings
of love and hatred. Fuji was impressive. Fuji knew what it was doing.

"It knows what it's doing?" Nitta seemed to find my words odd.
He smiled sagaciously.

Whenever Nitta came to visit me from then on, he brought
various other youths with him. They were all quiet types. They
called me "*Sensei*," and I accepted that with a straight face. I have

nothing worth boasting about. No learning to speak of. No talent. My body's a mess, my heart impoverished. Only the fact that I've known suffering, enough suffering to feel qualified to let these youths call me *"Sensei"* without protesting—that's all I have, the only straw of pride I can cling to. But it's one I'll never let go of. A lot of people have written me off as a spoiled, selfish child, but how many really know how I've suffered inside?

Nitta and a youth named Tanabe, who was skilled at composing *tanka* poems, were readers of Mr. Ibuse's work, and perhaps because of this they were the ones I felt most comfortable with and became closest to. They took me to Yoshida once. It was an appallingly long and narrow town, dominated by the mountains that loomed above. Cut off from the sun and wind by Fuji, it was dark and chilly and not unlike the meandering, spindly stem of a light-starved plant. Streams flowed alongside the streets. This is characteristic, apparently, of towns at the foot of mountains; in Mishima, too, steadily flowing streams are everywhere, and people there sincerely believe that the water comes from the snows melting on Fuji. Yoshida's streams are shallower and narrower than those in Mishima, and the water is dirtier. I was looking down at one of them as I spoke:

"There's a story by Maupassant about a maiden somewhere who swims across a river each night to meet some young scion of the nobility, but I wonder what she did about her clothes. Surely she wouldn't have gone to meet him in the nude?"

"No, surely not." The young men thought it over. "Maybe she had a bathing suit."

"Do you suppose she might've piled her clothes on top of her head and tied them down before she started swimming?"

The youths laughed.

"Or maybe she swam in her clothes, and when she met the scion she'd be soaking wet, and they'd sit by the stove till she dried. But then what would she do on the way back? She'd have to get the clothes all wet again swimming home. I worry about her. I don't see why the young nobleman doesn't do the swimming. A man can swim in just a pair of shorts without looking too ridiculous. Do you suppose the scion was one of those people who swim like a stone?"

"No," Nitta said earnestly. "I think it was just that the maiden was more in love than he was."

"You may be right. The maidens in foreign stories are cute like that—very daring. I mean, if they love somebody, they'll even swim across a river to meet him. You won't see that in Japan. Just think of . . . what was the title of that play? In the middle there's a river, and on one bank stands a man and on the other a princess, and they spend the whole play weeping and moaning. There's no need for the princess to carry on like that. Why doesn't she just swim to the other side? When you see it on stage, it's a very narrow river—she could probably wade across. All that crying is pointless. She won't get any sympathy from me. Now, in the *Asagao Diary* it's the Ōi River—that's a big river, and Asagao is blind, so you feel for her to some extent, but, even so, it's not as if it'd be impossible for her to swim across. Hanging on to some piling beside the river, ranting and blaming it all on the sun—what good is that going to do? Ah, wait a minute. There was one daring maiden in Japan. She was something. You know who I mean?"

"Who?" The young men's eyes lit up.

"Lady Kiyo. She swam the Hidaka River, chasing after the monk Anchin. Swam like hell. She was something, I tell you, and according to a book I read she was only fourteen at the time."

We walked along the road chattering drivel like this until we came to a quiet old inn on the outskirts of town that was run by an acquaintance of Tanabe's.

We drank there, and Fuji was good that night. At about ten o'clock, the youths left me at the inn and returned to their homes. Rather than going to sleep, I walked outside in my dotera. The moon was astonishingly bright. Fuji was good. Bathed in moonlight, it was a nearly translucent blue, and I felt as if I'd fallen under the spell of a sorcerer fox. Such a sparkling, vivid blue. Like phosphorus burning. Will-o'-the-wisp. Foxfire. Fireflies. Eulalia. Kuzu-no-Ha, the white fox in human form. I followed the road, walking a perfectly straight line, though I could have sworn I had no legs. There was only the sound of my *geta* clogs—a sound that had nothing to do with me but was, rather, like a separate living thing—reverberating with exceptional clarity: *clatter, clop, clatter, clop*. Stealthily I turned to look back. Fuji was there, burning blue and floating in space. I sighed. A valiant Meiji Royalist. Kurama Tengu. That's how I saw myself. I rather cockily folded my arms and marched on, convinced I was an awfully dashing fellow. I walked quite a long way. I lost my coin purse. It held about twenty silver fifty-sen pieces—it was heavy and must have slipped from the folds of my dotera. I was strangely indifferent. If my money was gone, all I had to do was walk to Misaka Pass. I kept walking. At some point, though, it occurred to me that if I retraced my steps I'd find my purse. Arms folded, I ambled back the way I'd come. Fuji. The Meiji Royalist. A lost coin purse. It all made, I thought, for a fascinating romance. My purse lay glittering in the middle of the road. Of course; where else would it be? I picked it up, returned to the inn, and went to bed.

I'd been bewitched by Fuji that night, transformed into a simpleton, a mooncalf, completely without a will of my own. Even now, recalling it all leaves me feeling peculiarly weary and languid.

I stayed in Yoshida just one night. When I got back to Misaka Pass, the woman who ran the place was all knowing smiles, and her fifteen-year-old sister was standoffish. I found myself wanting to assure them I'd been up to nothing naughty, and, though they asked me no questions, I related in detail my experiences of the previous day. I told them everything—the name of the inn I'd stayed at, how Yoshida's saké tasted, how Fuji looked in the moonlight, how I'd dropped my purse. The little sister seemed appeased.

"Get up and look, sir!" One morning not long afterwards, this same girl stood outside the teahouse shouting up to me in a shrill voice, and I grudgingly got up and stepped out into the corridor.

Her cheeks were flushed with excitement. She said nothing, only pointed toward the sky. I looked, and—ah!—snow. Snow had fallen on Fuji. The summit was a pure and radiant white. Not even the Fuji from Misaka Pass is to be scoffed at, I thought.

"Looks good," I said.

"Isn't it superb?" she said, triumphantly selecting a better word. She squatted down on her heels and said, "Do you still think Misaka's Fuji is hopeless?"

I'd often lectured the girl to the effect that this Fuji was hopelessly vulgar, and perhaps she'd taken it more to heart than I'd realized.

"Let's face it," I said, amending my teaching with a grave countenance. "Fuji is just no good without snow."

In my dotera I walked about the mountainside filling both my hands with evening primrose seeds, which I brought back to the teahouse and scattered in the back yard.

"Now, listen," I said to the girl, "these are *my* evening primroses, and I'm coming back next year to see them, so I don't want you throwing out your laundry water and whatnot here." She nodded.

I'd chosen this particular flower because a certain incident had convinced me that Fuji goes well with evening primroses. The teahouse at Misaka Pass is what one might call remote, so much so that mail isn't even delivered there. Thirty minutes' bouncing and swaying on a bus brings you to the foot of the pass and Kawaguchi, a poor little village if ever there was one, on the shore of the lake; it was at the post office here that my mail was held for me, and once every three days or so I had to make the journey to pick it up. I tried to choose days when the weather was good. The girl conductors on the buses don't offer the sightseers aboard much in the way of information about the scenery. But once in a while, almost as an afterthought, in listless near-mumble, one of them will come out with something dreadfully prosaic like: "That's Mitsu Pass; over there is Lake Kawaguchi; fresh-water smelt inhabit the lake."

Having claimed my mail one day, I was riding the bus back to Misaka Pass, sitting next to a woman of about sixty who wore a dark brown coat over her kimono, whose face was pale and nicely featured, and who looked a lot like my mother, when the girl conductor suddenly said, as if it had just occurred to her, "Ladies and gentlemen, you can certainly see Fuji clearly today, can't you?"— words that could be construed as neither information nor spontaneous exclamation. All the passengers—among them young salaried workers with rucksacks, and silk-clad geisha types with hair piled high in the traditional style and handkerchiefs pressed fastidiously to their lips—simultaneously twisted in their seats and craned their necks to gaze out the windows at that commonplace triangle of a mountain as if seeing it for the first time and to ooh and ah like idiots, briefly filling the bus with a buzzing commotion. Unlike all the other passengers, however, the elderly person next to me, looking as though she harbored some deep anguish in her heart, didn't so much as glance at Fuji, but stared out the opposite window at the cliff that bordered the road. Observing this, I felt a sense of almost benumbing pleasure and a desire to show her that I, too, in my refined, nihilistic way, had no interest in ogling some vulgar mountain like Fuji, and that, though she wasn't asking me to, I sympathized with her and well understood her suffering and misery. As if hoping to receive the old woman's motherly affection and approval, I quietly sidled closer and sat gazing vacantly out at the cliff with her.

Perhaps she felt somehow at ease with me. "Ah! Evening primroses," she said absently, pointing a slender finger at a spot beside the road. The bus passed quickly on, but the petals of the single golden evening primrose I'd glimpsed remained vivid in my mind.

Facing up admirably to all 3,778 meters of Mount Fuji, not wavering in the least, erect and heroic—I feel almost tempted to say Herculean—that evening primrose was good. Fuji goes well with evening primroses.

Mid-October came and went, and I was still making very little progress with my work. I missed people. Sunset brought scarlet-rimmed clouds with undersides like the bellies of geese, and I stood alone in the corridor on the second floor smoking cigarettes, intentionally not looking at Fuji, my eyes fixed instead on the autumn leaves of the mountain forests, crimson as dripping blood. I called to the proprietress of the teahouse, who was sweeping up fallen leaves in front.

"Good weather tomorrow, Missus!"

Even I was surprised by the shrillness of my voice; it sounded almost like a cry of joy. She rested her hands on the broom a moment and looked up at me dubiously, knitting her brow.

"Did you have something special planned for tomorrow?"

She had me there.

"No. Nothing."

She laughed. "You must be getting lonesome. Why don't you go mountain climbing or something?"

"Climb a mountain and you just have to come right back down again. It's so pointless. And whatever mountain you climb, what is there to see but the same old Mount Fuji? The heart grows heavy just thinking about it."

I suppose it was a strange thing to say. The proprietress merely nodded ambiguously and carried on sweeping the fallen leaves.

Before going to sleep I would quietly open the curtains in my room and look through the glass at Fuji. On moonlit nights it was a pale, bluish white, standing there like the spirit of the rivers and lakes. I'd sigh. Ah, I can see Fuji. How big the stars are. Fine weather tomorrow, no doubt. These were the only glimmerings I had of the joy of being alive, and after quietly closing the curtains again I'd go to bed and reflect that, yes, the weather would be fine tomorrow—but so what? What did that have to do with me? It would strike me as so absurd that I'd end up chuckling wryly to myself as I lay in my futon.

It was excruciating. My work . . . Not so much the torment of purely dragging pen over paper (not that at all, in fact, since the writing itself is actually something I take pleasure in), but the interminable wavering and agonizing over my view of the world, and what we call art, and the literature of tomorrow, the search for something new, if you will—questions like these left me quite literally writhing in anguish.

To take what is simple and natural—and therefore succinct and lucid—to snatch hold of that and transfer it directly to paper, was, it seemed to me, everything, and that thought sometimes allowed me to see the figure of Fuji in a different light. Perhaps, I would think, that shape was in fact a manifestation of the beauty of what I like to think of as "elemental expression." Thus I'd find myself on the verge of coming to an understanding with this Fuji, only to reflect that, no, there was something about it, something in its exceedingly cylindrical simplicity that was too much for me, that if this Fuji was worthy of praise, then so were figurines of the Laughing Buddha—and I find figurines of the Laughing Buddha insufferable, certainly not what anyone could call expressive. And the figure of this Fuji, too, was somehow mistaken, somehow wrong, I would think, and once again I'd be back where I started, confused.

Mornings and evenings gazing at Fuji: that's how I spent the cheerless days. In late October, a group of prostitutes from Yoshida, on what, for all I knew, may have been their only day of freedom in the year, arrived at Misaka Pass in five automobiles. I watched them from the second floor. In a flurry of colors, the girls fluttered out of the cars like carrier pigeons dumped out of baskets, and, not knowing at first in which direction to head, flocked together, fidgeting and jostling one another in silence, until at last their curious nervousness began to dissipate, and one by one they wandered off their separate ways. Some meekly chose picture postcards from a rack at the front of the teahouse; others stood gazing at Fuji. It was a dismal and all but unwatchable scene. Though I, a solitary man on the second floor, might feel for those girls to the extent that I'd be willing to die for them, there was nothing I could offer them in the way of happiness. All I could do was look helplessly on. Those who suffer shall suffer. Those who fall shall fall. It had nothing to do with me, it was just the way the world was. Thus I forced myself to affect indifference as I gazed down at them, but it was still more than a little painful.

Let's appeal to Fuji. The idea came to me suddenly. Hey, look out for these girls, will you? Inwardly muttering the words, I turned my gaze toward the mountain, standing tall and impassive against the wintry sky and looking for all the world like the Big Boss, squared off in an arrogant pose, arms folded. Greatly relieved, I forsook the band of courtesans and set out in a lighthearted mood for the tunnel down the road with the six-year-old boy from the teahouse and the shaggy dog, Hachi. Near the entrance to the tunnel, a skinny prostitute of about thirty stood by herself silently gathering a bouquet of some dreary sort of wildflowers. She didn't so much as turn to glance at us as we passed but continued picking the flowers intently. Look after this one, too, I prayed, casting an eye back at Fuji and pulling the little boy along by his hand as I walked briskly into the tunnel. Reminding myself it all had nothing to do with me, I strode resolutely on as the cold water that seeped through the ceiling dripped down on my cheeks and the back of my neck.

It was at about that time that my wedding plans met with a serious hitch. I was given to understand, in no uncertain terms, that my family back home was not going to lend their assistance. Once married, I fully intended to support my household with my writing, but I had been selfish and presumptuous enough to assume that my family would, at this juncture, come to my aid to the tune of at least a hundred yen or so, allowing me to have a dignified, if modest, wedding ceremony. After an exchange of two or three letters, however, it became clear that this would not be the case, and I was thoroughly at a loss as to what to do. Having come to terms with the fact that, as things stood, it was entirely possible that the young lady's side would call the whole thing off, I decided there was nothing for it but to make a clean breast of everything, and came down from the mountain alone to call at the house in Kōfu. I was shown into the parlor, where I sat facing the girl and her mother and told them all. At times it sounded, disconcertingly enough, as if I were reciting a speech. But I thought I at least managed to describe the situation in a relatively straightforward and honest manner.

The young lady remained calm. "Does that mean your family is opposed to the idea?" she asked, tilting her head to one side.

"No, it's not that they're opposed." I pressed softly down on the table with the palm of my right hand. "It just seems to be their way of telling me I'm on my own."

"Then there's no problem." The mother smiled graciously. "As you can see, we're not wealthy ourselves. An extravagant ceremony would only make us feel awkward. As long as you have real affection for her and you're serious about your work, that's all we ask."

Forgetting even to bow my head in reply, I gazed speechlessly out at the garden for some time. My eyes felt hot. I told myself I'd make this woman a devoted and dutiful son-in-law.

When I left, the young lady accompanied me to the bus stop. As we walked along, I said, "Well, what do you think? Shall we continue the relationship a while longer?" Sheer affectation.

"No," she said, laughing, "I've had enough."

"Aren't there any questions you want to ask me?" I said. A confirmed fool.

"Yes."

I was resolved to answer with the plain truth any question she might choose to ask.

"Has snow fallen on Mount Fuji yet?"

That threw me.

"Yes, it has. On the summit ..." My words trailed off as I glanced up and spotted Fuji before us. It gave me an odd feeling.

"What the hell? You can see Fuji from Kōfu. You trying to make a fool of me?" I was suddenly speaking like a hoodlum. "That was a stupid question. What kind of fool do you take me for?"

She looked down at the ground and giggled. "But you're staying at Misaka Pass, so I thought it wouldn't do not to ask about Fuji."

Strange girl, I thought.

When I got back from Kōfu, I found that my shoulders were so stiff I could hardly breathe.

"You know, you're lucky, Missus. Misaka Pass is a pretty good place after all. It's like coming back home."

After dinner, the proprietress and her little sister took turns pounding on my shoulders. The woman's fists were hard and penetrating, but the girl's were soft and had little effect. Harder, harder, I kept saying, until at last she got a stick of firewood and whacked on my shoulders with that. That's what it took to relieve the tension, so keyed up and intent on my purpose had I been in Kōfu.

For two or three days after that I was distracted and had little will to work; I sat at my desk and scribbled aimlessly, smoked seven or eight packs of Golden Bat cigarettes, lay around doing nothing, sang "Even a Diamond, Unpolished" to myself over and over, and didn't write so much as a page of the novel I'd been working on.

"You haven't been doing so well since you went to Kōfu, have you, sir?" One morning as I sat at the desk with my chin propped up on my hand, my eyes closed, turning all sorts of things over in my mind, the fifteen-year-old sister, who was wiping the floor in the alcove behind me, said these words with a tone of sincere regret, and a touch of bitterness.

Without turning to look at her, I said, "Is that so? I haven't been doing so well, eh?"

"No, you haven't," she said, still wiping the floor. "The last two or three days you haven't gotten any work done at all, have you? Every morning, you know, I gather up all the pages you've written and left lying around, and put them in order. I really enjoy doing that, and I'm glad when you've written a lot. I came up here last night to peek in and see how you were doing—did you know that? You were lying in your futon with the quilt pulled up over your head."

I was grateful to her for those words. This may be overstating it a bit, but to me her concern seemed the purest form of support and encouragement for one making every effort to go on living. She expected nothing in return. I thought her quite beautiful.

By the end of October, the autumn leaves had become dark and ugly, and then an overnight storm came along and left nothing behind but a bare, black, winter forest. Sightseers were few and far between now. Business dropped off, and occasionally the proprietress would go shopping in Funazu or Yoshida at the foot of the mountain, taking the six-year-old boy with her and leaving the girl and myself alone for the day in the quiet, deserted teahouse. On one such day I began to feel the tedium of sitting alone on the second floor and went outside for a stroll. I saw the girl in the back yard, washing clothes, went up to her, flashed a smile, and said, in a loud voice, "I'm so bored!" She hung her head, and when I peered at her face I got quite a start. She was nearly in tears and obviously terrified. Right, I thought, doing a grim about-face and stomping off along a narrow, leaf-covered path. I felt perfectly miserable.

I was careful from then on. Whenever the girl and I were alone in the place, I tried to stay in my room on the second floor. If a customer came, I would lumber downstairs, partially with the intention of watching out for the girl, and sit in one corner of the shop drinking tea. One day a bride, escorted by two elderly men in crested ceremonial kimono and *haori* coats, arrived in a hired automobile. The girl was alone in the shop, so I came downstairs, sat in a chair in one corner, and smoked a cigarette. The bride was decked out in full wedding regalia: long kimono with an elaborate design on the skirt, *obi* sash of gold brocade, and white wedding hood. Not knowing how to receive such singular guests, the girl, after pouring tea for the three of them, retreated to my corner as if to hide behind me and stared silently at the bride. A day that comes but once in a lifetime . . . No doubt the bride was from the other side of the mountain, on her way to be married to someone in Funazu or Yoshida, and had decided to rest at the top of the pass and gaze at Fuji. It made for a scene that, even to a casual observer, was provocatively romantic. In a little while the bride rose and quietly left the shop to stand near the edge of the cliff and take in the view at her leisure. She stood with her legs crossed—a bold pose. Awfully sure of herself, I was thinking, admiring her, Fuji and her, when suddenly she looked up at the summit and gave a great yawn.

"My!" Behind me, a small cry showed that the girl, too, had been quick to notice. Before long the bride got back in the car with her escorts and left, to scathing reviews.

"She's *used* to this, the hussy. Must be her second, no, at least her third time. The groom's down at the foot of the mountain waiting for her, no doubt, but she has them stop the car and gets out to look at Fuji. Don't tell me a woman getting married for the first time would have the nerve to do that."

"She yawned!" the girl eagerly concurred. "Stretching open that big mouth of hers . . . She ought to be ashamed of herself. Whatever you do, sir, you mustn't marry anyone like that."

It hardly befitted a man of my years, but I blushed. My own wedding plans were progressing smoothly, thanks to a certain mentor of mine who was taking care of everything. The ceremony, a dignified if meager affair with only two or three close family friends attending, was to be held at this man's house, and I, for my part, felt almost like a child inspired and encouraged by the affection of others.

Once November arrived, the cold at Misaka became hard to bear. A stove was set up downstairs.

"You must be freezing on the second floor. Why don't you work down here, beside the stove?" the lady of the house suggested, but I find it impossible to work with people watching, and declined.

She continued to worry about me, however, and one day she went to Yoshida and came back with a *kotatsu* for my room. Snuggling beneath the coverlet of that little footwarmer, I felt grateful from the bottom of my heart for the kindness of these people. But gazing at Fuji, which was already covered with two-thirds its full winter cap of snow, and the desolate trees on the nearer mountains, I began to see the meaninglessness of enduring much more of the penetrating cold at Misaka Pass and decided it was time to head for the lowlands. The day before I left, I was sitting on a chair in the shop wearing two dotera, one over the other, and sipping cheap green tea, when a pair of intellectual-looking young women in winter overcoats—typists, I guessed—approached on foot from the direction of the tunnel. Shrieking with laughter about one thing or another, they suddenly caught sight of Fuji and stopped as dead in their tracks as if they'd been shot. After consulting each other in whispers, one of them, a fair-skinned girl wearing glasses, came up to me with a smile on her face and said, "Excuse me, would you snap a photo of us, please?"

This flustered me. I'm not very good with gadgets, and I haven't the least interest in photography. What's more, I presented such a squalid figure in those two dotera that even my hosts at the teahouse had laughed and said I looked a proper mountain bandit, so I was thrown into quite a panic to be asked to perform such a fashionable act by those two gay flowers from (I presumed) Tokyo. But then, rethinking the situation, it occurred to me that even as shabbily dressed as I was, a discerning observer might easily detect in me a certain sensitivity and sophistication that would indicate at least sufficient dexterity to manipulate the shutter of a camera, and, buoyed up by this reflection, I feigned nonchalance as I took the instrument, casually asked for a brief explanation of how to work it, and peered into the view finder, inwardly all a-tremble. In the middle of the lens stood Fuji, large and imposing, and below, in the foreground, were two little poppies—or so the girls appeared in their red overcoats. They put their arms around each other and looked at the camera with sober, solemn expressions. It all struck me as very funny, and my hands shook hopelessly. Suppressing my laughter, I peered through the finder again, and the two poppies grew even more rigid and demure. I was having a difficult time aiming and finally swept the two girls out of the picture entirely, allowing Fuji, and Fuji alone, to fill the lens. Goodbye, Mount Fuji. Thanks for everything. *Click.*

"Got it."

"Thank you!" they said in unison. They'd be surprised when they got back home and had the film developed: only Fuji filling the frame, and not a trace of themselves.

The next day I came down from Misaka Pass. I stayed the first night at a cheap inn in Kōfu, and the following morning I leaned against the battered railing that ran along the corridor there, looking up at Fuji, about one-third of which was visible behind the surrounding mountains. It looked like the flower of a Chinese lantern plant.

I Can Speak

I can speak

On the following page appears an English composition
assignment that Dazai wrote in 1927. Corrections were made
by his teacher, an Englishman named G.P. Bruhl. It's
interesting that Shūji misspelled his name "Shuge," a
mistake similar to Keiji's "UMEKAWA" in "My Elder
Brothers." The essay departs considerably from the facts. It
reads (with Bruhl's corrections):

> A very brief history of his first half life. (Not biography,
> because he has still his future.)
> Shuge Tsushima, one of the most unfortunate Japanese
> boys, is the son of G. Tsushima who died five years
> ago and who had been very strict.
> G. Tsushima had many children—nine children; Shuge is
> the seventh son of them. Shuge was born on the 19th
> of June, 1909, in Aomori which is his father's native
> town.
> At his birth, he had been already given a malignant illness
> by his parents.
> As a child, he was the weakest of all children in the whole
> neighbourhood.
> In his seventh year, he was given like a mere chattel, to
> his father's sister in Mito, who had no child. His life
> during eight years which followed in Mito, was one hard
> struggle with homesickness. He was too weak to go to
> a middle school when he reached the age. He went to
> health resorts, and a year after he became healthy enough
> to go to a school.

P.–1

A very brief history of his first half life. (Not biography, because he has still his future.)

L. 1. 1.
Shuge Tsushima

Shuge Tsushima, one of the most unfortunate Japanese boys, is the son of G. Tsushima — who died five years ago, and who had been very strict.

G. Tsushima had many children — nine children; Shuge is the seventh son of them. Shuge was born on the 19th of June, 1909, in Aomori where which is his father's native town.

At his birth day, he had been already given a malignant illness by his parents.

As a child, he was the weakest of all many children in the whole neighbourhood.

In his seventh year, he was given

*About this time, his homesickness became more severe.
At last he left the Mito Middle School and escaped from
his aunt.*

*He came back to Aomori in which his childhood was
passed; but his old playfellows did not call on him. He
entered the Aomori M. School.*

*The lone sickly boy tried in vain to make friends. In
that school he was knocked about often by their inspector,
for he had become mean and crafty.*

*When he completed the course of the fourth form in
that school, he was qualified to become high school boy.*

And now he is attacked by doubtful melancholy.

But he is still young.

Now or never!

Let him march forth to his splendid future.

*Bruhl's comments: Very good, but why do you write about
yourself as "he"?? The subject concerns you alone, you should
have written in 1st person singular—"I".*

*Dazai stayed at a boardinghouse in Kōfu throughout
December, 1938, while making preparations for his marriage to
Ishihara Michiko.*

*The title of this story and the italicized words in the text are
in English in the original.*

———

Agony is the night of submission. The morning of resignation. What is life—the struggle to surrender? The endurance of misery? Thus youth is eaten by the worm, and happiness is said to be found in squalid alleyways.

My song had lost its voice. Idle in Tokyo, I had begun falteringly to write, not songs, but what you might call the grumblings of daily life, little by little learning from my own work the path my literature must follow, until at some point I thought, well, this is about the size of it, with something resembling a degree of self-confidence, and decided to start work on the novel I'd been thinking about for some time.

Last year, in September, I rented a room on the second floor of Tenka Chaya, a teahouse at the top of Misaka Pass in Kōshū, and there, little by little, I pushed ahead with my work. When I'd written nearly a hundred pages of manuscript, I read it over and found that it wasn't all that bad. Newly encouraged, I promised myself, on a day when a wild, wintry wind was blowing, not to return to Tokyo until I'd finished the novel.

It was a foolish vow. September, October, November ... the cold at Misaka Pass became hard to bear. I spent a succession of lonely, disheartened nights, vacillating over what to do. Having made that arbitrary promise to myself, I somehow had the feeling that to break it now by scurrying back to Tokyo would be a great sin. And so I remained atop the pass, thoroughly stymied. Then it occurred to me to move down to Kōfu. Kōfu was, if anything, even warmer than Tokyo. I could make it through the winter there with no problem at all.

I went. It was a great help. That odd-sounding cough cleared up. In a sunny room in a boardinghouse on the outskirts of Kōfu, sitting at my desk, I thought how glad I was that I'd come. Little by little I pushed ahead with my work.

Each afternoon, as I sat alone trying to write, I would hear a chorus of young female voices. I'd lay down my pen and listen. Across the street from the boardinghouse was a silk mill, and the girls there sang as they worked. The one who led the chorus had an extraordinary voice. A nightingale in the henhouse—that's the phrase that came to mind. What a *voice*, I'd think. I wanted to express my gratitude to her. I even thought of climbing the fence outside the mill to try to get a glimpse of the owner of that voice.

"You have no idea how your singing helps one wretched man get through each day, how heroically you have inspired me, and my work. I want to thank you from the bottom of my heart." I thought of scrawling this on a piece of paper and tossing it in through the window of the mill.

But if I did that, it might startle her. What if it made her so apprehensive that she lost her voice? That wouldn't do. It would be a crime if my gratitude had the opposite effect of muddling her pure and innocent song. Alone in my room I stewed and fretted.

Maybe it was love. On a cold and quiet night in February, from the street in front of the mill, came a sudden burst of rough, drunken words.

"D–Don't laugh at me. What's so funny? So I had a few drinks— I don't remember doin' anything to laugh about. *I can speak English.* I'm goin' to night school. Did you know that, big sister? You didn't, did ya. Mother doesn't know, either. It's a secret. See, I'm gonna be somebody. What's so funny? What the hell are you laughing for? Listen, Sis. I'm gonna be sent to the front soon. Don't be surprised when it happens. Even your drunk of a brother can do his part, y'know. No, no, not really. It's not for sure yet. But, look, *I can speak English. Can you speak English? Yes, I can.* Ah, English is good stuff, isn't it? Sis, tell me the truth, I'm a good boy, ain't I? I am, right? Mother, she don't know nothin'. . . ."

I opened the paper screen a crack and looked down at the street. At first I thought it was a plum tree in bloom. It wasn't. It was the little brother in a white raincoat.

He was standing with his back pressed flat against the fence, looking cold in the unseasonably light coat. Above the fence, a girl leaned out of a window of the mill, peering down at her drunken brother.

The moon was out, but I couldn't see either of their faces clearly. The sister's face was round and pale in the moonlight, and she seemed to be smiling. The brother had a dark complexion and appeared to be scarcely more than a child. *I can speak . . .* The force with which those drunken words hit me was almost painful. "In the beginning was the Word. . . . all things were made through Him." I felt as if the song I'd lost had come back to me. It was a trivial scene, but one I'll find difficult to forget.

Whether the girl that night was the one with the beautiful voice, I couldn't say. Probably not, I guess.

Dazai and Ishihara Michiko at their wedding at Ibuse Masuji's house,
January 8, 1939.

A Little Beauty

美少女

Bishōjo

———◆———

"Thinking back on my life till now," Dazai wrote in "Fifteen Years," a long, rambling essay published in 1946,

> *the only period when I enjoyed even a small amount of comfort and repose was when I was thirty and Mr. Ibuse helped arrange for me to marry my present wife. We rented the smallest conceivable house on the outskirts of Kōfu for six yen, fifty sen a month, and I had two hundred yen in royalties saved up. I didn't meet with anyone; each afternoon at about four o'clock I would begin leisurely drinking saké and eating boiled tofu.*

It was also an extremely productive time, during which he wrote, among other stories, "One Hundred Views of Mount Fuji," "Seascape with Figures in Gold," "No Kidding," "Canis familiaris," and "A Little Beauty."

———◆———

It's already been more than half a year since New Year's, when I rented this small house on the outskirts of Kōfu in Yamanashi and settled in to press ahead little by little with my humble work. By June, the torrid temperatures typical of summer in the Kōfu basin had begun to make their presence felt. Born and raised in the north country, I was stunned by this fierce, relentless heat that seemed to boil up from the bowels of the earth; just sitting

quietly at my desk I would have dizzy spells, the world growing
hushed and dark before my eyes. Never before in my life had I
come close to fainting simply because of the temperature.

My wife was suffering from a heat rash that covered her entire
body, and, having heard that the hot springs at Yumura Spa, just
outside the Kōfu city limits, were especially good for that sort of
thing, she'd begun to commute there each day. Our little six-and-a-
half-yen-a-month hut was on the northwest rim of Kōfu, surrounded by mulberry fields, and was only about a twenty minute
walk from Yumura. (Perhaps even less—fifteen minutes or so—if
you cut straight across the parade grounds of the 49th Regiment.)
Every morning, as soon as she'd cleared away the breakfast things,
my wife would take her bathing articles and set out for the baths.
According to her, the public spa at Yumura was very relaxed and
comfortable, and was frequented by elderly men and women from
the neighboring farming villages, none of whom, in spite of the
alleged special properties of the waters, had any skin ailments to
speak of, so that she herself took first prize in the unsightly skin
category. She said the bathhouse was done in tile and was clean
and sanitary, and though the water was not very hot, that was the
only drawback, and everyone sat in the bath for thirty minutes or
an hour, chatting about this and that, and, at any rate, it was like a
different world there, so why didn't I go along with her some time
and see for myself? Early in the morning, as you crossed the parade
grounds, you could smell the fresh grass, and your feet would get
soaked with the cold morning dew, and your heart would open up
with joy, and you felt like giggling to yourself, she said. I'd been
neglecting my work, citing the heat as a convenient excuse, and
was bored at the time, so I immediately embraced the idea of going
to have a look. At eight o'clock the next morning we set out, my
wife leading the way.

It was nothing to write home about. Not once, treading the grass
of the parade grounds, did I feel like giggling to myself. In the
garden in front of the public bath stood a rather large pomegranate

tree, its bright red flowers in full bloom. There are an awful lot of pomegranate trees in Kōfu.

The bathhouse had just recently been built; it was neat and clean and bright inside, with sparkling white tiles and plenty of sunlight. The bath itself was on the small side—about twelve square yards. Five other people were in it. When I slid in, I was astonished at how tepid the water was. It seemed scarcely warmer than tap water. I squatted down till I was up to my chin, then froze in one position. It was too cold to move. If I so much as stuck my shoulder out of the water, I felt a chill. I had to squat there as stiff and still as a dead man, forlornly reflecting on the absurd predicament I'd gotten myself into. My wife sat beside me, quietly composed, her eyes shut, looking as if she'd reached satori.

"This is awful," I grumbled. "You can't even move."

"But after about thirty minutes," she calmly replied, "you'll be dripping with perspiration. It gradually starts taking effect."

"Is that so." I resigned myself.

Unlike her, however, I could hardly sit there with my eyes closed, contemplating enlightenment, so I hugged my knees and surveyed the surroundings. There were two other family sketches in the bath. One consisted of a white-haired man of sixty or so and a woman of about fifty, both of whom possessed a certain quality of refinement and grace. They were an elegant old couple. Probably among the wealthier residents of the area. The old man had a handsome, prominent nose and wore a gold ring on his right hand. He was pink-skinned and plump and looked as if he might once have been quite the playboy. As for the woman, there was something chic about her that suggested she might not be opposed, say, to the occasional cigarette, but, at any rate, this elderly couple was not the problem. The problem lay elsewhere.

A group of three sat huddled closely together in the corner of the bath diagonally opposite me. One of them was an old fellow of about seventy with a dark, hard clump of a body and an uncannily wrinkled and shrunken face. Beside him was an old woman who looked about the same age and was small and skinny, with a chest as bumpy as a washboard. With her yellow skin and breasts like shriveled sacks of tea, she was altogether a pitiful sight to behold. Neither she nor the old man resembled anything human. They were like badgers peering warily out at the world from their cave. But crouched quietly in the water between this ancient pair, sheltered by them, was a young girl—their granddaughter, perhaps. And this one was magnificent. A pearl stuck fast in the protective embrace of two dusky, timeworn shells.

Not being the sort who can observe things out of the corner of his eye, I stared directly at this specimen. She looked about sixteen or seventeen. Possibly eighteen. Her skin was rather pale, but by no means was she sickly looking. Her firm, ample body made me think of ripening peaches. There was something in an essay by Shiga Naoya where he said that women are at their most attractive when they've just reached marriageable age and their bodies have just reached maturity. I remember reading this and thinking, phew, where'd he get the nerve to write something like that? But taking a long, hard look at this girl in all her lovely nakedness, I now realized there was nothing lecherous in Mr. Shiga's words and that here was something worthy of truly dispassionate, almost sublime, aesthetic appreciation.

The girl wore a forbidding expression. She had almond eyes and smooth, single-fold eyelids, and a thin crescent of white was visible below either iris. Her nose was unremarkable, but her lips were rather thick and turned sharply up at the corners when she smiled. There was something of the wild and untamed about her. Her fine hair was knotted at the back of her head. Crouching there in the water, enfolded by the two old folks, she seemed the picture of innocence. Though I stared directly at her for some time, she was indifferent, detached.

Gently, as if handling a priceless treasure, the old couple stroked the girl's back and massaged her shoulders. Every indication was that she was recuperating from some sort of illness. But in no sense

had it left her emaciated. Her smooth, firm skin gave her a look of
purity and cleanliness befitting a queen. Entrusting her body to
the old couple, she smiled to herself from time to time in such a
way that for a moment I actually thought she might be slightly
retarded. But when suddenly she rose to her feet, I wasn't thinking
any more: I was all eyes. It was hard to breathe for a few seconds.
The girl was well over five feet tall and of truly wonderful proportions. Just superb. Full, round breasts that might have fit snugly in
large coffee cups, taut, smooth stomach, and solid, shapely limbs.
She passed right before me, swinging her arms as she waded
through the water, without the slightest trace of embarrassment.
Her hands were small and pretty and so white as to seem nearly
translucent. Without getting out of the bath, she stretched to
reach the water faucet. Under the faucet was an aluminum cup
that she filled and drained any number of times.

"Yes, that's it, drink up, dear." The old woman cheered her on
from behind, her wrinkled mouth crumpling into a smile. "The
more you drink, the better you're going to feel."

At that point the other elderly couple chimed in with their opinion that, yes, this was certainly true, and they all smiled at one
another, and then, with no warning whatsoever, the elderly
gentleman of the gold ring turned to me and said, "You'd better
drink some, too. It's the best thing for whatever ails you," in a tone
of voice that suggested a direct order. This threw me into a dither.
What with my sunken chest and ghastly, protruding ribs, I must
certainly have looked to be someone recovering from a serious illness. Confounded as I was by the old man's command, however, I
knew it would be impolite to ignore him, so I forced a smile and
stood up. A chilly morning breeze swept over me and I shivered.
The girl wordlessly handed me the aluminum cup.

"Thanks," I said quietly, taking it and following her example by
remaining standing in the bath as I turned the faucet and mind-
lessly guzzled a cupful. It tasted of salt. Minerals in the water, no
doubt. Hardly the sort of thing I wanted to drink great quantities

of. I forced down three cupfuls, replaced the cup, and sank back down in the water up to my chin, looking, no doubt, as glum as I felt.

"I bet you feel better already," said Gold Ring triumphantly. I was at a loss for a response and unable even to force a smile. "Yes," I said, with a respectful nod.

My wife had her head down and was giggling. I, however, far from appreciating the humor of it all, was in a bit of a panic. I have the misfortune of being by nature incapable of making small talk with strangers, and I was so afraid that this elderly gentleman was going to try to engage me in conversation that I wanted only to get out of there as quickly as possible. The situation had gone beyond being absurd. I glanced at the girl, who was again nestled quietly between the protective old couple, her face raised toward the heavens and utterly expressionless. She took no notice of me whatsoever. I gave it up as hopeless and rose to my feet before the old fellow with the gold ring could try to speak to me again.

"Let's go," I whispered to my wife. "It's no warmer than it was at first." I stepped quickly out of the bath and began drying myself with a towel.

"I'll be out in a while," she said.

"Oh yeah? Well, I'm heading back."

From the dressing room where I was hurriedly putting on my kimono, I could hear the amiable chatter that now commenced in the bath. No doubt the oldsters had felt somewhat ill at ease with a queer fellow like me sitting there with my tightlipped affectation and ogling eyes; as soon as I was gone they all felt released from the awkward constraint I'd occasioned them, and the conversation began to flow. Even my wife had joined in and was now expounding on the subject of heat rash. I was a hopeless case, incapable of fitting in. Never mind me, I thought bitterly to myself, I'm just weird. As I was leaving, I glanced again at the girl. She was still sitting there, not moving a muscle, a radiant treasure watched over by her two swarthy guardians.

That girl was good. I knew I'd seen something special, and locked the memory away in a secret place in my heart.

The temperatures reached their zenith in July. Even the tatami mats were hot to the touch, and it was unbearable whether you were sitting or standing or lying down. I had a good mind to seek refuge at some spa in the mountains, but in August we were to move to a house just outside Tokyo, and since it was necessary to keep some money aside for that project, going to a summer resort was out of the question. I thought I was going to go mad. Then one day it occurred to me that a short haircut might cool and clear my head somewhat, and I set out in search of a barber shop. I wasn't going to be picky about the appearance of the place; any one I came to that wasn't full of customers would do, but the first two or three I stopped at seemed to be packed. I found a small shop on a sidestreet across from the local public bath and peeked through the window, but again there seemed to be customers waiting. I was about to retreat when the barber stuck his head out the window and said, "We can be right with you, sir. You want a haircut, right?" He had me pegged.

I smiled grimly, pushed open the door, and went inside. I hadn't particularly noticed it myself, but apparently my hair had grown disgracefully long and shaggy, and that, no doubt, was why the barber had guessed my intention though I'd done no more than glance through his window. It was embarrassing.

The barber was a waggish-looking fellow of forty or so with a close-shaved head, thick, round, black-rimmed spectacles, and protruding, puckered lips. His apprentice was a pale, skinny boy of seventeen or eighteen. I could hear two or three people talking beyond a thin curtain that separated the barber shop from a Western-style parlor, and I realized now that they were the people that, from outside, I had mistaken for customers.

When I sat in the chair, the breeze from a floor fan wafted against the hem of my kimono, and I breathed a sigh of relief. It was a neat and tidy little shop, with potted plants and goldfish bowls placed strategically about. Yes, indeed, I told myself, nothing like a haircut when the weather's hot.

"Cut it very short in the back, please." Being one who finds it difficult to speak at all to strangers, it took a great effort to say even this much. When I looked in the mirror, a vain, pretentious face glared back at me, mouth clamped shut in a queerly tense, pompous scowl. It must be a question of bad karma. What a pathetic destiny, I thought—unable even to enter a barbershop without putting on airs.

I was still peering at the mirror when my eye was caught for the first time by the reflection of a flower in the background—a girl in a blue summer dress sitting on a chair next to the window behind me. I didn't make much of this. It passed through my mind that perhaps she was the barber's assistant, or his daughter, and I gave her only a brief glance. I soon became aware, however, that every so often the girl was craning her neck to study my face in the mirror. Two or three times our eyes met. Restraining the impulse to turn around, I kept thinking I'd seen that face somewhere before. The girl, however, evidently satisfied now that I'd begun taking notice of her, no longer deigned to look at me. With an air of complete self-confidence, she sat with her elbow on the window ledge and her hand on her cheek, gazing out at the street. Cats and women—leave them alone and they'll cry for you; try to get close and they'll run away. The little bitch has instinctively mastered the art already, I was thinking in my vexation, when she languidly lifted a small bottle of milk from the table beside her and quietly drank it down.

That's when it hit me. She's been sick. It's her, it's the girl who was recuperating from something, the one with the wonderful body. Ah . . . It was the milk, that's what finally tipped me off. I felt like apologizing to her: Sorry—I'm better acquainted with your breasts than with your face. Now she was covered by a blue summer dress, but I was familiar with every nook and cranny of her superb physique, and it made me happy just to realize that. It was almost like being related by blood.

I made the blunder of smiling at the girl in the mirror. When she noticed this she not only declined to return the smile but stood up and walked slowly off toward the curtain and the parlor beyond. Her face was absolutely devoid of expression, and again I wondered if she wasn't something of an idiot. But I was satisfied. I'd gained one pretty little acquaintance. After having my hair clipped short by the man who was, presumably, the girl's father, I felt cool and refreshed and perfectly merry, and that's all there is to this naughty little tale.

With Ibuse Masuji at Shima Hot Springs in 1940. Photo by Ima Uhei.

Canis familiaris

畜犬談

Chikukendan

———————◆———————

In the afterword to a collection of stories that included "Canis familiaris," Dazai wrote that he

truly suffered over the problem of stray dogs in Kōfu. I began writing the story in perfect seriousness, in hopes of venting my fury, but, as I was writing, it gradually turned comical. It seems that when indignation goes beyond a certain point it ends up being funny. After I'd finished the story and read it over, I realized it had turned into a comedy, so I dedicated it to Ima Uhei, who was known as a master humorist in those days.

Michiko has written elsewhere:

At that time most people in Kōfu let their dogs run loose, and they were everywhere. Once when I was out walking with Dazai, he suddenly scrambled up on top of a pile of dirty, unmelted snow—about fifty centimeters high. He had sensed that a dogfight was about to begin on the street ahead of us and was seeking refuge. That's how much he feared and hated dogs. But one day he arrived home with a puppy following behind and said, "Give it an egg."

"Pochi" is a common name for dogs in Japan.

———————◆———————

I have confidence when it comes to dogs. I'm confident that eventually I'll be bitten by one. I have no doubt that one day a dog will sink its teeth into my flesh. I'm confident of it. In fact, it amazes me that I've managed to get by unscathed until now. Dogs, dear reader, are ferocious beasts. Is it not said that they've been known to bring down horses and to do battle with, and even defeat, the mighty lion? Small wonder, I say, nodding sadly to myself. Just look at those teeth. Long, sharp fangs like that are not to be scoffed at. On the street we see dogs poking their noses into garbage cans, feigning innocence and a self-effacing air, as if to show us that they're entirely unworthy of our notice, when in reality they're fierce beasts quite capable of toppling a horse. Since there's no telling when, in a fit of rage, any given dog might expose its true nature, they should all be kept securely chained down. It won't do to relax our guard for even a moment. When one sees the dog owner who, simply because it is he that supplies the table scraps, trusts the fearsome animal implicitly, calling to it in a playful voice ("Here, boy! Come on, boy!") and laughing uproariously at the sight of his beloved three-year-old child tugging the creature's ears, one can only shudder and cover one's eyes. What if the dog, with no more warning than a sharp yelp, were to suddenly take the child in its jaws? You can't be too careful with these beasts. The belief that a dog will not bite the hand that feeds it is nothing more than a sanguine, fatuous superstition. A creature with fangs like that is born to bite, and there can be no scientific proof that its owner is immune. What, then, is one to think of those who let such vicious animals run loose on the street?

In late autumn of last year, a friend of mine was added to the list of victims. It's a heartrending story. According to my friend, he was strolling along with his hands in his pockets, minding his own business, when he saw a dog sitting on the street before him. He says that the dog gave him an unsettling look out of the corner of its eye, but that, having done nothing to provoke the beast, he managed to pass by without incident. It was only after he'd passed that the dog suddenly barked and clamped on to his left leg. Instant catastrophe. My friend was stupefied at first, but before long he was choking back tears of vexation. Small wonder, I say, and nod sadly to myself. What recourse is there for a man in that situation? None whatsoever.

Dragging his wounded leg, my friend headed straight for a hospital to receive treatment. He was to commute to that hospital for the next twenty-one days. That's three weeks. Even after the wound had healed, he was obliged to receive daily injections to counteract a possible infection by the odious virus that causes rabies. To negotiate with the dog's owner for damages and so forth is not something a man as timid as my friend is capable of doing; the cost of the shots was by no means negligible, and, begging my friend's pardon, he is not the sort who has that kind of money to spare and undoubtedly had a terrible time just scraping it together. At any rate, this was a calamity of the first order. A disaster of staggering proportions. Neglect the shots for a single day and he could find himself with the ghastly disease known as hydrophobia, his face growing more and more canine in aspect as, delirious, he begins to bark and growl and crawl about on all fours. Imagine the anxiety and dread in my friend's heart as he received his injections. Being the well-adjusted man of the world he is, he underwent the ordeal of commuting to the hospital for twenty-one days—three weeks—without losing his composure and is now once again cheerfully going about his business, but if it had been me, I'm quite sure I would have seen to it that the culprit did not remain among the living. I am three or four times as vengeful as the average man and, in seeking my vengeance, can be five or six times as ruthless. I would have lost no time in pulverizing that dog's skull, gouging out its eyeballs, chewing them to a pulp and spitting them out, and, still not satisfied, would have then proceeded to poison every single dog in the neighborhood. To suddenly leap up barking and bite the leg of a perfect stranger who's minding his own business is inexcusably violent, anti-social behavior. Nor does the fact that we're talking about a dumb animal make such behavior any easier to forgive. It's because people let them get away with it, saying the poor things don't know any better, that we have a problem. Severe and merciless punishment is called for. Last fall, when I heard of my friend's disaster, my hatred for *Canis familiaris* reached an extreme; it became a consuming passion that burned like a hard, blue flame.

This January I rented a twelve-mat shack on the outskirts of Kōfu, in Yamanashi, and hid out there, plugging away at my inept stories. You see dogs wherever you go in Kōfu. The town is teeming with them. They loiter on corners, stretch out to snooze in the sun, or career recklessly through the streets and alleys; they howl and flash their fangs, gather in empty lots to hone their fighting skills by sparring and grappling, and band together at night to dash through the empty streets like gangs of desperadoes. Their numbers are so great that one wonders if there aren't at least two dogs for every household in Kōfu. Yamanashi is somewhat renowned for the *Kai* breed of dogs, but the mutts one encounters on the street are a far cry from being purebreds of any sort. Shaggy, redhaired types prevail, but they are all—every last one of them— worthless, dimwitted curs.

Being a latent dog-hater by nature, and one whose ill will toward dogs had only increased since my friend's tragedy, I was not one to be unwary in my dealings with the beasts, but with dogs swarming everywhere I went, dominating each alley and lying coiled up like snakes in every nook and cranny, mere precaution was scarcely adequate. I went through hell. I should have liked to wear a helmet, gauntlets, and shinguards whenever taking to the street. I hesitated to present such a bizarre figure in public, however, and one had also to think of civilian morale, so I was forced to come up with a different strategy. I contemplated long and hard. I have some grasp of human psychology, and have been known to predict the behavior of people with a certain degree of precision, but canine psychology is a lot more difficult. To what extent does human speech facilitate emotional interaction between man and dog? That's question number one. If words are in fact of no use whatsoever, then neither party has any choice but to read the other's gestures and expressions. Tail movement, for example, is crucial. But if you observe closely, you'll find that these movements of the tail are extremely complex and by no means easy to interpret.

I eventually lost hope with this tack altogether, and the strategy I finally chose was, I admit, bungling and inept. A pitiful, desperate grasping at straws. I decided to greet each dog I met with a beaming smile, by which I hoped to make it clear that I meant no harm. At night, when the smile might be difficult to discern, I would hum children's songs in an attempt to inform one and all that I was a man with a gentle heart. These tactics actually did seem to have some effect. As of this writing, I have yet to be attacked. But you can never be too careful. No matter how frightened I may be, I never run past a dog. I saunter slowly by with an obsequious simper, letting my head lilt gently from side to side as if I haven't a care in the world, when in fact I feel as if I'm suffocating and a dozen caterpillars are crawling up and down my spine. I despise myself for this cowardliness, mind you. I experience such self-disgust that I feel like bursting into tears. But, convinced as I am that the moment I drop the act I'll be bitten, I continue to grin pathetically at every dog I meet. Fearing that if I let my hair grow too long the dogs might regard me as suspicious and bark at me, or worse, I decided to be meticulously regular in my visits to the once-dreaded barbershop, and I abandoned my walking stick out of fear that the animals might mistake it for a weapon of aggression and leap to the offensive.

Unable to decipher canine psychology, I had been reduced to simply trying to curry the favor of every mutt that crossed my path, but I could never have predicted what was about to happen as a result. Dogs took a liking to me. As I walked down the street they would come up one by one, wagging their tails, and fall into step behind me. I gnashed my teeth in frustration. What perfect irony.

I'd have preferred the adoration of a herd of camels to that of dogs, for whom I had never felt any affection and whom I had recently come to dislike intensely. The frivolous hypothesis that to be loved is never unpleasant, however unpleasant the one who loves you, simply doesn't hold up in real life. There are times when your pride, your feelings, will not tolerate that love. It was unbearable for me.

I hate dogs. I am only too keenly aware of their true nature, the violent brutality that lurks within each and every one of them. Let a dog find someone to throw him table scraps once or twice a day and he'll turn his back on his friends, leave his wife and family, and take up residence alone under the new master's veranda, affecting a look of devotion; he'll bark and snarl at his old comrades, forget his own mother and father and sisters and brothers, and think of nothing but pleasing Master, kowtowing and bootlicking without the least sense of shame. Give him a kick and he merely skulks off with his tail between his legs, looking bewildered as the family laughs. It's not for nothing that we reserve the epithet "dog" for men of the lowest and ugliest characters. A dog, in spite of being equipped with legs strong enough to easily carry him ten leagues in a single day, and those gleaming white fangs that can deal death to a lion, has no scruples against letting his slothful, decadent nature get the better of him and, devoid of even a shred of dignity, surrenders to human domination without the slightest resistance, turning against his own kind, barking and nipping at any other dog that comes near in the hope that doing so will please his master.

Consider sparrows. Fragile, weaponless little creatures though they be, they have maintained their freedom and operate a society completely independent of humans; they are friendly to one another and spend their days in blissful poverty, singing their songs. The more I think about dogs, the more disgusting they seem. Dogs are repulsive. They remind me of myself in some ways, and that only repulses me all the more. I can't stand dogs. How, then, to describe what I felt when these very beasts decided to take a particular liking to me and began rolling up with wagging tails and lavish displays of affection? Horror? Chagrin? No, there are no words. Overawed by their savage nature, I'd been immoderately generous with my cajoling smiles, the cruel upshot of which was that the dogs thought they'd gained an admirer and immediately pegged me for a pushover. Moderation is essential in all things. Apparently I still haven't learned that.

Early spring. Before dinner I went for a walk in the direction of the parade grounds of the 49th Regiment, which was near my house, and hadn't gone far before two or three dogs fell in step behind me, and though I was in mortal fear, expecting them to begin chewing on my heels at any moment, I was by now resigned to having this sort of thing happen whenever I left the house and strolled slowly along, feigning calm indifference and suppressing the urge to flee like a scared rabbit. Behind me, the dogs began picking fights with one another, and though I pretended not to notice and deliberately refrained from looking back, I was in fact in a bit of a panic. Had I been carrying a pistol I would not have hesitated to shoot them. The dogs, however, perceiving only the bodhisattva without and not the demon within, never suspected the ill will I harbored and seemed ready to follow me anywhere. I made one complete lap around the parade grounds and headed for home with the dogs still in tow.

I'd been through this routine any number of times by now, and it was customary for the dogs to scatter and disappear as I neared my house, but on this particular day there was one distressingly tenacious and presumptuously familiar specimen who stuck with me. A jet-black, miserable-looking little puppy. Quite a tiny thing, really—the trunk of his body looked as if it might fit in the palm of my hand. But that was no reason to relax my guard. He was old enough to have all his teeth. Were he to bite me, I'd end up commuting to the hospital for three weeks. Twenty-one days. Young ones of this sort are given to caprice. They lack common sense, and one must therefore be doubly cautious. The little mutt was now beside me, now behind me, now in front, peering up at my face as he waddled along, and ended up seeing me all the way to my house.

"Hey," I called to my wife from the doorway. "This thing followed me home."

"My! Isn't he darling?"

" 'Darling' my foot. Get rid of it. Don't be too rough, though, or it'll bite you. Give it some candy or something."

Weak-kneed diplomacy. The dog instinctively detected the fear in my heart and lost no time in capitalizing upon it. The next thing I knew, he had brazenly taken up residence. Throughout March, April, May, June, July, and August he has remained at my house, and even now, with autumn in the air, he has not seen fit to leave. I can't tell you how many times this dog has brought me to grief. I just don't know what to do about him. For the sake of convenience, since he's here and won't go away, I've dubbed the beast "Pochi," but in spite of the fact that we've lived in close conjunction for half a year, I do not consider him one of the family. He is, as far as I'm concerned, an outsider. We don't get on well together. There is a decided lack of harmony. Sparks fly as we struggle to come to grips with each other's psychology. And to relax the tension with a warm, spontaneous smile is something neither of us is capable of doing.

He was still just a child when he arrived here, a comically despicable little rascal, and I must admit that there were times when, seeing him studying with a look of utter incredulity the ants that scurried over the ground or howling with fear at the sight of a toad, I burst into laughter in spite of myself and reflected that, for all I knew, his washing up on our shores may well have been the will of God. So I made a bed for him under the veranda, boiled his food until it was soft and suitable for an infant, sprinkled him with flea powder, and so on. But after a month or so, things took an ugly turn. He began to display his true nature, in all its beastly vulgarity.

This dog, I had no doubt, had been intentionally abandoned out on the far side of the parade grounds. When he entangled himself in my life that first day, he was pitifully skinny and his coat was in such bad shape that his rear end was virtually hairless. Precisely because I am the sort of man I am, I fed him sweets, prepared rice gruel for him, refrained from speaking harshly to his face, and generally treated him with the utmost civility. Anyone else would surely have given this hound the boot. Admittedly, these kindnesses of mine were inspired not by any sort of affection but, rather, by an innate hatred and dread of dogs. Be that as it may, however, it was because of me that this Pochi saw his fur restored and grew up to be a full-fledged adult male of his species. While it was never my intention to gain the dog's gratitude, still it struck me as not unreasonable to expect that he might in turn at least provide us with some small pleasure or entertainment, but apparently that was asking too much of an abandoned mutt. After gorging himself on the food I gave him, he would, perhaps with the intention of engaging in a bit of after-dinner exercise, begin chewing a perfectly good pair of clogs to pieces or lend an unwanted hand with the laundry, pulling things down from the clothesline in the garden and dragging them through the mud.

"That's not funny. I've had just about enough of these practical jokes. I don't recall anyone asking you to pull a stunt like that," I told him with no little irony one day, and though I spoke the words as gently as possible, I meant them to sting. Impervious to my sarcasm, however, the dog merely rolled his eyes about a bit and began friskily leaping up and pawing me. How infantile can you get? Though I didn't let it show, I was by now quite disgusted with the impudence of this beast and regarded him with something very close to contempt. The older he got, the more he revealed his uselessness. When he was still a puppy, he was somewhat better proportioned, and one wondered if he might not even have a touch of purebred something-or-other in him, but this proved to be sheer illusion. His torso continued to grow and stretch, but his arms and legs remained extraordinarily short, so that he came to resemble a tortoise. All in all, not a figure one could bear to gaze upon for very long.

Ugly as he was, however, he stuck to me like a shadow whenever I left the house. I have, perhaps, a bit more than my fair share of vanity, but it was no good my trying to affect cool indifference as I walked down the street when all the children I crossed paths with were pointing and laughing and making comments about "the funny-looking dog." I would try to make it seem as if the dog and I were perfect strangers by hurrying on ahead, but Pochi would stick with me, glancing continuously up at my face, now trotting in front, now falling behind, all but twining himself around me, so that there was no way anyone might have taken the two of us for strangers. The lord and his faithful vassal. Thanks to this dog, each time I now left the house it was with a darkened spirit and a heavy heart. It was good spiritual training for me, I suppose, and it wasn't all that unbearable as long as he contented himself with merely accompanying me on my walks. Worse things were to come, however, as the beast in him gradually surfaced.

He began to display a taste for fighting. While escorting me about, he took it upon himself to exchange greetings with every other dog that happened along. Greeting them, that is, by engaging them in mortal combat. Considering his age and the shortness of his legs, Pochi was surprisingly stalwart in battle. I once watched dubiously as he invaded a vacant lot claimed by five other dogs and took them all on at once. I thought he'd bitten off more than he could chew that time, but he managed somehow to dodge about with sufficient agility to avoid disaster. He was extremely overconfident and would have at it with any dog, regardless of size. When, from time to time, he found himself overpowered, he would make a slow but steady retreat, yapping and howling as he backed away. His voice would take on the quality of a scream, and you could see that beneath the jet-black fur his face had turned ghostly pale. I turned pale myself once when he attacked a German shepherd the size of a calf. As it turned out, however, there was no contest. The shepherd didn't take Pochi seriously and merely toyed with him, batting him about with its forepaws, thanks to which, of course, Pochi survived. But if you're a dog, apparently, suffering a single humiliation like that tends to strip you of your courage. After the shepherd incident, Pochi began to avoid getting into fights, which was fine with me, of course, since I do not approve of that sort of thing in the first place.

No, wait, that's not putting it strongly enough. I believe that tolerating fights between savage beasts on the public streets is a disgrace to any nation that would call itself civilized, and when I hear the deafening pandemonium of barbaric howls that accompany these battles, my rage and abhorrence are such that I feel from the bottom of my heart that death is too good for the bastards. I have no love for Pochi. I fear him and hate him, yes; but of love I feel nothing at all. I think it would be splendid if he'd just die. Trotting casually along behind me wherever I go, and then, as if he thought it his duty to me, greeting each dog we meet with that ghastly barking and howling, never once noticing that his master is literally trembling with fear—it makes me feel like jumping in a taxi, slamming the door behind me, and fleeing. It's one thing for the two dogs to have it out for themselves, but what if the other beast, whipped into a frenzy by the smell of blood, were to suddenly leap at Pochi's master? Don't tell me it couldn't happen. We're talking about bloodthirsty carnivores here. There's no telling what they might do. Should those horrible fangs pierce my flesh, I would be three weeks—twenty-one days—commuting to the hospital. Dogfights are hell. I warned Pochi any number of times.

"You are not to fight. If you simply must fight, do it far away from me. I'm not on your side. I don't even like you."

Pochi actually seemed to understand this to some extent, and looked a bit dejected whenever I brought the subject up. It was downright creepy. At any rate, whether my repeated admonitions had that effect or whether it was a result of his humiliating defeat at the hands of the shepherd, Pochi gradually turned effete and cowardly to the point of cravenness. If another dog barked at him when we were out walking, Pochi, straining every nerve to appear cultured and genteel in his master's eyes, would shudder and cast a sidelong glance of condescending pity at the other animal as if to say, "Oh, dear, how beastly," all but shaking his head and clucking his tongue, and finally look up at me with a prissy, sycophantic smile. It was the most disgusting thing I've ever seen.

"This animal doesn't have a single redeeming quality," I told my wife. "Now he won't make a move without first studying my face."

"It's because you won't leave him alone." My wife had been indifferent to Pochi from the start. She would grumble a bit whenever he pulled stunts like dragging the laundry through the mud, but afterwards she would do a complete turnabout, melodiously calling his name as she dished out his food. "Maybe his personality is beginning to disintegrate," she said, laughing.

"Oh. Just like his master, is that what you're trying to say?" My loathing for Pochi was growing by leaps and bounds.

In early July there was a change in the scenario. We had finally found a small house under construction in Mitaka, Tokyo, and had signed a contract with the owner to rent it for twenty-four yen a month, beginning as soon as construction was completed. The owner was to notify us by special delivery mail when the house was finished, and we began to prepare for the move. It goes without saying that Pochi was to be left behind.

"We might just as well take him with us." My wife didn't really care one way or the other. The Pochi problem was not high on her list.

"Out of the question. I didn't take the dog in because I think he's cute. I'm letting him stay here only because I'm afraid he'll try to get revenge if I kick him out. Don't you understand that?"

"Then why is it that whenever he's out of your sight for a moment you start raising such a fuss? 'Where's Pochi? Where's Pochi?'"

"Because it's even spookier when he's not around. How do I know he's not out with his comrades hatching some evil plot behind my back? He knows I hold him in contempt. Dogs are extremely vindictive animals, you know."

Now was my chance. All we'd have to do is leave the dog here, pretending he'd completely slipped our minds, hop on the train, and head for Tokyo. He wasn't likely to cross Sasagoto Pass and chase us all the way to Mitaka. We weren't going to abandon him. We were just going to forget to take him with us. That's no crime. And no reason for Pochi to bear a grudge. You can't take revenge on someone unless you've got a grudge.

"He'll be all right, don't you think? He's not going to starve to death or anything, right? There is such a thing as a curse from beyond the grave, you know."

Now even my wife looked a bit uneasy. "After all, he was an abandoned dog in the first place," she said.

"That's right. Hell, he won't starve. He'll figure out something. I can't take a dog like this back to Tokyo. Think how embarrassed I'd be in front of my friends. I mean, look at him. Look how long his body is. It's grotesque."

So it was settled: Pochi was to remain behind. Just at this point, however, the plot thickened again. Pochi developed a skin condition. A major skin condition. One hesitates to even attempt to describe it; it was a spectacle that could have made a strong man turn away in disgust. And as the heat grew more sweltering with each passing day, Pochi began to emit an odor that was not to be ignored. Now it was my wife who was ready to say uncle. At times like this, women are even more ruthless and daring than men.

"Think of the nuisance to the neighbors," she said. "You'd better kill him."

"Kill him?" I was shocked. "It's only a question of a few more days."

We prayed for the landlord's letter to come. He had said the house ought to be finished by late July, but July was now nearly over. We stood by each day with our things packed, expecting the letter at any moment, but it kept not coming. Just about the time I'd begun sending inquiries to the landlord, Pochi's skin condition came into full bloom. It was positively harrowing to behold. Pochi, too, seemed well aware of what a sorry sight he was, and began to show a preference for dark, shady places. When I found him, on occasion, stretched out in the sun on the front steps, I had only to disparage his appearance with a heartfelt "God, what a mess!" and he would immediately scramble to his feet, slink off with drooping head, and disappear beneath the veranda.

Still, whenever I left the house, he would tiptoe out and try to follow me. I wasn't about to be tailed by such a monstrous-looking creature, however, and would stop and stare at him, curling my lip in an unmistakable sneer. This worked extremely well. Pochi would seem suddenly to remember what a frightful sight he was, hang his head dolefully, and shamble back to his hiding place.

My wife, too, would now bring the Pochi problem up for discussion from time to time. "I just can't stand it any more," she'd say. "Even I'm beginning to feel itchy. I try not to look at him, but sometimes you can't help it. One little glance and it's all over. I've even started to see him in my dreams."

"It won't be long now." I figured we had no choice but to endure. Sick or not, he was still a potentially ferocious animal. Make the wrong move and he'd rip off a chunk of your flesh. "We'll probably hear from Mitaka in a day or two. Once we've moved, that's the end of it."

Finally we got a letter from the landlord. My heart sank when I read it, however. Because of the prolonged rain and a shortage of workers, it said, the house wouldn't be finished for another ten days or so. I was utterly dejected. I wanted to move as soon as possible, if only to rid myself of Pochi. I became so fretful and jittery that I couldn't get any work done and spent all my time drinking saké and reading magazines. Pochi's skin condition got more horrible with each passing day, and I, too, began getting itches here and there. I don't know how many times, late at night, I shuddered at the sound of Pochi scratching and writhing in misery outside. It was altogether too much for me. Often, in a spasm of frenzy, I thought I'd just do what had to be done and have done with it. When we got a second letter from the landlord asking us to wait another twenty days, all my jumbled feelings of anger and resentment focused at once on Pochi: I began to feel that he was the cause of all my troubles, that it was because of him that nothing seemed to proceed smoothly. Then one night I found my *yukata* infested with fleas, and that was the last straw. The rage I'd suppressed so long exploded, and I came to a monumental decision.

I decided to kill him. Under normal circumstances I would never have dreamed of such a violent course of action, particularly against a fearsome beast, but what with the intense summer heat and the boredom and frustration of doing nothing each day but wait for word from the landlord, combined with bouts of insomnia, I'd been driven to a state of agitated distraction. I cracked. When I discovered Pochi's fleas in my *yukata* that night, I immediately sent my wife out to buy a large slice of beef while I went to the pharmacy for a small quantity of a certain chemical concoction. That was all the preparation necessary. My wife was more than a little excited. We bent our heads together that night, the ruthless ogre and his spouse, conferring in whispered tones.

I got up at four the next morning. I had set the alarm, but was awake before it went off. The night sky was growing pale with the first light of dawn. The air was almost chilly. Carrying the goods in a bamboo sheath, I stepped outside.

"When you've done it, come right back." My wife stood on the front step calmly seeing me off. "You don't have to wait around till the end."

"Right. Here, Pochi!"

Pochi came out from under the veranda, wagging his tail.

"Come on!" I walked briskly off. Since I'd spared him the usual contemptuous glare, Pochi forgot his shame and trotted cheerfully along behind me. There was a thick fog. The town was asleep, the streets hushed. I hurried toward the parade grounds. On the way, we met up with a frightfully large, red-haired dog who began to bark ferociously at Pochi. Pochi put on his high-toned act, merely giving the animal a disdainful glance as if to say, "What *are* you carrying on about?" and passing quickly by with his nose in the air. The redhair, however, was a dastardly sort. Without any justification whatsoever, he attacked from behind, diving straight for Pochi's sad little testicles. Pochi spun about to face his attacker, but then hesitated and peeked up at me.

"Sic him!" I shouted. "He's a craven sneak! Tear him apart!"

Having received my permission, Pochi gave a mighty shudder and leaped like a rifle shot at the redhair's throat. Thus began a tumultuous battle, the two of them bouncing and spinning about like a single, whirling ball of fur. Though the redhair was twice Pochi's size, he was hopelessly outmatched, and it wasn't long before he beat a hasty retreat, whining and whimpering. He may have caught Pochi's skin disease as well. What a fool.

I was tremendously relieved when the fight was over. I'm not exaggerating when I say I'd watched with sweaty palms. It even seemed to me at one point that I was going to get entangled in the battle and probably wind up dead. It wouldn't have mattered, though, if I'd been torn to pieces. My only real concern was that Pochi fight his heart out, and I cheered him on with a strange intensity. Pochi chased the fleeing redhair a short distance, then stopped and glanced back at me, suddenly dispirited. He hung his head and slinked guiltily back to my side.

"Good boy! You showed him!" I said, and walked on. We clattered across a bridge and there we were, at the parade grounds.

I'd chosen this spot because this was where Pochi had first been abandoned. I was taking him back to his home to die.

I came to a halt and let the large slice of meat drop to the ground.

"Eat, Pochi." Not wanting to watch, I stood gazing off into the distance as I listened to him gobbling the meat. He would be dead within sixty seconds.

With shoulders hunched, I began to walk slowly away. The fog was still thick. Even the nearby mountains were only vague, dark shapes, and I couldn't make out the peaks of the Southern Japan Alps, or Fuji, at all. My clogs were soaked with dew. I hunched my shoulders even more. When I'd crossed the bridge and got as far as the middle school near my house, I turned and glanced back, and there stood Pochi. He avoided my gaze, looking ashamed of himself and hanging his head.

I'm a grown man. I felt not the slightest gush of sentimentality. Instantly I perceived what had happened. The poison hadn't worked. I nodded and told myself were back to a clean slate.

"It's no good. The stuff didn't work," I told my wife when I reached the house. "Let it go. He isn't guilty of any crime. Artists are supposed to be on the side of the underdog." I'd done some thinking as I walked home. "The artist is a friend to the weak. That's his first motivation and his ultimate goal. It's a plain, simple truth, but it's something I'd forgotten. And it's not just me. Everybody's forgotten that. I intend to take Pochi to Tokyo. If any of my friends make fun of the way he looks, I'll give them a good thrashing. Have we got any eggs?"

"Yes." My wife wore a sour expression.

"Give one to Pochi. If you've got two, give him two. You're just going to have to be patient. His skin will clear up soon enough."

"Of course," she said, still with the same sour look on her face.

Dazai in a formal kimono, with *hakama* trousers, *haori* coat, dark *tabi* socks, and *geta* clogs. In Mitaka, 1942.

Thinking of Zenzō

善蔵を思う

Zenzō o omou

———◆———

Kasai Zenzō (1887–1928) was a writer from Hirosaki, the town in Tsugaru where Dazai attended higher school. Dazai seemed to feel a special affinity with Zenzō—an impoverished and sickly man who sacrificed everything for his art and found it impossible to remain in Tsugaru. Kon Kan'ichi, the model for "Kōno Kaichi" in this story, later wrote an essay in which he says "Zenzō was clearly not very well thought of among the folks in his home town.... No one even seemed to be willing to associate with him." Kon also describes Dazai's behavior at the "Hometown Autumn" gathering as being pretty much as described in the story. Michiko backs this up in another essay:

> *Many of the things Dazai wrote seem to me to have been gross exaggerations or pure inventions that give the impression of being true, but the circumstances of the gathering of Tsugaru artists appear to have been more or less as depicted in "Thinking of Zenzō".... I remember him coming home by rickshaw that night and telling me how he'd blundered. The part about the rose-seller, too, is about fifty percent the truth as I witnessed it.*

———◆———

*J*ust speak your mind. Say what you have to say, without trying to cover anything up. No more jokes or silly grins. For once in your life, tell the truth.

—If I were to do as you suggest, I'd have to spend time in jail again. I'd have to leap into the sea again. I'd have to become a madman again. You wouldn't run away if that happened? Yes, I'm forever telling lies. But you are one person I've never deceived. You've never had any trouble seeing through my lies, have you? As for truly diabolical liars, there may be one or two among the people you most respect. Yes, that man. That man is repulsive to me. So great is my distaste for him, my determination not to become like him, that I've ended up making even the truth sound like lies. Muddying the waters. But I won't deceive you. Today, again, I'll tell you a story that's far from limpid, a story that sounds like a lie but is, in fact, the truth.

Sunrise is the child of sunset. Without the setting sun, dawn could never be born. Sunset is always trying to tell us this: "I've grown weary. You mustn't stare at me so. You mustn't love me. I am not long for this world. But tomorrow morning, in the eastern sky, a new sun will be born. Promise me you will be his friend and companion. I've brought him up with tender care. He's a fine, healthy child—so plump and round." When sunset makes this appeal to you, my friends, can you revile him with a mocking sneer, calling him sick or decadent? The bully who steps boldly forward with folded arms and a ready "Of course I can" is the biggest asshole alive. Fools like you just make this world all the harder to live in.

Forgive me. That was uncalled for. I'm in no position to stand above humanity, acting as prosecutor, or judge. I have no right to condemn others. I am a child of evil. Beyond redemption. I suspect my past sins are fifty or a hundred times greater than yours. And even now I continue to sin. However I try to watch myself, it's hopeless. Not a day goes by that I don't do something evil. I could prostrate myself before God, my hands bound together with ropes, and devote myself to prayer, but even then, before I knew it, I'd be committing some atrocious deed. I'm a man who ought to be whipped. Whip me till the blood spurts out; I would have no choice but to bear it in silence.

The sun didn't come into this world with that unsightly, embarrassed smile he wears at dusk. He arrived plump and round, bursting with innocent enthusiasm and the conviction that his every desire would be fulfilled; there was a glorious time when he blazed a lazy, carefree trail across the heavens. He's a weakling now, but he wasn't born that way. Awareness of evil—the evil in himself—has weakened him. "Once I sat on the throne of the king. Now I sit in my garden, admiring the roses." A friend of mine wrote these lines.

There are rosebushes in my garden, too. Eight of them. They aren't in bloom, however. I was tricked into buying these roses. The deception was so underhanded that it bordered on extortion and left me in an indescribable gloom.

In early September I moved from Kōfu to this house in Mitaka. The house is surrounded by farmland, and at some time around noon on my fourth day here, a farmer woman suddenly appeared in my yard and called out, "Excuse me, sir," in an oily, obsequious voice. I was writing a letter when she arrived, but laid down my pen and looked at her. She was a fat woman of about thirty-five or -six. Her full-cheeked, darkish face resembled a giant chestnut, and her narrow slits of eyes gleamed as she flashed white teeth in a repellent smile. Sensing that something disagreeable was about to happen, I didn't respond, but merely waited for her to speak. She gave me a deep bow, peering up obliquely at my face.

"Excuse me, sir," she said again. "We're the farmers who own the fields around here. A new house is going to be built in one of the fields, and these roses here, you see, we had to dig 'em up, poor things, because they were on the land where the house is going to be. We hate to let 'em go to waste like that, so we were wondering if you wouldn't let us replant 'em in your garden. We've had 'em for six years—look how thick the roots are—and each year they put out beautiful roses. Heck, we work right here in these fields, so we'll drop by every so often and look after 'em for you. We have dahlias, tulips, all sorts of flowers in our fields, sir, anything you like, you just tell us and we'll come plant 'em in your garden for you. We wouldn't ask you to take our flowers if we didn't think you were good people. We like this place, and we know you're good people, and that's why we're asking you."

She spoke in a restrained sort of growl, giving it all she was worth. I knew she was lying, however. My landlord owns all the fields in our neighborhood. The landlord himself had told me this when I rented the house. I knew everyone in his family, too. The old man, his son, the son's wife, and one grandchild. There wasn't any foul, disingenuous "farmer woman" like this in the picture. No doubt she figured that, having moved in just four days before, I'd be ignorant of all this and easily duped. Even her costume was a joke. An unsoiled livery coat, a neatly tied lavender undersash, a bandana on her head, dark blue gloves and matching leggings, brand new straw sandals, quilted undershirt—it was all too perfect. The stereotype of a farmer woman, something you'd expect to see on stage. There was no doubt in my mind that she was an impostor, and that this was a con job of the sleaziest sort. What was truly nauseating was that there was even an air of crass coquettishness about her, in her attitude and voice. But I was incapable of snapping at her or running her off.

"It's good of you to go to all that trouble. Do you mind if I have a look at them?" The politeness of the words that came out of my mouth startled me. I felt a powerless, weary sort of resignation—it was just my luck to have been pegged as a potential sucker—and I even forced a smile as I stepped out onto the veranda. I myself am a fulsome weakling; it's not for me to point the finger at others. The roses were wrapped in straw matting, eight of them, each a little over a foot tall. None of them had any flowers. There weren't even any buds.

"Are you sure they'll—"

"They'll bloom, they'll bloom," she said before I'd even finished the question, opening her narrow eyes as widely as possible. Her eyes were moist, as if brimming with tears. That clinched it. She was a swindler. When people are lying, their eyes always water— it's a rule with no exceptions. "And what a lovely smell they give off, yes indeed. This one's cream. This one's pink. This one's white . . ." She babbled on. A characteristic peculiar to liars is their inability to remain silent for a single moment.

"Do all the fields around here belong to you?" I asked this question gingerly, as if touching an open wound.

"Yes, sir. Yes, they do," she said in a rather harsh tone, nodding twice, then a third time.

"So you're building a new house. When?"

"They'll start any day now. They say it's going to be a splendid big one, too. Ha, ha, ha." She laughed with masculine bravado.

"Oh, it's not your house, then? You sold one of the fields to someone?"

"That's right, yes. We sold one of them off."

"How much does a *tsubo* of land go for in this area? Not cheap, I suppose."

"Oh, a *tsubo* costs, what, a good twenty, thirty yen, I guess. Heh, heh." Even as she chuckled, she was beginning to perspire about the forehead. She was giving it everything she had.

I gave up. I decided not to tease her any more. I, too, once told transparent lies that I continued to cling to firmly in spite of the knowledge that people could see right through them. And I remember those strange, hot tears that welled up in my eyes as I did so.

"All right. Plant them for me, if you will. How much do you want?"

"Money? Goodness, I didn't come here to sell 'em to you. It's just that we feel sorry for the poor roses," she said, her entire face lighting up with a smile. Then she leaned toward me and lowered her voice. "Let's say fifty sen apiece."

I called to my wife, who was sewing in the next room. "Pay this person, will you? I just bought some roses."

The imitation farmer woman planted the rosebushes, thanked us insincerely, and made her getaway. I stood on the veranda, gazing blankly at the eight plants.

"That woman was an impostor," I told my wife. I could feel my face turning bright red. I felt hot down to my earlobes.

"I knew that from the beginning," she said calmly. "I was going to go out and turn her down, but you stepped on the veranda and asked to have a look. I wasn't about to play the evil witch to your Prince Charming."

"I hate to lose the money, though. Four yen—it's outrageous. Talk about being burned. It's fraud, that's what it is. I feel like throwing up."

"Oh, well. At least we have the roses."

We have the roses. Obvious as this fact was, it lent me a wondrous sense of courage. For the next four or five days, I devoted myself to those plants. I gave them the water left over from washing the rice. I made stakes to support them. I carefully removed each dead leaf. I pruned the branches. I eradicated every last one of the little green, leafhopper-like bugs that infested them all. *Don't die. Don't die. Send down your roots,* I prayed with an anxious trembling in my breast. And, indeed, somehow they managed to survive.

Morning, noon, and evening I stood on the veranda, gazing with dwindling hope at the fields beyond the hedge. How happy it would have made me if that woman had proved not to be a fake, if she had suddenly appeared in the fields. "Forgive me. I was convinced you were an impostor. To distrust others is a terrible thing, isn't it?" Thus, with a great joy in my heart, I would have apologized, perhaps even shedding tears of gratitude to God. Never mind the tulips and dahlias. I don't need anything like that. All I want is to see you suddenly pop up in this field, hard at work. That would be my salvation. Come out, come out, show your face. I'd stand on the veranda for the longest time, sweeping my gaze over the fields beyond the hedge, but all I'd see were the potato leaves waving and flapping in the autumn wind and, occasionally, the old landlord strolling slowly about with his hands clasped behind his back, looking things over.

I'd been taken. There was no question about it now. I had to pin all my hopes on the flowers these scraggly plants would produce. The fruits of non-resistance. I was half resigned to the probability that the flowers wouldn't be much. Some ten days later, however, a friend of mine, a not very famous Western-style painter, made the trek out to our hut in Mitaka and gave me a most unexpected piece of information.

But I'm getting ahead of myself. It was around the same time all this was happening that I received an invitation from the Tokyo office of a newspaper of some repute in Aomori Prefecture, the land of my birth.

"We trust this finds you well. Autumn has come to Tsugaru, and both the golden fields of rice and the apple orchards with their crimson fruit are about to yield abundant harvests for the fourth consecutive year. It is in keeping with the spirit of our gratitude for this blessed good fortune that we have decided to sponsor a gathering of those Aomori natives involved in the arts in Tokyo. We sincerely hope you can find time out from your undoubtedly busy schedule to spend an evening with us exchanging impressions of Tokyo and reminiscing about our homeland . . ." And so on. This gently worded invitation was printed on one half of a prepaid, return postcard, along with the time and date of the gathering. I wrote "Will attend" and sent the postcard back.

Why would a man like me, who has long regarded his home town with horror, accept such an invitation? There are three reasons. The first has to do with the fact that, from the time I was a child, I've always been terrified of large gatherings, an unfortunate flaw in my personality that, far from being corrected with age, has only grown more pronounced as I've grown older, to the extent that I make excuses to avoid even gatherings at which my attendance is absolutely essential. The upshot of this is that I'm seen as being lax in fulfilling my obligations to others and have even acquired a reputation for being stuck up. I had therefore recently decided that from now on I would make every effort to perform my duty as a citizen by presenting myself before others when called upon to do so and expressing my feelings as clearly and sincerely as possible.

The second reason was that I was indebted to a man named Kawauchi, who was the editor-in-chief at the newspaper that had sent out the invitations, and whom I had caused a certain amount of concern during my illness five years ago. Mr. Kawauchi was an acquaintance of mine from higher school and has always stealthily supported my writings in spite of the abuse they receive at the hands of critics. After I'd fallen ill, I borrowed money like mad from all sorts of people, and though I've been repaying those loans little by little ever since, I still haven't managed to settle them all. It was during this period that, half-deranged, I sent a letter to Mr. Kawauchi asking him, too, for money. He promptly sent a reply that, as it turned out, was a flat refusal, but for which I was, nonetheless, grateful. Though I was nothing but a destitute pen-pusher, this gentleman took the trouble to explain quite frankly his own circumstances and to say that since it would go against his grain to waffle and hesitate when it was clear that he would be unable to honor my request, he had decided to turn me down in no uncertain terms. There was, behind his words, a tangible sense of manly dignity that I, even in the midst of my suffering, was grateful for. I haven't forgotten that. No doubt the invitation was Mr. Kawauchi's doing. Were I to make some excuse and fail to attend, he might assume that I had turned the invitation down because he hadn't lent me the money that time. Well, no, surely he wouldn't think that, but if by some chance he should have the slightest suspicion that such were the case, it would be more painful for me than death. By no means do I hold a grudge against him. The truth is that I still feel indebted to him for that letter. For this reason too, then, I had to attend the gathering at all costs.

The third reason lay in the wording of the invitation itself. "The golden fields of rice and the apple orchards with their crimson fruit ..." I, too, am a child of Tsúgaru. Reading these words, I could see, right before my eyes, the mountains and rivers of my homeland. I've been back only once in the past decade. During the winter eight years ago ... Ah, that too was a painful time. I'd been summoned by the Aomori Public Prosecutor's Office, and alone I boarded an express train for Aomori at Ueno Station. I spent the night near Asamushi Hot Springs, and in the morning, beneath oppressive, low-hanging clouds as black as ink, I watched snow flutter down on the dark gray sea with its leaden swells squirming and waves exploding on the shore in hard, jagged fragments like broken glass. Ah, I thought, never again! I resolved that nothing would ever bring me back to this place. I went to Aomori and presented myself at the public prosecutor's office, where I was thoroughly grilled and investigated. When, at about midnight, I was finally released and stepped out the back door of the courthouse, wind-whipped snow beat against my cheeks like a thousand arrows and lifted the skirt of my cloak to sting my entire body. Standing there on the frozen, empty street in the land of my birth, feeling as forlorn as a solitary strolling player, or the little match girl, I began to boil with rage and to ask myself—So this is my home, is it? This is that dear old homeland of mine? Down those dark, unpeopled streets where the only sound was the roar of the wind I hurried with hunched shoulders, leaning forward into the white, wildly spinning spirals of snow, and made my way back to Aomori Station. Stopping only to eat a bowl of Chinese noodles at a stall in front of the station, I got back on the train for Ueno and returned without having met a single soul from my old home town. This was the only glimpse I'd had of the land of my birth in the last ten years. Now, dazed from years of suffering, I completely forgot my loathing for the place when I read those cajoling words about golden fields and crimson fruit and giddily wrote down "Will attend."

With each passing day after I'd sent my reply, however, I was increasingly gripped with anxiety, an anxiety inspired by the notion of "worldly success." It was as a local boy who'd made good as an artist that I'd been invited by the newspaper—was it not a bit like the prodigal son returning home in robes of gold? Quite an honor, really. That meant I'd become a man of distinction, did it not? Once such thoughts had occurred to me, I could scarcely help but become flustered. Surely I, whose foul reputation was legend, was being made the object of a dirty prank—they were deliberately treating me as a prominent figure so that, behind my back, they could stick out their tongues, nudge each other, wink, and snicker. Having convinced myself that this was, indeed, the scenario, it was impossible for me to maintain my composure. There's not a single person back home who reads my works. Or, if they do read them, no doubt they merely focus with a pitying smile on the vile nature of the main character, recounting his flaws to others with exasperated shakes of the head, scornfully deriding me for bringing shame upon our homeland.

Once, four years ago, when I briefly met my eldest brother in Tokyo, he told me to stop sending my books to the relatives. "Not even I want to read them," he said. "When the relatives read what you write, how do you think they . . ." He didn't finish, but bowed his head, as if the words had caught in his throat, but he'd said enough to make things perfectly clear to me. I don't intend to send another one of my books back home as long as I live. Even the literary figures there—with the single exception of Kōno Kaichi—regard me as a laughable fool. And those artists with no connection with literature—the painters and sculptors and so on—no doubt they, too, readily take to heart the denunciations of my work they read in the newspapers and smile with a superior, rueful air. This isn't persecution mania. Nor is it, by any means, merely my cynical

way of looking at things. The truth is that it may be even worse
than I'm making it out to be. And that's among my comrades in the
arts. How much lower do you suppose my reputation is among the
other people in my home town? Sitting around their hearths:
"Well, I hear the youngest Tsushima boy has been making quite a
disgrace of himself down there in Tokyo." That's about as far as it
goes, I imagine; then they stir the coals, boil the tea, and switch the
topic of conversation to the upcoming autumn festival or
whatever.

Meanwhile, unaware of this pathetic state of affairs, the
lamebrained, destitute writer receives an invitation from his
hometown newspaper and promptly accepts, chuckling with glee
and thinking, well, well, it looks as if I'm a success after all. How
pitiful can you get? Success? Robes of gold? More like the ass
in a lion's skin. A proper laughingstock. Once I'd realized this, I
was frantic with shame. What have I done? I should have said I
couldn't attend. Or, no—it wasn't a question of will or won't attend—by the mere act of sending a reply, I was branding myself a
craven whore. To feign ignorance of the invitation and hide in
some corner blushing, hunched-up and trembling, would have
been the proper course of action, the only one suited to a man like
me.

I hated myself passionately for the feebleness, the slovenliness
that had made me accept the invitation. Now it was too late. Now,
as a result of my own dimwittedness, I had no choice but to pluck
up my courage, climb into my best *hakama* trousers and appear at
the gathering with my head held high. Let them laugh, let them do
their worst, I will be impervious to them, acting out the role of the
prominent man of letters, perhaps I'll even deliver a long speech—
thus, with something like desperation, my fighting spirit raged
within me. Strength is what counts in this world, I told myself; if a
man plows doggedly ahead, he will at length cease to be laughed at.
Ah, the superficiality of it all, the shamelessness! Suddenly six is
nine, the once-reviled man is the object of praise and sniveling

reverence, people begin to curry his favor and stealthily send him tributes. But though I tried to work myself into a lather, telling myself I'd march in there in my hakama and launch into a speech, I knew it was out of the question. I've caused people a lot of grief. I haven't written anything worthwhile. It's all bluster. Dishonesty. Cravenness. Lies. Lechery. Cowardice. I don't need to wait for God's judgment, I'm already constantly spilling out lame excuses.

Allow me to confess the truth. I wanted to see myself in a hakama. Getting all worked up, causing my own heart to pound by imagining myself making some great, earthshaking speech, and then coming suddenly back to my senses and realizing what a worthless nobody I am, I'd begin to wish I could crawl into a hole and disappear, but then, once again, my breast would swell and, unable to shake my worldly attachments, I'd think—well, at least let me wear a hakama in public. If I'm going to appear, it might as well be in a proper hakama. I'd better not smile much, since I look like hell with all these missing teeth, so I'll keep my lips tightly pursed, my jaw firmly clenched, and when I speak, I'll speak clearly, apologizing for staying out of touch with everyone for so long. If I do that, who knows—maybe the folks from my home town will think to themselves, why, the youngest Tsushima boy's a fine gentleman, nothing like the rumors we've heard. I'll go. I'll put on a hakama and go. I'll extend my greetings to everyone in a clear, brisk voice, then sit in my seat in the last row, modest and restrained, and people will think I'm a splendid fellow, and they'll tell other people, and the word will spread and eventually be whispered even in my home town, five hundred miles away, bringing a quiet smile to the lips of my sickly mother. This is the chance of a lifetime. I'll go, I'll put on a hakama and go, I told myself, my breast swelling yet again with excitement. I'm just not capable of forsaking my home town. For all the scorn it has heaped upon me, I just can't bring myself to turn my back on my home town. The one burning desire I've kept in my heart these four years since I recovered from my illness was now a raging fire. Somewhere in the deepest recesses of my soul I've always treasured the thought of the prodigal son's glorious return. I love my home town. I love everyone in my home town!

The appointed day arrived. It poured rain from morning on, but that didn't dissuade me. I have a hakama. It's a rather good one, too. Silk. I only wore it once, at my wedding ceremony, after which my wife wrapped it elaborately in oilpaper and stored it in the bottom of our trunk. My wife thinks it's a formal hakama. She came to this conclusion all by herself: I wore it to our wedding, so it must be a formal hakama. I was broke at the time, however, and in no position to buy a proper formal hakama, so I made do with a plain silk one. Thinking it would be a pity to destroy this illusion of my wife's, however, I've never told her the truth of the matter. At any rate, this was what I wanted to wear to the gathering. This was to be my robe of gold.

"Get out that good hakama of mine, will you?" I couldn't bring myself to say "formal."

"The formal hakama? Oh, you mustn't wear that. Who ever heard of wearing a formal hakama with a splash-pattern kimono? It'd be strange." I have only one thing to wear for special occasions—an unlined splash-pattern kimono. I used to have a summer *haori* coat also, but it disappeared at some point.

"It won't be strange. Get it out." I considered telling her the truth, that it wasn't a formal hakama, but I held back.

"It'll look funny."

"I don't care. I want to wear it."

"No, really, you mustn't." She was sticking to her guns. There was a touch of egoism involved here. She wasn't about to let the hakama I wore on our wedding day be defiled. "You have a perfectly good serge."

"Forget it. I walk around in that thing, I look like the narrator at a silent movie. It's soiled, too. Unwearable."

"I ironed it this morning. It goes much better with your kimono."

My wife couldn't understand why I was being so adamant. I considered explaining it to her, but it seemed like too much trouble.

"The formal hakama," I said, finally coming right out with the lie. "The formal hakama will look better. In this rain, the serge will be a wrinkled mess in no time."

"Wear the serge." My wife's voice had a pleading tone to it now. "Wrap it up and carry it so it won't get wet. You can put it on when you get there."

"Right." I threw in the sponge.

I had her wrap the serge hakama and a pair of white *tabi* socks in cloth, tucked up the hem of my kimono, and walked out into the rain with an umbrella and a vague sense of foreboding.

The gathering was at a well known Western restaurant in the middle of Hibiya Park. It was scheduled to start at five-thirty, but I, having had bad luck with my bus connections, didn't arrive until after six. I whispered a few words to the boy in charge of handing out the slippers, and he directed me to a small room near the entrance where I could change my clothes. In the room, a pale-faced kid of about ten wearing a fancy white suit was sitting sloppily on the floor, stuffing his cheeks with confectioneries while a tutor gave him a lesson in arithmetic. Probably the owner's darling son. The tutor was a plump, self-composed woman of twenty-seven or -eight with white skin and round glasses. I retied my kimono, then opened my bundle and put on the white socks, and as I was fiddling with my serge hakama, the tutor, undoubtedly moved by this pitiful sight, silently got up, walked over to me, and helped me get into the thing. She tied the sash in front in a neat bow. I thanked her and hurried out of the room, then walked slowly and deliberately up the stairway, stopping halfway to undo her handiwork. I was not about to walk around with that soiled, wrinkled sash tied in a pretty bow.

As soon as I set foot in the reception room I grew rigid with tension. Now was my chance. The time to reclaim my good name, disgraced in my home town these ten long years, had come. A prominent figure, I told myself, carry yourself like a prominent figure. Someone tapped me on the shoulder. I turned, and there stood Kōno Kaichi. Forgetting all about my rotten teeth, I beamed at him. Kōno Kaichi has been my friend for ten years, and it's not because we're from the same part of the country that we associate with each other. I sought out his friendship because he is a faithful, pure, and honest artist. Kōno Kaichi grinned back at me, and I smiled even more broadly. All those vows about being modest and restrained had already slipped from my mind.

Everyone sat down. I ended up in the rearmost seat, literally. In the confusion and bustle, nodding to this person and that, I ended up sitting in the very last seat. Well, perhaps it was partially a conscious choice. Not, it seems to me, a choice made out of deference to the others at the gathering, but rather out of a certain sense of rebellion. It was even, I suspect, with an arrogant sort of disdain, but I can't say for sure. At any rate, I ended up in the rear, and I was perfectly comfortable there. This is just fine, I thought, quite frankly pleased with how things were progressing. Now to win back my good name.

It was not to be, however. I deported myself despicably. It was an absolute disaster.

What a truly, truly hopeless man I am. There's nothing worthwhile about me. I'm a spoiled child when it comes to my home town. When I come in contact with that hometown atmosphere, I grow limp, my selfishness gets the better of me, I lose all self-control. I become so useless that it's amazing even to me. My will power goes out the window, my brakes fail. My heart pounds frightfully, every joint in my body goes slack, and it becomes impossible for me to put on airs. Though delicacies of every description were served, one after the other, I was too full of emotion to eat. All I did was drink. Guzzled the saké like mad. Because of the rain, all the windows were shut and the room was hot and muggy, and as the alcohol flowed through my veins I began to huff and puff, and my face, no doubt, took on the hue of a boiled octopus.

This wouldn't do. At this rate, my reputation back home would only sink even lower. It saddened me to think how vexed and mortified my mother and eldest brother would be if they could have seen me at that moment, but my brakes had failed completely. I just kept drinking. I was being positively infantile.

At thirty-one, without a trace of boyish charm remaining, here I was playing the baby—it was grotesque to an extreme. The drunker I got, the more pathetic I became, telling myself I disavowed the gathering altogether, hatching cocky schemes to flaunt my role as a heretic, then reconsidering, thinking, no, no, these are all respectable men, preeminent in their fields, honest, humble, kindhearted artists who have lived lives of hardship and adversity. The only craven one here is me. Ah, what a coward you are, I told myself, how like an old woman gone to seed! If you were so opposed to the idea of this sort of gathering, why did you deck yourself out in a hakama and come? Anyone can see through that abject fretfulness of yours.

At any rate, I was a mess, squirming in my seat, unable to relax, incessantly swaying from side to side and drinking cup after cup of saké. I thoroughly overindulged in the stuff, and as it coursed through my veins, my entire body grew so hot that steam must have risen from the top of my head.

The self-introductions began. They were all famous people. Japanese-style painters, Western-style painters, sculptors, playwrights, dancers, critics, popular singers, songwriters, cartoonists, all with the dignity befitting the *crème de la crème*, pronouncing their names with cool grace and throwing in the occasional lighthearted jest. With blustering bravado I applauded loudly at incongruous moments and repeatedly shouted "Hear, hear!" though I was scarcely listening, undoubtedly shocking all present into feeling a mixture of repulsion and abhorrence as they wondered who that drunken stumblebum in the rear corner might be. I was perfectly aware of this, but my brakes were gone.

One man after another introduced himself, the order continuing from one seat to the next, winding through the room and gradually approaching the rear. Considering the condition I was in, what in the world was I going to say when my turn came? Disoriented as I was, a long speech was unthinkable. It would be received as the blatherings of an incorrigible drunk and make me the object of even greater scorn. Then, out of the blue, there appeared before my eyes a little river in spring, fed by melting snows. Lush, green dropwort growing on either bank. Ah! I do have things to say. I have lots to say. It's just that suddenly I don't feel like saying them. I just don't want to. Hell with it. I don't care if my home town never understands me. I'm resigned to that. I give up on the robes of gold.

Even as the alcohol swirled through my disordered brain, however, I cast about for ideas. I decided I would merely thank the newspaper people for the feast, then turn and walk out. The only thing I could do with heartfelt honesty, without any hypocrisy, was to express my gratitude and leave it at that. But then a voice inside me told me to reconsider, that if I only said "Thanks for the meal" and left, it would sound base and slavish, as if I were proclaiming an inability to buy my own food and drink, and now I was at a loss again.

My turn came. I swayed to my feet, trying to order my thoughts on the spur of the moment and smiling with something like the coquetry of an old hag, so disgusting I could have thrashed myself. I didn't want to use the name Dazai. That name would only meet with indifference and scorn. It wouldn't be fair to my poor works, or to my readers. "I'm the youngest son of the Kanagi Tsushimas ..." Ah, but if I say that, I'll be exposing my mother and eldest brother to public disgrace. I knew that a certain calamity had recently befallen my eldest brother. For the past five or six years, in fact, my family had met with one misfortune after another, not to mention all the trouble and shame I'd caused them. Forgive me.

"I'm the youngest son of the Kanagi . . ." This is what I tried to say, but the words got tangled on my tongue and it was clear that almost no one could hear me.

"Once more!" From the front issued a thick voice shouting these words, and my deranged, aimless frustration focused on that voice and exploded.

"Shut the fuck up!" I said under my breath. At least I thought it was under my breath, but when I sat down and gazed around the room, I saw that a deathly chill had fallen over the entire assemblage. It was all over now. I'm beyond salvation. Word of what a hooligan I am would be shouted from the rooftops throughout my home town.

I won't go on about how scandalously I behaved after that. To make such unabashed confessions is suspiciously like asking my readers for succor and comfort, and may even be inspired by the ignoble desire to lighten the burden of my sins. I must bear my transgressions in silence and await the judgment of God. I have only myself to blame. Let's just say I exposed all the corruption of my soul in one fell swoop. On the way home, in the pouring rain, I hired a rickshaw at Kichijōji Station. The rickshaw puller was a decrepit old man. Soaked to the skin, he tottered along, huffing and puffing and groaning with the strain. I shouted at him the entire way to my house.

"What the hell's wrong with you, groaning like that? Where are your guts, man? Run! Faster!" I was laying my true, satanic nature bare.

That night I finally realized the truth. I'm not the sort who gets ahead in the world. I have no choice but to resign myself to that. I must now unequivocally abandon the dream of a triumphant return in robes of gold. I shall proceed with calm composure, bearing always in mind the old adage that green pastures are where you find them. I may remain a mere street-corner musician to the end of my days. Only those who want to listen to my moronic, obstinate music—only they should listen. Art cannot order people around. Art dies the moment it acquires authority.

The following day that friend of mine who's studying Western-style painting came to my hut in Mitaka, and I told him about my fiasco of the night before and of the resolution I'd made to myself. This friend of mine had also been driven from his home town, a place on an island in the Inland Sea.

"A home town is like a mole on your face," he said. Once you start letting it bother you, there's no end. You can cut it off, but the scar will always remain." This friend has a mole the size of a kidney bean under his right eye.

Uncomforted by his half-hearted words of solace, I'd thrown my head back and was gloomily blowing cigarette smoke at the ceiling.

That's when it happened. My friend, having spotted the eight rosebushes in the garden, informed me of a remarkable fact. Those roses, he said, were outstanding specimens.

"Are you sure?"

"I should say so. They must be a good six years old. You'd have to pay as much as a yen apiece for roses like that at the growers' market." My friend is someone who's expended a lot of time and energy on roses. In the little garden at his house in Ogikubo he has forty or fifty rosebushes.

"But the woman who sold them to me was a fraud," I said, and gave him a brief account of how I'd been swindled.

"People who make their living selling things tend to lie even when they don't need to. She was probably desperate to get you to buy them. Missus, could you lend me a pair of shears?" My friend stepped down into the garden and began fervently pruning away the superfluous branches.

"Maybe she was from my homeland, that woman," I said. My cheeks felt warm for some reason. "So she wasn't entirely a fraud, eh?"

Taking a seat on the veranda, puffing at my cigarette, I felt not a little contented. God exists. Surely He exists. Green pastures are where you find them. Behold the fruits of non-resistance. I considered myself a fortunate man. They say to experience sorrow at any price. That the blue sky is most beautiful when seen through a prison cell window. And so on. I gave thanks. And for a moment, this thought flashed through my mind: As long as these roses are living, I am king of my own heart.

Eight Scenes from Tokyo

東京八景

Tōkyō Hakkei

———◆———

Dazai wrote "Eight Scenes from Tokyo" during a ten-day stay at the Fukudaya Inn in Yugano, Izu, in July 1940. "Mr. S.," who appears near the end of the story, is Satō Haruo. "H." is, of course, Hatsuyo.

———◆———

For those who suffer

It's a dreary little mountain village in southern Izu with nothing but hot springs to recommend it. Maybe a total of thirty houses. One would expect lodging to be inexpensive in such a desolate place, and it was for that reason alone that I'd chosen it. I arrived on July 3, 1940. At the time, my finances were such as to allow me a certain breathing space. That's not to say, however, that anything but darkness lay ahead. For all I knew, I might suddenly find myself unable to write. Two months of producing nothing and I'd be right back where I started—penniless. It was a limited, pitiful sort of breathing space when I thought about it, but it was a breathing space, something I hadn't experienced in ten years.

Dazai on the veranda of his house in Mitaka, spring 1940.

I first moved to Tokyo in the spring of 1930. Not long afterwards, I began sharing a house with a woman named H. Each month I received a generous allowance from my eldest brother back home, but although H. and I constantly cautioned each other against extravagance, we inevitably had to pawn something or other by the end of the month, fools that we were. It was to be six years before I parted with H. I was left with a futon, a desk, an electric lamp, a wicker trunk—and ominously large debts. Two years later, through the gracious offices of a certain mentor of mine, I took part in an ordinary arranged marriage. Two more years had passed, and now, for the first time, I was able to take a bit of a breather. I'd published nearly ten volumes of my paltry work, and I had the feeling that if I simply applied myself assiduously to writing, and submitted things to editors whether invited to or not, I'd be able to sell, say, two out of every three pieces. From now on this was going to be a real, grown-up job, devoid of any sort of romantic charm. Still, I wanted to write only what I wanted to write.

Forlorn and tenuous as this breathing space was, I was thrilled to have it. It would allow me at least a month of writing what I liked without having to worry about money. The reality of such good fortune was hard to accept, and the uneasy blend of rapture and anxiety it inspired only served to prevent me from getting down to work, much to my distress.

"Eight Scenes from Tokyo." I'd long intended to find the time to write that story, slowly and painstakingly. In painting those scenes, I hoped to depict my ten years of life in the city. I'm thirty-two this year. According to the standard Japanese view of things, that puts me on the verge of middle age. I consult my own flesh, my own passions, and find myself, alas, unable to deny it. Mark this well: your youth is gone. You're a grave and solemn-faced man in his thirties. "Eight Scenes from Tokyo." I would write that, a farewell to my youth, without pandering to anyone.

"He's grown more and more plebeian, hasn't he?" I sometimes get wind of such mindless backbiting, and each time I do, I hear my heart's vehement response: I was plebeian from the beginning. You didn't notice? You've got it all backwards. When I prepared to make literature my life's work, the fools agreed I'd proved a pushover. I could only smile to myself. Perennial youth is the realm of the actor. It doesn't exist in the world of letters.

"Eight Scenes from Tokyo." Now, I thought, was the time to write it. I had no pressing assignments. I was more than a hundred yen ahead. This was no time for pacing my narrow room in vain, sighing contorted sighs of rapture and anxiety. I must be constantly on the advance.

I bought a large map of Tokyo and boarded the train for Maibara at Tokyo Station. This wasn't to be a pleasure trip. I was going to carve out a monument of once-in-a-lifetime importance. Or so I kept telling myself. At Atami I transferred to a train bound for Itō, from Itō I boarded a bus for Shimoda, and, after a bouncy ride south along the eastern coast of the Izu Peninsula, I got off at this miserable thirty-shack mountain village. Surely lodging wouldn't be more than three yen a night in a place like this. Four inns—all of them shabby, depressing little affairs. I chose the F— Inn, somehow under the impression that it might be slightly less objectionable than the others. A coarsely mannered, mean-spirited chambermaid showed me upstairs, and, when I saw the room, I felt, in spite of my years, like weeping. I remembered the room I'd had in a boardinghouse in Ogikubo some three years before. Even by Ogikubo standards, my quarters there were the lowest of the low. But the six-mat space I was shown at this inn was even more wretched and miserable.

"Is this the only room you have?"

"Yes. All the others are taken. But this room is nice and cool."

"Is it."

Every indication was that I was being taken for a fool. Perhaps it was my clothing.

"The rates are four yen or three-fifty, depending. Lunch is separate."

"Make it three-fifty. I'll let you know whenever I want lunch. I have some studying to do, and I'll be staying about ten days."

"Can you wait a moment?" She went downstairs and returned shortly to say, "I'm afraid if it's a long stay, we'll have to ask for the money in advance."

"I see. How much shall I give you?"

"Well," she mumbled falteringly, "any amount would be . . ."

"How about fifty yen."

"Mmm."

I laid all my bills out on the desk, exasperated.

"Here, take it all. There's ninety yen there. I'll buy cigarettes with what I've got left in my purse." Why, I thought, had I come to a place like this?

"Thank you." She gathered up the bills and left.

You mustn't get angry, I told myself. There's important work to be done. I forced myself to suppose that the reception I'd just been given was all a man in my position was due, and dug pen, ink, and paper out of the bottom of my bag.

This, then, was where my first breathing space in ten years got me. But this wretchedness, too, was ordained by fate, I solemnly reminded myself, and settled down to work.

This wasn't to be a pleasure trip. A difficult task lay before me. That night, under the dim electric lamp, I unfolded my big map of Tokyo and spread it out on the desk.

How many years had it been since I'd spread out a map of Tokyo? Ten years ago, when I first started living in the city, I was ashamed even to buy such a map for fear that doing so would brand me a country bumpkin, and it was only after much vacillation that I finally made up my mind and bought one, asking for it in a deliberately churlish and self-deprecating tone of voice. Having succeeded in buying the thing, I stuffed it in my pocket and stomped back to my boardinghouse. That night, too, I had shut myself up in my room and quietly spread out the map. Red, green, yellow—like a lovely painting. I held my breath and gazed at it.

The Sumida River. Asakusa. Ushigome. Akasaka. It was all there. And I could get to any of these places in no time at all, whenever I wanted. I felt as if I were beholding a miracle.

Now, with the outline of Tokyo, like a mulberry leaf partially eaten by silkworms, spread out before me, all that came to mind were images of the people there and their different ways of life. To this charmless, featureless plain, people from all over Japan roll up in droves to push and shove and sweat, to fight for an inch of ground, to live lives of alternating joy and sorrow, to regard one another with jealous, hostile eyes, females crying out to males, males merely strutting about in a frenzy. Suddenly, out of the blue and apropos of nothing, these doleful lines from the novel *The Tale of a Genius* flashed into my mind.

"*And love?*

"*To behold a beautiful dream, and behave in a manner most foul.*"

Words that have nothing in particular to do with Tokyo.

Totsuka. This is where I first stayed. The youngest of my elder brothers was renting a house here and was studying sculpture. I had graduated from Hirosaki Higher School that year, 1930, and enrolled in the French department at Tokyo Imperial University. I couldn't understand a word of French, yet I wanted to listen to lectures on French literature and had a vague sort of reverence for Professor Tatsuno Yutaka. I rented a room in the back of a newly built boardinghouse, three blocks from my brother's place. Though neither of us put it into words, we tacitly agreed that, brothers or not, there would be a distinct possibility of unpleasantness were we to live under the same roof, and so chose to live separately, albeit in the same section of Tokyo. Three months later, this brother of mine died. He was twenty-seven. I continued to lodge in the boardinghouse after his death. From my second semester on, I rarely attended classes. I was assisting, with cool indifference, in that shadowy movement which the world most held in horror. Scornfully, I dealt with the bombastic prose that claims to play a major role in that movement. I was, during this period, pure politician.

It was in the fall of that year that H., at my request, came from the country to join me. I'd met H. in the early autumn of my first year at Hirosaki Higher School and had continued to see her throughout my three years there. She was an innocent young geisha. I rented a room for her above a carpenter's shop in Higashi Komagata, in Honjo Ward. As yet I had never slept with her. My eldest brother came to Tokyo to discuss the problem this woman presented. The two of us, brothers who'd lost our father seven years before, sat talking in the dimly lit room in Totsuka. My brother wept to see the diabolical changes that had so abruptly come over me. I agreed to leave the woman in his hands, on the condition that she and I eventually be permitted to marry. Much greater than the suffering of the haughty younger brother who gave her up, no doubt, was that of the elder brother who took her away. I first slept with H. on her last night in Tokyo. The next day my brother took her back home to the country.

Throughout it all, H. acted as if she were simply along for the ride. I received one letter, stating in stiff, businesslike language that she had arrived safely, and that was the last correspondence I had from her. She seemed terribly unconcerned, and that was a source of discontent for me. Here I am, I thought, sending all my relatives into shock, fighting for this woman though it means giving my own mother a taste of the horrors of hell, and she just sits back with her mindless self-assurance—it's despicable. She should write to me as often as once a day, I thought; she doesn't love me enough. But H. just didn't like to write letters. I gave up hope. From early morning till late at night I bustled about doing my job for the movement, never once refusing to do what I was asked. When I gradually became aware of the limits of my capabilities in that direction, it only doubled my sense of despair.

A woman in a bar behind the Ginza fell in love with me. There is a period in every man's life when people find him attractive. A period of squalor. I persuaded the woman to leap into the sea with me at Kamakura. When you're defeated, I thought, it's time to die. My work for that ungodly movement had begun to get the better of me. Simply for fear of being called a coward, I'd accepted more work than I was even physically capable of. And H. was thinking only of her own happiness. You're not the only woman in the world. This is your punishment for not understanding how I suffer. Serves you right.

Being alienated from my family was the hardest part. The most immediate cause of my suicide attempt was the realization that, because of my relationship with H., my mother, my brother, and even my aunt had completely given up on me. I've written any number of times about the person who died. It's a black spot on my entire life. I was put in a detention cell. An investigation resulted in a stay of prosecution. This was near the end of 1930. My family treated with gentle kindness the younger brother who'd failed to die. My eldest brother paid off H.'s redemption fee, freeing her from the geisha house, and in February of the following year she was sent to me. My brother was always fastidious about keeping his word. H. arrived with a carefree look on her face. We rented a house in Gotanda, near the subdivision on the old Shimazu estate, for thirty yen a month. H. diligently set to work housekeeping. I was twenty-three; she was twenty.

Gotanda, my moron period. I was utterly without a will of my own. I hadn't the slightest desire to start life over again. I tried to humor and amuse those friends who occasionally came to call, and that was all I did. Far from being ashamed of my criminal record, I was actually rather proud of it. It was truly a time of ignominious imbecility. I attended school only rarely. Despising all forms of exertion, I spent my days gazing indifferently at H.'s face. I was a fool. I did nothing. I slid back into my old activities with the movement, but there was no passion in it this time. The idle nihilist: that was me in my first house in Tokyo.

That summer we moved to Dōbōchō in Kanda. Then, in late autumn, to Izumichō, also in Kanda, and early the following spring to Kashiwagi in Yodobashi. Nothing worthy of mention happened. For a time I wrote haiku, using the venerable-sounding pen name Shurindō. I was an old man. I was twice placed in detention cells as a result of my work for the movement. Each time I was released, I followed the advice of friends and changed houses. I felt neither enthusiasm nor abhorrence for what I was doing. My lethargy was such that I simply did whatever those around me thought best. I spent my days with H. in vapid indolence; we were like two animals in a cave. She was in rare form. Two or three times a day she'd tear into me, using the foulest language, but afterwards she'd forget her anger entirely and sit down to study English. The English was my idea, and I'd made a study schedule for her, but she didn't seem to learn much. She got to where she could more or less sound out Roman letters, and then, at some point, she stopped. Even in her own language she was still quite hopeless at carrying on correspondence. She just didn't like doing it, and I had to write rough drafts of letters for her. She seemed to enjoy playing the outlaw's moll. She was never overly distraught even when I was hauled off by the police, and some days she actually seemed thrilled with what she judged to be the heroism of that infamous ideology. Dōbōchō, Izumichō, Kashiwagi: I was twenty-four years old.

In late spring, not long after moving to Kashiwagi, it became necessary for me to move once more. I fled just as the police were about to call me in. This time it was a rather complicated affair. I invented a story to get my brother to send me two months' allowance at once, and used that money for moving. After dividing up my household effects and leaving them in the care of various friends, I found an eight-mat room above a lumber merchant's shop in Hatchōbori, Nihonbashi, and moved in with only those things I could carry. I became a man named Ochiai Kazuo, a native of Hokkaido. I was, quite naturally, miserable. I was very careful with what money I had, and tried to suppress my anxiety with the feckless reasoning that things would probably all work out somehow, but I was totally unprepared to face whatever tomorrow might bring. I couldn't do anything. From time to time I went to school and stretched out for hours on the lawn in front of the lecture halls. On one such day, an economics student who'd graduated from the same higher school as I told me something awful. Listening to him was like trying to swallow boiling water. Impossible, I thought, it can't be true. I even despised the fellow for telling me such a thing. All I would have to do to get at the truth would be to ask H. I hurried back to Hatchōbori, to our room above the lumber shop, but I found it difficult to broach the subject. It was an afternoon in early summer. The sun poured in through the western windows, and it was hot. I sent H. out for a bottle of Oraga beer. Oraga was twenty-five sen at the time. I drank that bottle and asked for another, and H. shouted at me. Being shouted at helped me pluck up my courage, and I managed to relate to her, in as casual a tone as possible, all I'd heard that day from the economics student. H. said the whole story "smelled green"—an expression from back home— and briefly furrowed her brow as if in anger. That was all; she then went on quietly sewing. There was no hesitation or ambiguity in her reaction. I believed her.

But that night I read the wrong book. Rousseau's *Confessions*. When I got to the part where Rousseau agonizes over his wife's past, I couldn't bear it. I began to doubt H.'s word. Questioning her again, I finally got her to spit it all out. Everything the economics student had told me was true. In fact, it was even worse than he'd said, and I began to fear that if I kept digging I'd find there was no end. I told her I'd heard enough.

When it came to matters of this nature, I was hardly in a position to point the finger. What about that incident in Kamakura, after all? Nonetheless, my blood boiled. Until that day I had protected and cared for H. as my greatest treasure, my only pride. I'd been living my life for her. I sincerely believed I'd rescued her from the geisha house while she was still undefiled. I had gallantly accepted

H.'s version of the facts and had even boasted to my friends that she'd managed to guard her chastity until we were together precisely because she was the spirited, willful woman she was. There were no words to describe how I now saw myself; not even "half-wit" fit the bill. The idiot son. I'd had no idea what kind of creature a woman was. I didn't hate H. for having deceived me. Listening to her confession, I even felt sorry for her and was tempted to stroke her gently on the back. It was a pity, that was all. I felt awful. It was as if my entire life had been smashed to bits. I felt, in short, that I couldn't go on. I turned myself in to the police.

I survived the prosecutor's investigation and was soon loose again on the streets of Tokyo. I had no place to return to but H.'s room, and lost no time in going to her. It was a pathetic reunion: smiling cravenly at each other and weakly taking each other's hands. We moved from Hatchōbori to Shirogane Sankōchō, in Shiba Ward. We rented a one-room cottage that adjoined a large, vacant house. My eldest brother, though utterly disgusted with me, quietly continued to send money from home. H. was in good spirits, as if nothing untoward had happened at all. I, however, seemed to be gradually awakening from my idiotic daze. I composed my last will and testament, my suicide note. One hundred pages that I entitled "Memories." "Memories" is now considered my maiden work. I wanted to set down, without the least ornamentation, all the evil I'd done since childhood. This was in the autumn of my twenty-fourth year. I sat in the cottage gazing out at an abandoned garden overgrown with weeds, utterly devoid of the ability to laugh or smile. It was, once again, my intention to die. Call it affectation if you will. I was full of myself. I regarded life as a drama. Or, rather, I regarded drama as life. I was no longer of use to anyone. H., who had been all I could call my own, bore the marks of other hands. I hadn't a single thing to live for. I resolved that I, as one of the fools, one of the doomed, would faithfully play out the role in which fate had cast me, the sad, servile role of one who must inevitably lose.

But life, as it turned out, wasn't drama. No one knows for sure what will happen in the second act. The character tagged for destruction sometimes stays around till the final curtain. I had written my little suicide note, the testament of my infancy and boyhood, the first-hand account of a hateful child, but that testament, rather than freeing me, became a burning obsession that cast a faint light into the empty darkness. I couldn't die yet. "Memories" alone wasn't enough. Having revealed that much, I now wanted to set it all down, to make a clean breast of my entire life until then, to confess everything. But there seemed no end to it. First I wrote about the incident at Kamakura. No good. That didn't say it all, somehow. I wrote another piece, and still I was unsatisfied. I sighed and began another. It was a series of little commas; the final period never came. I was already being devoured by that ever-beckoning demon. Trying to empty the sea with a teacup.

1933. I was twenty-five. I was supposed to graduate from university in March. Far from graduating, however, I didn't even sit for the examinations. My family back home was unaware of this. I'd done a lot of foolish things, but surely I wouldn't fail to graduate, surely I was not so untrustworthy as to deceive them on that score—or such seemed to be their unspoken assumption. I did a magnificent job of betraying them. I had no desire to graduate. But to deceive someone who trusts you is to enter a hell that can take you to the brink of madness. I lived in that hell for the next two years. I appealed to my eldest brother, telling him that next year, next year for certain, I'd graduate, and begging him to give me one more year; he did, and I betrayed him again. I was to do the same thing the following year. Determined to die, and suffering the fierce introspection and self-scorn and fear that that determination engendered, I lived on, engrossed in writing the series of self-centered tales that I called my suicide note. As soon as this is finished, I told myself.

Perhaps those works were, in fact, nothing but callow, pretentious sentimentalism, but it was sentimentalism that I wrote with my life on the line. Whenever I finished a story, I placed it with the others in a large manila envelope. On the front, in ink, I brushed the words *The Final Years*. That was the title I intended to give the collection of suicide notes. Meaning, of course, that the end was near.

A buyer had been found for the big vacant house in Shiba, and we had to move. My allowance from home had decreased considerably since I'd failed to graduate from university, and I had to be even more frugal than before. Amanuma, in Suginami Ward. I rented a room on the second floor of the house of an acquaintance, a fine, upstanding citizen who worked for a newspaper company. I was to live under this man's roof for the next two years and to cause him no end of trouble and worry.

I had less intention of graduating than ever. I was a fool with a single compulsion—to finish that collection of stories. Fearful of being rebuked by my host and H., I bought time by lying, telling them I'd be able to graduate the following year. Once a week or so I put on my student's uniform and left the house. I'd go to the library, check out this book and that, leaf through them, toss them aside, doze off for a while or scribble a rough draft for a story, and when evening came I'd go back to Amanuma. Neither H. nor our host suspected anything. On the surface all was well, but inwardly I was in a desperate rush. Every moment counted. I wanted to finish my writing before my family stopped sending me money. Ah, but it was quite a battle. I'd write something, then tear it up. That demon was now gnawing hideously away at the very marrow of my bones.

A year passed. I didn't graduate. My family was furious, but I made my by now customary appeal. Next year I would graduate no matter what, I unhesitatingly lied. There was no other way to keep the money coming. I could hardly tell anyone my true situation. I didn't want to create any accomplices. I wanted to be regarded as the archetypal prodigal son, acting entirely alone. I believed that only in this way could those around me avoid being implicated. "I just need one more year to finish my suicide note"—obviously I couldn't tell them that. To be tagged a self-absorbed, poetic dreamer was the last thing I wanted. And if I'd come out with such an outrageous declaration, my family would have been forced to stop sending me money whether they wanted to or not. If they knew my real intentions and continued to support me, the world might have accused them of helping me die. I wouldn't stand for that. I had to deceive them, to play to the hilt the part of the cunning and treacherous little brother—this, at least, was my rationalization, and it was conceived in absolute seriousness. Once a week I still put on my uniform and went to school. It was beautiful how H. and the newspaper fellow believed in my imminent graduation. I was backing myself into a corner. Day after day was black as night. I am not an evil man! To deceive others is to live in hell.

That spring, to make commuting to his office easier, my acquaintance found a new residence in Amanuma, behind the marketplace. It was near Ogikubo Station. He invited us to move in with him, and we rented a room on the second floor of the new house. I had trouble sleeping each night. I drank cheap liquor. I coughed up prodigious amounts of phlegm. I thought I might be coming down with an illness of some sort, but that, of course, was neither here nor there. All I wanted was to finish the collection of works in that manila envelope as soon as possible. It was an egocentric, pretentious idea, I suppose, but I thought leaving that behind would be my way of apologizing to everyone. It was the very best I could do. By late autumn it appeared to be finished. Out of twenty-odd pieces I selected fourteen, and tossed the rest in with the pages I'd discarded. There was enough paper to fill a suitcase. I took it all out into the garden and burned it to ashes.

"Why? Why did you burn them?" H. asked me suddenly that night.

"Don't need them any more." I smiled.

"Why did you burn them?" she said again. She was crying.

I began putting my affairs in order. I returned the books I'd borrowed and sold my letters and notes to a scrap dealer. I slipped two letters into the *Final Years* envelope. Now I seemed to be ready. Dreading the thought of sitting around face to face with H., I went out each night to drink cheap liquor.

It was at about this time that a friend from school asked me if I'd be interested in helping start a little literary magazine. I was more or less indifferent. I said I'd be willing to do it if he'd call the magazine *The Blue Flower*. What started as a joke soon became a reality. Kindred spirits appeared from near and far. With two fellows in particular I became quite close. This is how I burned up, if you will, the last of my youthful passions. A mad dance on the eve of death. Together we'd get drunk and take apart feeble-minded students. There were fallen women we loved like our own flesh and blood. H.'s wardrobe was cleaned out before she knew it. *The Blue Flower*, a magazine of belles-lettres, came out in December. After only one issue, all the other members dispersed, fed up with our crazed, directionless frenzy. That left only the three of us. We were dubbed "the three fools." But we three were friends for life. I learned a great deal from those two.

March of the next year came around; soon it would be graduation time again. I went for an employment interview at a newspaper company, and tried to show H. and the fellow we lived with that I was cheerfully looking forward to my graduation. Joking about how I was going to become a newspaper reporter and lead a normal, mediocre life, I brought laughter and cheer to our little household. My ruse would eventually be exposed, of course, but I wanted to maintain the illusion of peace and harmony even one day, even one moment, longer. Dreading above all the thought of giving people such a frightful shock, I acted out the temporizing lie as if my life depended on it. I was forever doing that: backing myself further into a corner as I contemplated my own death. Though it would all, in the end, be out in the open, the shock and rage only magnified by the deception, I could never bring myself to spoil the party by telling the truth, and thus I continued to sink deeper into the hell I'd created with my lies. I had no intention of entering a newspaper company and stood no chance of passing the examination anyway. The foundation of my great imposture was about to crumble. The time had come to die. In mid-March, I went to Kamakura alone. It was 1935. I planned to hang myself in the mountains there.

This was the fifth year since I'd caused such a ruckus by jumping into the sea at Kamakura. Being able to swim, it wasn't easy for me to drown myself, so I chose hanging, which I'd heard was infallible. Humiliatingly enough, however, I botched it. I revived and found myself breathing. Perhaps my neck was thicker than most. I went back to Amanuma in a sort of daze, with sore, red welts around my throat. I'd tried to prescribe my own fate and failed. But once I'd tottered home, I found a strange and marvelous world opening before me. H. greeted me at the door and patted me gently on the back. Everyone else, too, treated me with compassion. "Thank goodness, thank goodness," they said. I was dumbfounded, amazed at the kindness of people. My eldest brother was also waiting for me, having rushed to Tokyo. He berated me roundly, but I felt an overwhelming affection for him. I don't think I'd ever experienced such wondrous feelings before.

A most unexpected fate was waiting to unfold, however. Only a few days later I developed an intense pain in my abdomen. I suffered through it for a day and a night without sleep, and used a hot water bottle to try to ease the pain. When I began to lose consciousness, a doctor was sent for. I was loaded, bedding and all, aboard an ambulance and taken to a hospital in Asagaya. I was operated on immediately. It was appendicitis. In addition to having waited too long to call a doctor, warming the area with a hot water bottle had only made it worse. Suppuration had spread to the peritoneum, and it was a difficult operation. Then, on the second day after surgery, I coughed up any number of blood clots: my chronic chest problems had suddenly surfaced with a vengeance. I was now more dead than alive. Even the doctors had quite frankly given up hope for me. But the sinful, incorrigible patient began, little by little, to recover. Within a month, the incision on my stomach, at least, had healed. As a patient with an infectious disease, however, I was transferred to a hospital in Kyōdō. H. stayed at my side constantly. She laughingly reported that the doctor had told her she mustn't even kiss me.

The director of the hospital was a friend of my eldest brother's. I was given special care. We rented two large sickrooms and moved in with all our household effects. May, June, July . . . Just about the time the mosquitoes began to proliferate and white mosquito netting was hung over the beds, I moved, on the hospital director's orders, to Funabashi, near the seashore in Chiba. We rented a new house on the outskirts of town. The change of air was intended to help me recuperate, but this, too, turned out to be the wrong place for me. My life was undergoing a hellish upheaval. In the hospital in Asagaya, I'd acquired an odious habit, the use of a certain painkiller. The doctors had first given it to me to ease the pain when changing the dressing on my incision each morning and evening. Before long I couldn't sleep without the drug. I was extremely susceptible to the torment of insomnia, and was soon asking for injections at night. Since the doctors there had given up hope for me, they always kindly gave in to my requests. When I was transferred to the Kyōdō hospital, I persistently implored the director there to let me have the drug. He would reluctantly concede about every third time I pleaded with him. By now I didn't need the stuff to eliminate physical pain, but to blot out my shame and ease my distress. I no longer had the strength to withstand the misery in my own heart. After we moved to Funabashi, I complained to the town doctor of my insomnia and my need for the drug, and demanded a prescription. Later I coerced the timid fellow into giving me a certificate that allowed me to buy the drug directly from the pharmacy. Before I knew it, I was dismally addicted, and in no time at all I was hard up for money. My brother was sending me ninety yen a month for living expenses. Not surprisingly, he rejected my requests for a temporary increase. It stood to reason: what had I done to repay him for all his affection but toy with my own life in a reckless manner?

By autumn of that year, when I began occasionally to show myself in Tokyo, I presented the figure of a ragged and half-mad derelict. I remember it all, all the wretched scenes from that time. It's not something you forget. I was the basest, most reptilian young man in Japan. My reason for going to Tokyo was always to borrow ten or twenty yen. I once wept at a meeting with a magazine editor. I had editors shout me down, angered by my importunacy. Nonetheless, I had, at the time, reason to believe I could sell some of the things I'd written. While I was lying in the hospitals in Asagaya and Kyōdō, I'd managed, with the help of friends, to get two or three of the "suicide notes" from that manila envelope published in good magazines, and the response—the words of support as well as those of denunciation—was too much for me; it only made me more confused and distraught. I sank deeper into my drug addiction and, driven to desperation by the various forms of agony I suffered, would brazenly walk into magazine offices and ask to see an editor, or even the president, from whom I would try to solicit an advance. I was so crazed by my own suffering that I became blind to the obvious fact that other people, too, were living for all they were worth. In the end I managed to sell all the stories in the envelope. Now I had nothing left to sell. I wasn't capable of producing something new right away. I'd exhausted my material.

The literary world pointed at me and said I had talent but lacked morality, but I believed it was the other way around: I had the seeds of morality, but no talent. I do not possess what is called "literary genius." I know no technique other than to ram ahead with my entire being. I'm boorish and unrefined. One of those who adheres with misguided scrupulousness to the rigid ethic of earning one's own livelihood, but who despairs of living up to that ethic and ends up behaving in the most shameless, self-degrading way. I was raised in a strictly conservative household. Debt was the worst of sins. To pay off my debts I went deeper in debt. To help blot out the humiliation I felt, I increased my dosages of the drug. My payments to the pharmacy did nothing but balloon. I remember walking the Ginza one day sobbing and whimpering in broad daylight. I wanted money. I had borrowed cash—at times "extorted" was more like it—from nearly twenty people. I couldn't die. Not till I'd paid back every last loan.

People stopped associating with me. A year after moving to Funabashi, in the fall of 1936, I was bundled into an automobile and taken to a hospital in Itabashi Ward, Tokyo. It was a mental asylum, and I awoke the next morning in one of the cells there.

I stayed a month, and was finally released on a sunny autumn afternoon. H. had come to meet me, and together we got into a taxi.

Though we hadn't seen each other for a month, we remained silent. We rode along for some time before H. spoke.

"You're through with drugs now, I hope." She sounded angry.

"From now on, I trust no one," I said. This was the only thing I'd learned in the hospital.

"That's right." Ever the practical one, H. seemed to interpret my words as having to do with financial matters. She nodded emphatically. "You can't rely on other people."

"I don't trust you, either."

She looked disconcerted and hurt.

While I was in the hospital, H. had moved our things out of the house in Funabashi and was now living in an apartment in Amanuma. I settled in there. I'd been commissioned to write manuscripts for two magazines, and I began writing the night I was released. I wrote the two pieces, collected my money, and set out for Atami, where I drank immoderately for a month. I was at a loss as to what to do. It had been arranged that I was to receive a monthly allowance from my brother for three more years, but I still had all the debts I'd accumulated before entering the hospital. I'd planned to get some good writing done in Atami and, with the money I got for it, to pay back those debts that weighed most heavily on my mind, but, far from being able to write anything, I found it so impossible to face up to the gloom and desolation around me that I could do nothing but drink. I was thoroughly convinced of my own worthlessness as a man. As it turned out, all I accomplished in Atami was to get deeper in debt. Worthless, whatever I tried to do. I was utterly defeated.

I returned to the apartment in Amanuma and lay my body down, all hope abandoned. I was already twenty-nine, and I had nothing. One *dotera* to wear. H.'s possessions, too, were limited to the clothes on her back. I imagined we'd more or less reached the bottom. We lived in insectlike silence, completely dependent upon the money my brother sent each month.

But we had yet, as it turned out, to hit bottom. In early spring of that year, a rather close friend of mine, a Western-style painter, came to me to discuss something that took me completely by surprise. Listening to what he had to say, I felt as if I were suffocating. H. had erred, sadly.

I remembered how flustered she'd become at my offhand, abstract remark in the taxi the afternoon I was released from that accursed hospital. I had caused H. a lot of grief, but I'd always intended to stay with her till the day I died. Because I'm inept at expressing affection, however, neither H. nor the painter had understood this. It was one thing to hear the painter out, but quite another to know what to do. I didn't want anyone to get hurt. I was the oldest of the three parties involved, and I wanted to remain calm and come up with the proper course of action for each of us, but in fact I was quite overwhelmed by it all and so lost my composure, became so faltering and tearful, as to invite scorn from both of them. I was incapable of action. As time went by, the painter gradually distanced himself from the situation. Even in the midst of my own agony, I couldn't help pitying H. She showed signs of wanting to do away with herself. I, too, was one who, when things became hopeless, thought of death. We would die together. Surely even God would forgive us. In a spirit of camaraderie, like brother and sister, we set out on a journey. Minakami Hot Springs. That night, amid the mountains there, we attempted suicide. I was determined not to let H. die, and took some trouble to see that she didn't. H. survived. So did I, however, having been brilliant enough to botch things again. We'd used sleeping pills.

At long last H. and I parted. I hadn't the courage to try to hold her any longer. Some may say I deserted her. Fine. I could see the foul and ugly hell that awaited me were I to go on making a pretense of perseverance in the name of some empty humanitarian ideal. H. went back to the country to live with her mother. I didn't know what became of the painter. I stayed on in the apartment alone. I learned to drink rotgut. My teeth began to decay and fall out. My face became a gross and vulgar mask. I moved to a boardinghouse near the apartment. It was the lowest class of boardinghouse, and I felt it suited me. *This is my farewell look at the world/Standing at the gate in moonlight/Miles of withered fields/Lingering pines*. In my four-and-a-half-mat room I'd drink; drunk, I'd often step outside, lean against the front gate and mutter some such hodgepodge of poems.

No one associated with me except for two or three close friends with whom it was mutually difficult to part. Gradually I began to realize what the world at large thought of me. An ignorant, arrogant scoundrel; an imbecile; a base and cunning, lecherous dog; a con man pretending to genius, living the high life till he's hard up for money, then threatening the folks back home with phoney suicide attempts. I'd abused my virtuous wife, keeping her as one would a dog or a cat and finally throwing her out. These and other descriptions of my character were sneeringly, contemptuously circulated, and I was ostracized and treated as an outcast, a leper. Once I realized this, I stopped going out. In my room, on nights when I had nothing to drink, I would take a certain faint pleasure in munching on rice crackers and reading detective stories. Not a single assignment came from magazines or newspapers. Nor did I have any desire to write. I wouldn't have been able to anyway. But the debts I'd acquired during my sickness . . . No one pressed me to repay them, but those debts tormented me even in my dreams. I had now reached thirty.

I wonder what the turning point was. What was it that made me decide I must go on living, that gave me the strength others take for granted? Perhaps it was my family's run of misfortune. Immediately after he'd been elected to the Diet, my eldest brother was indicted for election fraud. I've always been in awe of my brother's sternly principled character; surely it was not he who'd acted improperly, but some evil person connected with him. My elder sister died. My nephew died. A cousin died. I got wind of these things indirectly. I'd had no direct communication with anyone back home for some time. News of this unhappy sequence of events lifted me, little by little, from my prostration. I'd always been self-conscious about the size of our family home, and the handicap of being a rich man's child had driven me to reckless desperation. The horrible sense of dread at having such unmerited fortune had made me, since earliest childhood, a craven and pessimistic sort. It was my belief that rich children must eventually fall into an especially large and elaborate hell, as befitted their status. Only a coward would try to escape. I was a child of bad karma and would die accordingly. But then, one night, I realized that now, far from being the wealthy scion, I was unmistakably one of the lowest rabble; I hadn't even a proper set of clothes. Money from home was to be cut off at the end of that year. I'd already been removed from the family register. The home in which I'd been born and raised, moreover, had reached a low in its fortunes. I no longer had any special privileges of birthright for which I was obliged to feel small. I had nothing, in fact, but debts. There was that realization, and one other thing. The fact that, as I lay in my room devoid even of the will to die, I was growing wondrously healthy and robust—

this, too, must be mentioned as an important factor in the change that came over me. One might also cite my age, the war, a re-appraisal of history, loathing for my own dereliction, humility toward literature, the existence of God, and so on, but explanations of what turns one around always sound hollow somehow. However closely the explanation may seem to fit the facts, there's always the hint of a gap, a fabrication somewhere. People do not necessarily think and consider in a prescribed way before choosing the path they'll walk. For the most part they simply wander, at some point, into a different meadow.

In the early summer of that, my thirtieth year, I began, for the first time in my life, to aspire to making a living with my pen. Rather late, if you think about it. In my empty four-and-a-half-mat room, I wrote for all I was worth. When there was rice left over in the boardinghouse pot after dinner, I'd stealthily scoop it up and pat it into riceballs in case I got hungry working late into the night. I wasn't writing suicide notes now: I was writing in order to live. A certain mentor of mine encouraged me. When everyone else ridiculed and despised me, that one writer alone quietly, consistently, gave me his support. I had to repay him for the priceless trust he'd placed in me.

In due course I finished "Old Folks." It was an honest account of the time H. and I went to Minakami Hot Springs to die. I was able to sell it immediately. One of the editors I knew had not forgotten me and had been waiting for me to submit something. Rather than squander the money thus acquired, I redeemed my dress kimono from the pawn shop and set out on a journey. The mountains of Kōshū. To reaffirm the change in my heart and mind, I intended to begin a long novel. I was in Kōshū for one entire year. I didn't complete my novel, but I did manage to write and publish more than ten stories. I heard voices of support from all sides. The "literary world" was a place I was grateful for, and blessed, I thought, were those who could spend their lives there. Shortly after New Year's, 1939, with that mentor of mine acting as go-between, I took part in an ordinary arranged marriage. Or, no, it wasn't so ordinary: the groom hadn't a penny to his name. We rented a two-room house on the outskirts of Kōfu City. Rent was six and a half yen a month. I published, in succession, two volumes of collected works. We began to get ahead, if just barely. It was quite an undertaking, but little by little I managed to pay off the debts that so weighed on my mind. In early autumn of that year my wife and I moved to Mitaka, outside Tokyo. It was Tokyo no longer. My life in Tokyo had ended the day I left Ogikubo with a single bag and headed for the hills of Kōshū.

I live solely by my writing now. On signing the registers at inns when I travel, I have no hesitation about listing "writer" as my occupation. If I suffer, I don't talk about it much. I may suffer even more than before, but I wear a smile. The fools say I'm becoming "plebeian." Each day, a giant sun sets over Musashino, hissing and boiling as it sinks.

I was eating a dreary meal, sitting with legs crossed in a three-mat room from which I could see the sunset, and said to my wife, "Being the type of man I am, I'm never going to be successful or rich. But this home of ours is something I intend to maintain and protect." It was then that I hit upon the idea for "Eight Scenes from Tokyo." Pictures from the past whirled around inside me like images from a revolving lantern.

Mitaka was outside Tokyo, but nearby Inokashira Park was counted as one of the city's famous scenic spots, so I saw no problem with including the Musashino sunset among the "Eight Scenes." Now to decide the other seven, I thought, flipping through the photo album of my heart. But I discovered that, for me, what might become art was not the scenery of Tokyo, but the "I" inside the scenery. Had I been deluded by art? Had I deluded art? Conclusion: Art is "I."

The rainy season in Totsuka. Twilight in Hongō. The festival in Kanda. The first snow in Kashiwagi. Fireworks in Hatchōbori. The full moon over Shiba. Evening cicadas in Amanuma. Lightning on the Ginza. Cosmos in the garden of the Itabashi mental hospital. Morning mist in Ogikubo. Sunset over Musashino ... The memories were dark flowers that danced and scattered in the wind and resisted order. And wasn't limiting it to exactly eight scenes a trite and vulgar thing to do? I was soon to encounter two more, one this spring and one this summer.

On April 4 of this year I paid a visit to my illustrious mentor, Mr. S., in Koishikawa. I'd caused him considerable distress during my sickness some five years back, and it had ended with his severely rebuking me and consigning me to what amounted to excommunication. Then, at New Year's this year, I'd gone to see him to pay my respects and to ask his forgiveness. I hadn't been in contact with him since then, and was now calling to ask that he act as sponsor at a party celebrating the publication of a book written by a good friend of mine. He consented, and we spoke about paintings and the works of Akutagawa Ryūnosuke and so on. "I know I've been rather hard on you," he said in that slow and measured way he has of speaking, "but I'm pleased now to see that the result has, in fact, proven favorable." We went to Ueno together by taxi. At an art museum there, we viewed an exhibition of Western-style paintings. Most of them were not very good. I was standing before one when Mr. S. came up beside me and peered closely at the canvas.

"Weak, isn't it?" he said in a detached sort of way.

"It's no good at all," I pronounced.

It was by that Western-style painter of H.'s.

We left the museum and headed for Kayabachō, where he took me to a private screening of the film A Beautiful Dispute, and after that we went to the Ginza for a cup of tea. Thus we whiled away the entire day. When evening fell, I walked with Mr. S. toward Shinbashi Station, where he said he would catch a bus home. On the way, I told him about my plan to write "Eight Scenes from Tokyo." I was talking about the sunset over Musashino when Mr. S. came to a halt on the bridge in front of Shinbashi Station.

"It makes quite a picture, doesn't it?" he said in a low voice, pointing at the Ginza bridge.

"Ah." I, too, stopped to admire it.

"Quite a picture," he said again, as if to himself.

This, too, I thought, should be included among the Eight Scenes: not so much the view, but the viewers themselves, Mr. S. and his excommunicated, delinquent disciple.

It was some two months later that I came upon yet another felicitous scene. We received a special-delivery letter one day from my wife's younger sister. "T. departs tomorrow. I'm told we'll be able to see him briefly at Shiba Park. Please come there tomorrow morning at nine o'clock. I'd like you to explain my feelings to him. I'm such a fool, I haven't said anything at all."

This sister-in-law of mine is twenty-two, but so tiny that one might easily mistake her for a child. Last year, following a formally arranged meeting, she and T. became engaged, but directly after the exchange of betrothal gifts T. was inducted into the army and assigned to a regiment in Tokyo. I had met the young, uniformed soldier once and had spoken with him for half an hour or so. He was a bright, alert, and well-mannered youth. Now, apparently, he was about to be sent to the front.

Less than two hours after we received the special delivery letter from my sister-in-law, another one arrived. "After thinking it over," she wrote, "I realize that my request was frivolous. You needn't say anything to T. But please do come to see him off."

My wife and I burst out laughing. It was clear what a dither the girl was in. She'd moved in with T.'s parents just two or three days before.

The next morning we got up early and set out for Shiba Park. A great crowd of well-wishers had congregated on the grounds of Zōjō-ji, the temple there. I stopped an elderly man in a khaki uniform who was busily wending his way through the crowd and learned from him that T.'s unit would stop in front of the huge main gate, but only for a five-minute rest before heading out. We stepped outside the temple grounds and stood in front of the gate to await them. Before long, my wife's sister, carrying a small flag, arrived with T.'s parents. It was the first time I'd met the parents. We weren't officially relatives yet, and I, always incompetent in social situations, failed even to introduce myself properly. I merely nodded to them and turned to my sister-in-law.

"Well?" I said. "Are you managing to stay calm?"

"Oh, nothing to it." She laughed brightly.

"What's the matter with you?" My wife scowled at her. "Cackling away like that."

An awful lot of people were there to see T. off. In front of the enormous gate stood six large banners bearing his name—the workers from his family's factory had taken time off to send him on his way. I walked away from everyone and stood to one side. I felt I was being looked down upon. T.'s family was wealthy. I had teeth missing and my clothes were a disgrace. I wore neither hakama nor hat. The impoverished writer. Some slovenly relative of the boy's fiancée—no doubt that's how T.'s parents regarded me. When my wife's sister came up to speak to me, I sent her away, saying, "You've got an important role to play today. Go stand with your father-in-law."

We waited a long time for T.'s unit to show up. Ten o'clock, eleven, twelve . . . Still they hadn't arrived. Sightseeing buses full of schoolgirls passed by. On the door of each bus was a piece of paper with the name of the girls' school written on it. I saw the name of a school back home. As far as I knew, my eldest brother's daughter was a student there. She might be on that bus, I thought. Maybe, as the bus passed, she was gazing innocently at the figure of her idiot uncle standing stolid and impassive before that famous Tokyo landmark, the main gate of Zōjō-ji, without realizing who it was. Twenty or so such buses came and went, and each time one passed, the lady tour guide would point in my direction and launch into an explanation. I feigned indifference at first, then tried a few poses. I folded my arms in a casual manner reminiscent of the statue of Balzac, and it was then that I began to feel as if I myself had become one of the famous landmarks of Tokyo.

It was nearly one o'clock when shouts of "They're here!" were heard, followed immediately by the arrival of a truck loaded with soldiers. T. had learned to drive and was behind the wheel. I stood at the rear of the crowd and idly looked on.

"Please?" My sister-in-law, who'd materialized beside me at some point, whispered this and pushed me forward. Snapping out of my reverie. I looked up to see that T. had come down from the truck and was saluting in my direction. I was, apparently, the first one he'd spotted. I hesitated and looked around before realizing that it was indeed me he was saluting, then squeezed through the crowd toward him with the girl in tow.

"Don't worry about us," I told him. "This one's not very bright, as you can see, but her heart's in the right place. You've got nothing to worry about. We'll all watch out for her." Untypically, I said these words without so much as a smile. I looked at the girl, who stood stiff and tense, chin raised. T. blushed somewhat and raised his hand again in a silent salute.

"Don't you have something to say?" I asked the girl, grinning now.

She looked down at the ground and said, "No, nothing."

The order to prepare for departure came moments later. I started to slip back into the crowd, but again I was pushed forward by my sister-in-law. She guided me to a spot near the cab of the truck, where only T.'s parents were standing.

"Good luck, and don't worry!" I shouted. T.'s father turned and looked at me. I detected a flash of irritation in that stern man's eyes that seemed to say: Who is this intrusive fool? But I didn't flinch. Was not the last bastion of a man's pride his ability to state that he has known near-fatal suffering? I was of no use to the army, and impoverished to boot, but now was not the time for diffidence. The Tokyo landmark shouted again, in an even louder voice.

"Nothing to worry about!"

Should by any chance some difficulty arise concerning T.'s marriage to my wife's sister, I told myself it was I, the social outlaw for whom appearances were of no importance, who would fight for the couple to the bitter end.

Having acquired that scene at Zōjō-ji's main gate, I felt as if my story had taken shape, like a bow drawn as taut as a full, rising moon. A few days later, armed with a map of Tokyo, pen, ink, and paper, I set out in high spirits for Izu. And what has come of my stay at this hot springs inn? It's been ten days since I arrived, and I still seem to be here. I must be up to something.

Dazai and his first daughter, Sonoko, in Mitaka, summer 1944.

Early Light

薄明

Hakumei

In November 1944, just two months after Dazai's son, Masaki, was born, B29s bombed Tokyo for the first time. In March 1945 the bombings grew intense, and Dazai sent his family to stay at the Ishihara house in Kōfu, where Michiko's younger sister, Ai, had been living alone. On April 2 the house in Mitaka was struck by a bomb. It was not damaged very badly, but Dazai was half buried in dirt when the wall of the pit he was taking shelter in collapsed. He went to join his family in Kōfu a few days later. Incendiary bombs were dropped on Kōfu during the early morning hours of July 7.

When our house in Mitaka, Tokyo, was damaged in the bombings, we moved to Kōfu, my wife's hometown. Her younger sister had been living alone in the family house there.

This was in early April of 1945. Allied planes passed frequently enough through the skies over Kōfu but hardly ever dropped any bombs. Nor was the war zone atmosphere as intense as it was in Tokyo. We were able to sleep without our air raid gear for the first time in months. I was thirty-seven. My wife was thirty-four, my

daughter five, and my son two, technically, though he'd just been
born in August of the previous year. Our life up to that point had
not been easy by any means, but we had at least remained alive and
free of serious illnesses or injuries. Having survived so much
adversity, even I felt a desire to go on living a bit longer, if only to
see how things would turn out with the world. Stronger than that,
however, was the fear that my wife and children would be killed
before I was, leaving me alone. Just to think about that possiblity
was unendurable. I had to see to it that they survived, and that
meant adopting the most prudent measures. I had no money,
however. Whenever I did get my hands on a fair sum, I would
promptly drink it away. I have the serious defect known as a drinking habit. Liquor at that time was an expensive indulgence, but
whenever friends or acquaintances visited me, I was unable to stop
myself from whisking them off to guzzle great quantities of the
stuff, just as I had in the old days.

So much for prudent measures. Even as I envied those who'd
long since evacuated their families to the distant countryside, I, for
lack of means and out of sheer indolence, remained forever dilly-
dallying in Mitaka, until at last we were visited by a bomb and I lost
all desire to stick it out any longer and moved the family to Kōfu.
Now, sleeping without my air raid gear for the first time in nearly a
hundred days, I was able to breathe a small sigh of relief, reflecting
that, though further hardships undoubtedly lay ahead, for the time
being at least there'd be no need to bundle up the children in the
middle of a cold night and scramble into the bomb shelter.

We were now, however, a family who'd lost their own home, and
this put us in an awkward position. I felt as though I'd been
through my share of tribulations in life, but moving into someone
else's house with two small children in tow allowed me a taste of
various distinctive new ones. My wife's mother and father had
both passed away, her elder sisters had married and left, and
though the youngest of the siblings, a boy, was officially the head
of the household, he had entered the navy right after graduating

from university two or three years before, leaving the youngest
sister, a girl of twenty-six or twenty-seven, alone in the house in
Kōfu. She corresponded regularly with her brother, apparently consulting with him in minute detail about all the household affairs. I,
of course, was the elder brother-in-law of these two, but, elder or
not, I obviously had no voice in managing those affairs. Far from being in a position of authority, in fact, I'd been nothing but a burden
to this family ever since my wife and I had married. I was not, in
other words, a man to be relied upon. It was only natural,
therefore, that I be excluded from consultation, and since I, for my
part, had not the slightest interest in the family "assets" or
whatever, this was a mutually satisfactory arrangement. But, being
older than both the navy boy and his twenty-six or twenty-seven-
year-old sister (twenty-eight, maybe—I never really checked), I was
worried that we might unintentionally trample on their pride, or
that they might be leery of my trying to outsmart them and get my
hands on those assets—though surely no one would be *that*
distrustful—and the truth is that I felt constantly on guard, as if I
were moving through a lush, moss-covered garden, hopping gingerly from one stepping-stone to the next. I even thought how much
easier it would be on all of us if only there were a still older man in
the house, one who'd accumulated more experience in the real
world.

This negative sort of concern for the feelings of others can wear
a man out. I borrowed the six-mat room facing the rear garden to
work and sleep in and arranged for my wife and children to sleep in
the room that housed the Buddhist altar. I paid a fair rent for the
rooms and made sure that I contributed our share to the purchase
of food and what not, and when I had visitors I took care not to use
the parlor, but showed them into my workroom. I am a drinker,
however, and visitors from Tokyo were not infrequent, the upshot
of which was that, even as I maintained every intention of honor-
ing the privileges due the actual owners of the house, I in fact ended up taking any number of inexcusable liberties. My sister-in-law

actually treated us with considerable diffidence and was a great help with the children, but, though there was never an unpleasant, head-on confrontation, we were a family that had lost its home, and while oversensitivity to that fact may have been the true cause of my discomfort, there was, nonetheless, the feeling of forever walking on thin ice. What this all added up to was that, thanks to our evacuation to the country, both the sister and ourselves were put under a debilitating strain. Still, our situation was better than most, it would seem; one can only guess what it was like for those evacuees in even worse circumstances.

"Don't evacuate. Stick it out in Tokyo till your house is burned to the ground: you'll be better off."

I wrote this advice in a letter to a close friend who remained with his family in Tokyo.

We'd come to Kōfu in early April, when it was still chilly and the cherry blossoms, considerably later than those in Tokyo, had just begun to open. We were there throughout May and June, when the heat unique to the Kōfu basin began to make itself felt. The deep green leaves of the pomegranate trees took on an oily sheen in the intense sunlight, and soon their bright red flowers burst into bloom, and the little green grapes grew plumper each day, gradually forming long, rangy bunches that hung heavily from the trellises; and it was just at about that time that a commotion began to sweep through the city of Kōfu. The entire town was abuzz with the rumor that the bombings were to be directed at small and medium sized cities, and that Kōfu, too, would burn. Everyone began making preparations to flee, loading their carts with household goods and dragging their families off into the mountains; you heard the sounds of footsteps and carts incessantly, even late at night. I had from the beginning been resigned to the fact that Kōfu too would eventually be hit, but to load our belongings on a cart and evacuate to the mountains with my wife and children to beg lodging from strangers when I'd scarcely had time to enjoy the relief of sleeping without air raid gear—that was asking too much.

I thought we should stay where we were. If the incendiary bombs started dropping, my wife, carrying the baby on her back and leading the five-year-old by the hand, could flee to the fields on the outskirts of town while my sister-in-law and I stayed behind and protected the house, fighting the flames as best we could. If it burned down, it burned down; working together, we could build a little shack on the ruins and take our stand.

This was the plan I suggested, and everyone agreed to it. We dug a pit to bury food, a set of kitchen utensils, umbrellas, shoes, toiletries, a mirror, needles and thread—all the barest necessities, to avoid being reduced to utter wretchedness should the house be destroyed.

"Bury these, too." My five-year-old daughter held out a pair of red *geta* clogs.

"Ah, yes. In they go," I said, taking the clogs and stuffing them into one corner of the pit. I felt for a moment as if I were burying a person.

"At least now we're all together," my sister-in-law said. She was, perhaps, experiencing the faint glow of happiness one is said to feel on the eve of annihilation. No more than four or five days later, in fact, the house went up in flames. It came a good month earlier than I'd expected.

For the previous ten days or so, the two children had been going to a doctor for eye problems, namely epidemic conjunctivitis, or "pinkeye." The boy's condition wasn't all that bad, but his sister's grew steadily worse. Within about a week—two or three days before the bombing—she had temporarily lost all use of her eyes. Her eyelids were so swollen it distorted her features, and when you forcibly pried the lids apart, you saw an inflamed, festering mess that resembled the eye of a dead fish. Thinking that perhaps this was no mere pinkeye but a virulent bacterial infection of some sort that had already done permanent damage, I took her to a different doctor, but again it was diagnosed as conjunctivitis. It would take quite a while to clear up entirely, we were told, but it would clear up.

Doctors frequently make mistakes, however. In fact, they're mistaken more often than not. I've never been one to put undue faith in anything doctors say.

I just hoped she'd regain her eyesight soon. I drank heavily, but couldn't get drunk. One night I even vomited on the way home from a place I'd been drinking at, and I'm not joking when I say that as I squatted there by the roadside I pressed my palms together in prayer. *Please let her eyes be open when I get home.* When I reached the house I heard her singing innocently. Thank God, I thought, dashing inside, only to find her standing there alone with her head bowed in the dimly lit room, singing to herself.

I couldn't bear to watch her. My child went blind because I'm a penniless drunk. If I had led the life of a proper, upstanding citizen, perhaps this calamity would never have occurred. The sins of the father are visited on the child. It was divine retribution. I went so far as to tell myself that if this child's eyes remained closed for the rest of her life, I would give up all thoughts of literature and personal glory to be permanently at her side.

"Where are your footsies, baby? Where are your handsies?" When she was feeling happy she'd play with her baby brother like this, groping for him blindly. What if there were an air raid now, with her in this condition? The thought made me shudder. We'd have no choice but to run for it, with the baby on my wife's back and this child on mine. But it would be impossible for my sister-in-law to protect the house all by herself. She, too, then, would have to flee with us. Judging by what the Allied planes had done to Tokyo, one had to assume that the city of Kōfu would be completely destroyed, including, surely, the doctor's office we were taking the girl to. And the other clinics as well; there wouldn't be a single doctor left in town. Then where would we be?

"I don't care what they do to us. It just seems to me they might be so kind as to wait another month or so before they do it."

Later on the very night I'd smilingly announced this opinion at the dinner table, we heard the air raid sirens for the first time, simultaneous with the familiar thundering explosions and a lighting up of the sky all around us. They'd begun dropping the incendiary bombs. I heard a series of splashes: my sister-in-law was throwing tableware into the small pond near the veranda.

It was the worst possible time for the attack to come. I boosted my blind child up on my back. My wife did likewise with the baby boy, and we each ran outside clutching a futon. We ran about ten blocks, taking shelter in ditches two or three times along the way, before we came to open fields. No sooner had we spread both futon out on a field of freshly mown barley and sat down to catch our breath than a shower of fire fell from the sky directly overhead.

"Get under the futon!" I shouted to my wife and threw my own futon over me, lying face down with my daughter still clinging to my back. I thought how painful a direct hit would probably be.

We were spared that, but when I threw off the futon and sat up for a look, I saw that we were surrounded by a sea of fire.

"Get up and put out the fire! Put out the fire!" I yelled, not only to my wife but in a voice loud enough for all the others lying on the ground around us to hear, and we began smothering the flames with our mats and blankets. It was almost amusing how easily they went out. Though my daughter could see nothing, she must have sensed that something extraordinary was going on; she clung silently to my shoulders, without uttering so much as a whimper.

"Are you all right?" I asked my wife, walking up to her once the flames were pretty much under control.

"Yes," she said quietly. "Let's hope this is as bad as it gets." For her, apparently, incendiary bombs were nothing compared to the explosive variety.

We moved to another spot in the field to rest, and no sooner had we done so than it began to rain fire again. This may sound strange, but it occurred to me that perhaps there is a splinter of divinity in each of us after all. Not only our family but everyone who'd taken refuge in that field escaped injury. We all busied ourselves snuffing out the sticky, greasy, flaming globs with futon or blankets or dirt, then sat back down to rest.

My sister-in-law left for the house of a distant relative in the hills some four miles from the city to try to get food for the following day. My wife and the children and I sat on one of the futon and used the other to cover ourselves. We decided this was as good a place as any to hold our ground. I was exhausted. I'd had just about enough of running hither and thither with the girl on my back. The children were now lying quietly on the futon, asleep, while their parents gazed vacantly at the glow of Kōfu going up in flames. The roar of the airplanes had decreased considerably.

"I guess it's about over," my wife said.

"Yeah. Well, none too soon for me, I'll tell you."

"I suppose the house burned down."

"Well, you never know. It'd be nice if it was still there."

I figured it was hopeless, but wouldn't it be wonderful if by some miracle the house was still standing?

"Not likely, though," I said.

"No, I suppose not."

It was hard to abandon the last flicker of hope, however.

A farmhouse was blazing away right before us. It took an incredibly long time to burn to the ground. One could almost see the history of that house going up in flames along with its roof and pillars.

The night faded into a pale dawn.

We carried the children to the national school, which hadn't burned. They let us rest in a classroom on the second floor. The children began to wake. Even after waking up, of course, the girl's eyes remained closed. Groping about, she amused herself by climbing up on the lecturer's platform and what not. Her condition seemed scarcely to weigh on her mind.

I left the wife and children there and set out to check on the house. It was a tremendous ordeal just walking through the streets, what with the heat and smoke from the smoldering houses on either side, but by following a roundabout path, changing course any number of times, I somehow managed to reach our neighborhood. How happy I would be if the house were still standing! But, no, it couldn't possibly be. I told myself I shouldn't get my hopes up, but the phantom of that one-in-a-million chance kept raising its head. I came in sight of the black wooden fence around the house.

It was still there!

But it was only the fence. The house itself was completely destroyed. My sister-in-law was standing in the ruins, her face black with soot.

"Hi. How are the children?"

"They're fine."

"Where are they?"

"At the school."

"I've got some riceballs. I had to walk like mad, but at least I got some food."

"Thanks."

"Let's keep our spirits up. Look at this. Most of the things we buried are fine. We'll be all right for the time being."

"We should have buried more stuff."

"It's all right. With all this, we'll be able to hold our heads up high wherever we go for help. I'm going to take some food to the school. You stay here and rest. Here, have some riceballs. Take as many as you like."

A woman of twenty-seven or twenty-eight is in some ways more mature than a man of forty or more. She was a rock, a model of composure. Her perfectly worthless brother-in-law proceeded to rip a few planks from the fence, lay them on the ground in the field in back, and sit down with legs crossed to stuff his cheeks with the riceballs she'd left. I was completely without resources or plan. But, whether good for nothing or just plain stupid, I didn't give a thought to what we were to do. The only thing that really concerned me was my daughter's eye problem. How in the world would we go about treating it now?

Before very long my wife and sister-in-law arrived. My wife had the baby on her back, and my sister-in-law was leading my daughter by the hand.

"Did you walk all the way here?" I asked my daughter.

"Uh-huh," she said, nodding.

"Is that right? That's really something. The house burned down."

"Uh-huh." She nodded again.

"It looks like the doctor's place is gone, too," I said, turning to my wife. "What are we going to do about her eyes?"

"We had them washed out this morning."

"Where?"

"A doctor came by the school."

"Really? That's great."

"No, just the best they could do. A nurse did it."

"Oh."

We took shelter for the day at the house of a schoolfriend of my sister-in-law's on the outskirts of town. With us we carried the food and the pots and pans we'd unearthed from the pit. Smiling at my sister-in-law, I pulled a watch from my pocket.

"We've still got this. I grabbed it before I ran out of the house."

It was my brother-in-law's pocket watch. I'd found it in the desk some time before and taken it out for my own use.

"Good going." She smiled back at me. "You surprise me. This really adds to our assets."

I was rather proud of myself. "It can be pretty inconvenient if you don't have a timepiece, you know." I pressed the watch into my little girl's hand. "See?" I said. "It's a watch. Put it up to your ear. Hear it go tick-tick-tick? Look at that," I told my wife and her sister. "It even makes a good toy for blind kids."

My daughter was standing perfectly still with her head cocked and the watch pressed against her ear when suddenly it slipped from her hand. It made a clear, tinkling sound as it hit the ground. The crystal was smashed to pieces. It was beyond repair. One could hardly expect to find a shop selling watch crystals.

"Oh, no," I said, my heart sinking.

"Dummy," my sister-in-law muttered, but I was relieved to see that she didn't seem particularly distressed about suddenly losing what was virtually the only "asset" she had left.

We cooked dinner in a corner of the garden at the schoolfriend's house, then retired early in a six-mat room inside. My wife and her sister, tired as they were, seemed unable to sleep and were quietly discussing what we should do.

"Hey, there's nothing to worry about," I told them. "We'll all go to my family's place up north. Everything's going to be fine."

They fell silent. From the beginning, neither of them had put much stock in any opinions of mine. They were apparently devising plans of their own now and didn't even deign to reply.

"All right, I know you don't have any faith in me." I smiled sourly. "But, listen, trust me just this once. That's all I'm asking."

I heard my sister-in-law giggle in the darkness, as if I'd said something totally outlandish. Then she and my wife continued their discussion.

"Fine. Suit yourselves," I said with a chuckle of my own. "Not much I can do if you won't trust in me."

"Well, what do you expect?" my wife suddenly snapped. "You say such preposterous things, we never know if you're joking or serious. It's only natural that we don't rely on you. Even now, with things the way they are, I bet all you can think about is saké."

"Don't be ridiculous."

"But if we had some, you'd drink it, wouldn't you?"

"Well, I don't know, maybe I would."

The two ladies decided that, at any rate, it wouldn't do to impose on our present hosts any more than we already had, and that, come morning, we'd have to look for somewhere else to stay. The following day we loaded our things on a large cart and went to the house of another of my sister-in-law's acquaintances. This house was quite a spacious affair. The man who owned it was about fifty and seemed a gentleman of sterling character. He lent us a ten-mat room. We also found a hospital nearby. The gentleman's wife told us that the prefectural hospital in Kōfu had been destroyed and had relocated to a building here on the outskirts of town. My wife and I each shouldered a child and set out, taking a shortcut through the mulberry fields, and reached the hospital, at the foot of the mountains, in about ten minutes.

The opthalmologist was a woman.

"The girl can't open her eyes at all. We're thinking about heading for my family's house in the country, but it's a long trip by train, and we don't even want to attempt it if her condition might get worse on the way. We're really at our wits' end." Wiping the sweat from my face, I fervently described the girl's symptoms, hoping to induce the lady doctor to do everything in her power to help us.

"What, this?" she said breezily. "This will clear up in no time."

"Really?"

"It hasn't affected the eyes themselves at all. I'm sure you'll be able to travel in four or five days."

My wife broke in to ask if there were any injections that could be given for this sort of thing.

"There are, yes, but . . ."

"Please, Doctor," said my wife, bowing deeply.

Whether the injection worked or the infection had simply run its natural course I couldn't say, but my daughter's eyes opened on the afternoon of the second day after we visited the hospital.

"Thank goodness, thank goodness," was all I could say, and I said it over and over. The first thing I did was take her to see what was left of the house.

"See? It burned all up."

"Yeah," she said, with a big smile on her face. "Burned all up."

"Everything's gone. Mr. Rabbit, our shoes, the Odagiri house, the Chino house, they all burned up."

"Yeah, they all burned up," she said, still smiling.

The house in Kanagi where Dazai was born.

Garden

庭

Niwa

———

*Emperor Hirohito announced Japan's surrender in a national
radio broadcast on August 15, 1945, a mere two weeks after
Dazai and his family arrived in Tsugaru.*

*Dazai repeatedly referred to himself as a "freeloader" at his
family home, but the fact that he stayed there for some fifteen
months before returning to Tokyo would seem to indicate that
he enjoyed basking in the hometown atmosphere he had pined
over for so long. During the time he was there the youngest of
his elder sisters died, the GHQ of the Occupation forces
ordered the breaking up of estates held by wealthy landowners
(including, of course, the Tsushimas), his grandmother died,
and his eldest brother, Bunji, was elected to the House of
Representatives.*

*"Garden" deals with the touchy relationship between Dazai
and Bunji largely by setting it against that of the historical
figures Hideyoshi and Rikyū, and some explanation may be in
order.*

*Toyotomi Hideyoshi (1536–1598) was the military genius
who unified Japan after the death of his predecessor, the
powerful daimyō Oda Nobunaga. The son of a farmer,
uneducated and ugly, he had nonetheless succeeded in
becoming Nobunaga's right-hand man. Hideyoshi, in spite
of his taste for extravagance and ostentation—exemplified*

by his construction of the enormous Osaka Castle—was also attracted to sadō—the "Way of Tea." Sadō was a zen-influenced ethical and aesthetic system that amounted to an entire way of life.

Sen-no-Rikyū (1522–1591) was the greatest tea master of all, and Hideyoshi was Rikyū's patron. Countless tales describing their relationship and the subtle niceties of Rikyū's impeccable aesthetic judgments have been handed down over the centuries and have virtually attained the status of folklore. One such tale has Rikyū visiting a friend who lives in the quiet, simple way favored by tea masters. The friend goes outside and knocks a lemon down from a tree, then proceeds to use it to flavor the soybean paste he serves Rikyū. Rikyū is charmed and impressed by this quaint offering, but when he is also served fine saké and rice cakes, he perceives that the apparently spontaneous, unaffected manner of his host was in fact premeditated, and he promptly leaves in disgust. Many similar stories depict Rikyū getting the best of Hideyoshi.

Hideyoshi seems to have become a bit unbalanced late in his life, and a lot of heads rolled (including that of his nephew, whom he had previously designated his heir). His mixture of admiration for and envy of Rikyū finally exploded when (according to one version of the story) Rikyū had a wooden statue of himself placed atop the main gate of Daitokuji Temple. Appalled at the presumptuousness of this, Hideyoshi ordered Rikyū to commit suicide.

———◆———

Our house in Tokyo was damaged by a bomb, so we moved to my wife's family home in Kōfu, but when that, too, was burned to the ground in the bombings, the four of us—myself, my wife, and our five-year-old daughter and two-year-old son—had no choice but to head for the house in Tsugaru where I was born. My father and mother had both passed away, leaving my eldest brother, more than ten years my senior, in charge of the household. Some may wonder why I didn't return to my home town sooner, without waiting to twice be the victim of calamity, but the fact is that in my twenties I did all sorts of things to bring disgrace upon my relatives, and I was hardly in a position now to go barge brazenly in on my brother. Nonetheless, having twice been bombed out of house and home, and with two small children to think of, I felt I had to give it a shot, so in late July, after I'd sent a telegram saying we were on our way, we left Kōfu.

It was a fairly grueling journey, and it took a full four days and nights before we finally arrived at the house in Tsugaru. Everyone greeted us with a smile. There was even a bottle of saké waiting for me on my dinner tray.

But here, too, in this little town at the northern tip of Honshu, aircraft buzzed through the skies spewing bombs. The day after I arrived I began helping build a shelter in a nearby field.

Then, just a short time later, the Emperor came on the radio to announce our surrender.

The day after the announcement, my brother began weeding his garden. I lent a hand.

"When I was young," he said, pulling up a clump of weeds, "I thought an overgrown garden had a certain charm of its own, but since I've gotten older, it bothers me to see so much as a single weed out here."

I wondered if that meant that I, even at my age, was still young. I still like old, untended gardens overgrown with weeds.

"But even a garden no bigger than this one," my brother went on, muttering as if to himself, "if you want to keep it looking nice, you've got to have a gardener out here every day. And protecting the shrubs from the snow in winter's another big job."

"It's really a lot of trouble, isn't it," the freeloading younger brother timidly chimed in.

"It used to get done all right," the elder brother said soberly, "but what with the lack of help these days, and all the commotion over the air raids, a gardener's been out of the question. It may not look like much now, but this garden wasn't just thrown together at random, you know."

"No, I don't suppose it was." The younger brother doesn't have much interest in this sort of thing. He is, after all, a barbarian who can gaze at an overgrown, untended garden and think it beautiful.

As the elder brother was explaining what style the garden belonged to, where that style had originated, and how it had found its way to Tsugaru, the conversation gradually came around to Sen-no-Rikyū.

"Why don't you fellows write about Rikyū? I think it would make a good story."

"Ah," I said noncommittally. When the talk turns to literature, even the freeloading younger brother can display a bit of the finicky reticence of a specialist.

"That was quite a man, I'll tell you," the elder brother continued, undaunted. "Not even Hideyoshi could ever get the better of him. Surely you've at least heard the story of the lemon bean paste?"

"Ah," the younger brother replied, keeping it vague.

"The unlearned man of letters," he said with a scowl, having apparently decided I didn't know anything. When my brother scowls, his face is scary enough to give you the chills. He thinks I'm a frightfully uneducated person, that I never read any books, and this seems to displease him more than anything else about me.

The freeloader, thrown into a flurry by his own blunder, smiled and said, "It's just that I don't really like Rikyū very much, somehow."

"He was a complex man, that's why."

"Exactly. There are things about him I can't understand. Even though he seemed to be scornful of Hideyoshi, he couldn't bring himself to break away from him. To me, there's something impure about that."

"It was because of Hideyoshi's charisma," he said, having at some point recovered his good humor. "It's hard to say which of them was superior, as a person. They were locked in a fierce struggle. Diametrically opposed in every way. Hideyoshi came from a poor background and had the looks to match—small and skinny, with a face like a monkey—and no education. Yet he, with his taste for grandiose, ornate architecture, was responsible for the flowery splendor of late sixteenth-century culture. Rikyū, on the other hand, came from a fairly wealthy family, he was stoutly built, imposing, handsome, and well educated, yet he preferred simple, quiet elegance, the thatched hut. That's what makes the opposition between them so interesting."

"But Rikyū was Hideyoshi's vassal, right? He was, what, the tea server. The outcome was decided from the beginning, wasn't it?" I said, still smiling.

"That wasn't what their relationship was about at all. Rikyū had more real power than most feudal lords, and those lords who were what you might call intellectual were more devoted to him and his refinement than they were to the unschooled Hideyoshi. Which is why Hideyoshi couldn't help but feel uneasy."

Men are strange creatures, I thought as I tugged at the weeds. A man like Hideyoshi, with all his political power, loses out to Rikyū in terms of aesthetic refinement—couldn't he just laugh it off and forget about it? Can't a man be satisfied without having to beat everybody at everything? And as for Rikyū, why did he have to make so sure he got the better of his own master, the man he was supposed to be serving? There was no way Hideyoshi could ever understand the nihilism behind aesthetic refinement. Rikyū could have just wandered off and spent his life traveling, like Bashō and all those people, couldn't he? The image of him sticking by Hideyoshi's side, obviously not thoroughly repelled by the man's power, winning a few, losing a few, both of them locked in a desperate struggle, I simply don't see the point of it all. If Hideyoshi was such an appealing character, why couldn't Rikyū just show him some artless affection and devote his life to serving him?

"There's no scene in the story that has the sort of beauty to move people." Maybe it's because I'm still young, but I'd find it tiresome to write stories without any such scenes.

My brother laughed, as if he were thinking how naive I am.

"That's where you're wrong," he said. "I guess you're not capable of writing it. You ought to study the adult world a bit more. But then, you're the unlearned man of letters, aren't you."

He stood up looking resigned and gazed at the garden. I did the same.

"It looks much better, doesn't it?" I said.

"Mm."

Rikyū's not for me. I for one have no desire to score points off my brother while I'm sponging off him. Rivalry is a shameful thing. Freeloading or not, it's never occurred to me to compete with my brother. The outcome was decided at birth.

My brother's lost an awful lot of weight lately. He's been sick. And yet there's a persistent rumor that he'll run for the Diet, or be elected governor. The people in my family are worried about his health.

A lot of visitors come to the house. My brother shows them to the parlor on the second floor and talks with them all, and he never complains of being tired. Yesterday a lady chanter of *Shinnai* ballads came. She's said to be the number one disciple of the great Fuji Tayū. She plucked a samisen and chanted for my brother in the room on the second floor with the gold-leaf sliding screens. He let me sit with him and listen. She did "Morning Crow" and "Sold into Bondage." Sitting in the formal posture, my knees went numb, and it was quite painful. I also felt as if I were catching a cold. But my sickly elder brother didn't seem the least bit uncomfortable, and requested two more ballads: "The Prophetic Dream," and "The Jester's Love Suicide." When she finally finished, we all moved to the parlor, and it was then that my brother voiced his opinion.

"It's a pity you've had to evacuate to the country and farm a plot of land, but it can't be helped with the times being what they are. However, as long as you keep your heart set on your craft, it won't deteriorate even if you lay down the samisen for a year or two.

You've got your future ahead of you. I'm sure your talents will only improve."

Though an utter layman in these matters himself, he calmly, confidently passed judgment on this woman who's famous even in Tokyo as a master of her art. It was quite a speech. One almost expected to hear shouts of "Bravo!" from the gallery.

The Japanese writers my brother seems to respect at the moment are Nagai Kafū and Tanizaki Jun'ichirō. He's also an avid reader of Chinese essayists. Tomorrow, I understand, the Chinese-born *go* master, Seigen, is coming to visit him. They're going to have a leisurely discussion, not about *go*, apparently, but about social conditions and the state of the world and so on.

This morning the elder brother got up early, and now he's already out working in the garden. Meanwhile, the barbarian younger brother, who seems to have caught a cold listening to the *Shinnai* balladeer yesterday, is sitting in the guest house hugging a hibachi, trying to decide if he should help with the weeding or not, and turning all sorts of arbitrary, self-serving notions over in his mind. Like, maybe this Seigen fellow is one of those who sees nothing wrong with an overgrown, untended garden.

Summer, 1946, in Kanagi.

Two Little Words

親という二字

Oya to iu niji

---

*The Japanese word for "parent" (or "parents"), oya, is a
two-syllable word written with a single Chinese character,
which is the point of the* senryū *poem quoted at the beginning
of this story. Admittedly, the joke doesn't work quite as well in
English.*

*Senryū are satirical versions of the seventeen-syllable haiku.
The* Yanagidaru *is a series of collections of* senryū *compiled in
the eighteenth and nineteenth centuries, and Dazai was an
avid reader of these collections.*

> *"Those two little words:
> 'Papa.'"* So says the father
> who can't read or write.

What a pathetic scene this *senryū* evokes.

"Wherever you go, son, whatever you do, always
remember these two little words: Papa."

"'Papa' is one word, Dad."

"H'm? Oh. Well, even if it is one word. Or three words, for that
matter."

So much for the lecture on filial piety.

But I'm not setting out to analyze verses from the *Yanagidaru* here. It's just that I was reminded of this poem recently, when I met up with a certain illiterate old man.

Those who've lost their homes in the air raids know how often you end up having to go to the post office. I was bombed out of house and home twice and finally fled to my eldest brother's place in Tsugaru to freeload off him, and since I've been here I'm constantly heading down to the post office to deal with government insurance and public bonds and so on. What's more, a Sendai newspaper is about to begin serializing a novel of mine called *Pandora's Box*, a story of lost love, and what with sending off the manuscripts by mail and conducting the necessary discussions by wire, these trips have recently become even more frequent.

It was on the bench at the post office that I got to know the old man I refer to.

It's always crowded there. I was sitting on the bench awaiting my turn.

"Mister. Write this for me, will ya?"

He was a timorous but also somehow crafty-looking old fellow, tiny as an elf, with a face to match. That he was a heavy drinker I knew at a glance, being one myself. The skin of his face was pale and coarse, and his nose was red.

I nodded, stood up, and walked over to the inkwell.

He showed me his postal savings passbook, a withdrawal slip (he called it the "take-out form"), and his personal seal.

"How much?" I said.

"Forty yen."

I wrote "forty yen" on the withdrawal slip, then copied down the passbook number and the name and address. An old address in Aomori had been crossed out on the passbook, and the new one, in Kanagi, was written underneath. I idly wondered if he'd lost his home in the air raids, and, as I later found out, that was exactly the case. The name on the passbook was a woman's: Takeuchi Toki. I didn't give much thought to that, merely assuming that Toki was his wife's name. It wasn't, though.

He presented the slip at one of the windows, then came back and sat beside me on the bench. After a while, the clerk in charge of cash payments called out the name from a different window.

"Takeuchi Toki-san."

"Yup," said the old man. He stood up and walked to the counter.

"Are you Takeuchi Toki?" the clerk said.

"No I ain't. She's my daughter. Yup. My youngest."

"It's best if she comes in person," the clerk said as he handed over the money.

Walking back toward me with the cash in his hands, the old man shrugged his shoulders slightly and gave me a crafty smile.

"She can't come in person," he told me. "She's dead."

From that day on I was to run into this old man at the post office time and again. As soon as he'd see me he'd flash a peculiar smile. "Mister," he'd always say. "Write it for me, will ya?"

"How much?"

"Forty yen."

It was always the same.

Each time we met I'd hear a bit more of his story. Just as I'd suspected, he was a drinker, and apparently whenever he took out forty yen he'd convert it to liquor the same day. It's still easy to get black market liquor up here.

His only son had gone off to the war, and so far he hadn't returned. His elder daughter lived in Kanagi, having married a local cooper. Before the big air raids he and his younger daughter had been living alone in Aomori, but when the house was destroyed she suffered critical burns. He got her to a doctor, but she died a short time later, whispering, "Mr. Elephant is coming, Mr. Elephant is coming," in her delirium.

"She must've been dreaming about elephants, eh, Mister? What a funny thing to dream about, eh? Hee! Hee!"

I thought he was laughing. Hell, he was crying.

I wondered if what he'd taken to mean "Mr. Elephant" (zō-san) wasn't actually "increased production" (zōsan). The daughter, Takeuchi Toki, had been a government worker for years. Perhaps the phrase "Increased production is coming" had some special meaning in the government offices and was one she'd used often in her work. But, at any rate, the illiterate father's interpretation—that she'd been dreaming of elephants—was a thousand times more pathetic.

I got pretty emotional and blurted out something a bit unconnected. "I tell you, those shit-eating bastards, with their primping and posing and pompous speeches, have gone and destroyed the whole country. If they'd all been timid, bashful little fellows, we wouldn't be in this mess today."

I realized it was an asinine sort of diatribe, but as I was spewing it out, tears came to my eyes.

"Takeuchi Toki-san," said the clerk.

"Yup."

The old man stood up, and I had an almost overwhelming urge to slap him on the back and tell him to go ahead and piss it all away on booze.

Oddly enough, however, only a few days later I was telling myself the same thing: What the hell, piss it all away on booze.

My savings passbook wasn't in my daughter's name, of course, but I wouldn't be surprised if the numbers inside were a good deal less substantial than those in Takeuchi Toki's. To give a precise figure as to how much cash it amounted to would be too dreary, so I won't, but the fact is that I had put that money in a postal savings account to avoid being reduced to completely wretched circumstances if, for some reason, I should suddenly be forced to leave my brother's house. Recently, however, I'd met up with a certain gentleman who said he could let me have ten bottles of whiskey. There was only one problem—it was going to cost me my entire savings. It didn't take me long to decide. What the hell, I thought, I'll piss it all away on booze. I'll get by somehow, whatever happens afterwards. If it turns out I can't get by—well, even if it comes to that, I'll probably get by somehow.

I'm going to be thirty-eight next year, but in many ways, as you can see, I'm still a completely hopeless case. On the other hand, however, if I manage to get through an entire lifetime pulling stunts like this, won't that, in itself, be a rather spectacular achievement? Such, at least, was the nonsense I was turning over in my mind as I set out for the post office.

"Mister."

The old man was there. I went to the counter to get a withdrawal slip.

"I don't need a take-out form today. I'm making a deposit," he said, showing me a fairly thick bundle of bills. "My daughter's insurance money came through. I'm going to put it in her account."

"That's great. But today *I'm* here to take money out."

It was awfully strange. We conducted our transactions, and the money I received at the withdrawal window was none other than the same stack of bills the old man had just deposited. I felt I'd done him a terrible disservice, somehow.

And when I handed that money over to a certain gentleman, I suffered the odd illusion that I was buying whiskey with Takeuchi Toki's insurance money.

A few days later, when the goods had been delivered and safely stored in our closet, I turned to my wife.

"This whiskey contains the life-spirit of a twenty-six-year-old virgin. I'll bet drinking it will give my novel a really erotic sort of luster," I told her, and began explaining all about my meeting with the sad, illiterate old man.

Before I'd gotten halfway through the story, however, she stopped me.

"Lies, lies, it's all lies. You're just making up one of those stories you tell whenever you're ashamed of yourself." Our two-year-old son came crawling up to her. "Isn't he, baby," she said, lifting him to her knee.

Merry Christmas

メリイクリスマス

Merii kurisumasu

Dazai returned to Tokyo with his wife and children in
November 1946, taking up residence once again in the house
in Mitaka. "Merry Christmas" was the first story he wrote on
his return. The real-life models for "Jinba-san" and
"Shizueko" were a woman named Hayashi Tomiko and her
daughter, Seiko. Tomiko was the ex-wife of a painter named
Hayashi Shizue. She was ill at the time Dazai wrote this story
and died about two years later, some six months after Dazai's
own death.

That the central incident in "Merry Christmas" is pure
fiction (although the setting and characters are quite real) is
perhaps signaled by Dazai's naming the "I" character
"Kasai"—a persona he had used in two or three other stories
earlier in his career.

Tokyo presented a picture of effervescent gloom. Though I imagined as I traveled back to the city that something like
this might serve as the first line of my next story, I found
on my return that, as far as I could see, "life in Tokyo" was the
same as ever. I'd spent the previous year and three months at my
childhood home in Tsugaru, returning with the wife and children

April 1947, at the broiled eel stand Wakamatsuya, near Mitaka Station. The man with Dazai is, presumably, the stallkeeper.

in mid-November of this year, but when I got back it was as if we'd merely been away on a little trip of, say, two or three weeks.

"Tokyo after a prolonged absence seems neither better nor worse; the character of the city hasn't changed at all," I wrote to someone back home. "There are physical differences, of course, but on the metaphysical level the place is as always. It reminds one of the old saying: Only death can cure a fool. A little change wouldn't hurt; in fact, one even feels justified in expecting it."

Not that I'd changed much myself. I spent a lot of time aimlessly walking the streets in a plain kimono and inverness.

In early December I entered a movie theater in the suburbs (perhaps the term "moving picture house" would be more appropriate—it was an appealingly run-down little shack) and watched an American film. When I came out it was already six o'clock and the streets were covered with a smoky white evening mist, through which darkly clad people hurried about, already thoroughly caught up in the year-end bustle. No, life in Tokyo hadn't changed at all.

I went into a bookstore and bought a volume by a famous Jewish playwright. Stuffing the book in my pocket, I turned toward the entrance, and there, standing on her tiptoes and looking like a bird about to take flight, was a young woman who was staring at me.

Blessing or curse?

To meet up with a woman you once pursued but no longer feel any affection for is the worst of misfortunes. And, in my case, most of the ladies I know fit that bill. Most? *All*, is more like it.

The one from Shinjuku? God, not that one ... It could be, though.

"Kasai-san?"

The girl said my name in a voice no louder than a murmur, lowered her heels, and gave a short bow. She was wearing a green hat, with the ribbon tied below her chin, and a bright red raincoat. As I studied her she seemed to grow younger, until her face matched the image of a certain twelve or thirteen-year-old girl in my memory.

"Shizueko."

A blessing.

"Let's get out of here. Or did you want to buy a magazine or something?"

"No. I came to look for a book called *Ariel*, but that's all right."

We stepped out onto the crowded street.

"You've grown up. I didn't recognize you."

That's Tokyo for you. This sort of thing happens.

I bought two ten-yen bags of peanuts from a street stall, put away my wallet, thought for a moment, then pulled out the wallet again and bought another bag. In the old days I'd always brought this girl a gift whenever I went to visit her mother.

Her mother was the same age as I. And she was one of the very few women from my past—no, make that the *only* one—whom, even now, I could have bumped into unexpectedly without becoming panic-stricken or nonplussed. Why? Well, she was of what they call "aristocratic birth," she was lovely, and she was frail of health ... but, no, such a set of criteria is merely vain and captious and hardly qualifies her as "the only one." She had divorced her tremendously wealthy husband, had suffered a downturn of fortunes, and lived in an apartment with her daughter, surviving on her modest assets. But, no. I haven't even a smidgen of interest in women's life histories, and in fact I have no idea why she parted with her wealthy husband or what exactly is meant by "modest assets." And if I were told, I'm sure I would promptly forget. Perhaps it's because I've been so consistently made a fool of by women, but I assume even the most pathetic female life story to be a pack of arbitrary lies and am no longer capable of shedding a single tear in response. In other words, such criteria as being well born, being beautiful, having fallen on hard times—such romantic conditions as these have nothing to do with the reason I single her out as "the only one."

The real reasons, four in number, are as follows. One: She was a stickler for cleanliness. Whenever she returned home after being out, she never failed to wash her hands and feet at the front door. I mentioned that she'd suffered a downturn of fortunes, but her tidy two-room apartment was always spic and span from one end to the other, and the kitchen and all the cooking and eating utensils, in particular, were spotless. Two: She wasn't the least bit infatuated with me. There was no need to get into the chasm-like rut of the dreary war of the sexes that accompanies lust, none of the agitated, lecherous confusion of "Is she attracted to me? Or is it just my vanity speaking? Shall I feel her out? Or is it all in my mind?" As far as I could tell, this woman was still in love with the husband she'd divorced, and deep in her heart she clung firmly to a sense of pride at having once been his wife. Three: She was sensitive to my moods and feelings. When everything in this world is getting me down, to the point that I feel I can't bear it any longer, it's no fun being told things like, "Well, you certainly seem to be prospering these days." Whenever I went to this woman's apartment, we were always able to converse about topics that perfectly matched my immediate circumstances and state of mind. "It's always been like that, in every age, hasn't it?" I remember her saying once. "If you tell the truth, they kill you. Saint John, Jesus Christ himself . . . and for John, of course, there was no resurrection. . . ." And she never once uttered a word about a single living Japanese writer. Four, and this is perhaps the most important of all the reasons: There was always an abundance of liquor at her apartment. I don't think of myself as especially stingy, but at those depressing times when I find myself with outstanding bills at all the bars I know, my feet just naturally lead me to places where I can drink all I like for free. Even as the war dragged on, and liquor became harder and harder to come by in Japan, there was always something to drink at that person's apartment. I would show up bearing some cheap gift for the daughter, then drink myself into a stupor before leaving.

These four reasons, then, are my answer to the question of why that person was "the only one." If someone were to reply to the effect that what I have just described is in fact one form of love, I would be able to do nothing but gaze back blankly and say, "Well, maybe so." If all male–female friendships are a form of love, then perhaps this, too, was love, but I never underwent any sort of anguish in regard to this person, and neither of us was fond of histrionics or complications.

"How's your mother? Same as ever?"

"Oh, yes."

"Not sick or anything?"

"No."

"You're still living with her, aren't you?"

"Yes."

"Is your place near here?"

"But it's a mess."

"No matter. Let's go get your mother, drag her out to a restaurant, and do some serious drinking."

"All right."

As we spoke, the girl seemed to grow less and less chipper. At the same time, though, with every step she took, she looked more and more grown-up to me. She was born when her mother was eighteen, and her mother, like me, was thirty-eight, which would make this girl . . .

My ego ballooned. It is possible, certainly, to be jealous of one's own mother. I changed the subject.

"*Ariel*?"

"It's really the strangest thing!" Just as I'd planned, she now became quite animated. "Before, when I'd just entered girls' school, you came to our apartment, it was summer, and you and mother were talking, and the word 'Ariel' kept coming up, and I didn't have any idea what it might mean, but for some reason I just couldn't forget that word, and . . ." Suddenly, as if she'd grown tired of her own chatter, her voice trailed off and she fell silent.

After we'd walked a bit further, she said, "It's the name of a book, isn't it," and fell silent again.

My head swelled even more. That clinches it, I thought. The mother wasn't in love with me, nor had I ever felt lust for her, but as for the daughter, well, I thought, you never know.

Her mother was a person who, reduced to poverty or not, could not live without delicious food, and even before the war against America and England began, she and her daughter had already evacuated to a place near Hiroshima where good food was plentiful. Shortly after the move I'd received a postcard from her, but I was having my share of difficulties at the time and didn't feel much of a need to write back immediately to someone who was taking it easy in the country. Before I ever did get around to writing, my own circumstances had begun to change radically, and now it had been five years since I'd had any contact with them.

Tonight, seeing me after five years, completely unexpectedly, which would be more pleased—the mother or the daughter? I, for some reason, suspected that the girl's pleasure would prove to be deeper and purer than that of her mother. If so, it was necessary for me to make my own affiliation clear. It would not be possible to affiliate myself equally with both. Tonight I would betray the mother and join forces with the girl. It wouldn't matter if, for example, the mother were to scowl with disapproval. It couldn't be helped. It was love.

"When did you come back to Tokyo?"

"October of last year."

"Right after the war ended, then. It figures. No way a selfish person like your mother could put up with living in the sticks any longer than she had to."

If there was a rough edge to my voice as I badmouthed the mother, it was only to ingratiate myself with the daughter. Women—no, *people*—have a strong sense of rivalry with one another. Even parents and children.

The girl didn't smile, however. It appeared that to bring up the subject of her mother at all, whether in praise or derision, was taboo. I could only conclude that hers was a particularly bad case of jealousy.

"What great luck, running into you like this." I changed the subject without missing a beat. "It was as if we'd agreed to meet at the bookstore at a certain time."

"I know," she said, falling easily this time for a little sugary sentiment. I was on to something now.

"Watching a movie to kill the time, then going to that bookstore five minutes before we were to meet . . ."

"A movie?"

"Yeah, I like to see a film once in a while. This one was about a tightrope walker in the circus. It's interesting to see a performer portray a performer. It brings out the best in even a lousy actor, because he's a performer himself. The sadness of entertainers just oozes out of him, whether he realizes it or not."

As a topic for conversation between lovers, you can't beat movies. They're perfect.

"I saw that movie, too."

"Just at the moment the two of them meet, a wave comes rushing between them, and they're separated once more. That part was good. Things like that can happen in life, you know— some little mishap, and you never see each other again."

Unless you can say treacly things like this without hesitation, you'll never make it as a young woman's lover.

"If I had left that bookstore a minute earlier, we might never have met again, or at least not for another ten years or so." I was trying to make our chance meeting seem as romantic as possible.

The street became narrow and dark, and there were muddy spots as well, so we could no longer walk side by side. The girl walked in front and I followed with my hands stuffed in the pockets of my inverness.

"How much farther?" I asked. "Half a *chō*? One *chō*?"

"Well, I never really know how far a *chō* is supposed to be."

I, too, actually, am pretty hopeless when it comes to judging distances. But to show one's stupidity is taboo in love.

"Are we within a hundred meters?" I said with a cool, scientific air.

"Well . . ."

"Meters are easier to grasp, right? A hundred meters is half a *chō*," I told her, but felt a bit uneasy about it. I did some calculating in my head and realized that a hundred meters was about one *chō*. But I didn't correct myself. Clownishness is taboo in love.

"Anyway, it's right over there."

It was a terribly shabby, barrack-like apartment. We entered and walked down a dim hallway to the fifth or sixth door, where I saw the aristocratic family name: Jinba.

"Jinba-san!" I called through the closed door. I was sure I heard a reply. Then a shadow moved across the glass.

"Ha! She's home!"

The girl stood bolt upright, all the color went out of her face, and she twisted her lips in a grotesque way. Then, suddenly, she burst into tears.

Her mother had been killed during the air raids on Hiroshima, she told me. She also said that, in the delirium of her death throes, her mother had called out my name.

The girl had returned to Tokyo alone and was now working in the legal office of a Progressive Party Dietman, a relative on her mother's side.

She was going to tell me all this, but hadn't been able to get the words out, so she'd gone ahead and led me to the apartment, not knowing what else to do.

Now I realized why it was that she'd looked so downcast whenever I mentioned her mother. It wasn't jealousy, and it wasn't love.

We didn't go in the room, but headed back out to the busy area near the station.

Her mother had always loved broiled eel.

We ducked under the curtain of an eel stall.

"Yes, sir! What'll it be?"

We stood at the counter. There was one other customer, a gentleman sitting on the far side of the stall, drinking.

"Large servings? Or small ones?"

"Small ones. Three of them."

"Yes, sir!" the young stallkeeper said in a hearty growl. He seemed a genuine "old Tokyo" type.

As he vigorously fanned the coals in his clay stove, I said, "Put them on three separate plates."

"Yes, sir! And the third person? Coming afterwards?"

"There are three of us here now," I said without smiling.

"H'm?"

"There's this person, and me, and standing between us there's a beautiful woman with a worried look on her face. Don't you see her?" I smiled a bit now.

I don't know what he made of this, but the young stallkeeper grinned, lifted a hand to his forehead, and said, "I can't top that!"

"Do you have any of this?" I said, raising an imaginary cup to my lips with my left hand.

"The very finest there is! Well, not that good, I guess."

"Three cups," I said.

Three plates of eel were set out before us. We left the one in the middle alone, and began eating from the other two. Soon three brimming cups of saké arrived.

I drank mine down in a gulp.

"Let me help," I said in a voice loud enough for only Shizueko to hear. I lifted her mother's cup and gulped it down, then took from my pocket the three bags of peanuts I'd bought earlier. "I'm going to drink a bit tonight. Stick with me. You can eat these while I'm drinking," I said, still keeping my voice down.

Shizueko nodded, and neither of us spoke for some time.

As I silently drained four or five cups in a row, the gentleman on the other side began boisterously joking with the stallkeeper. His jokes were truly inane, amazingly inept, and absolutely devoid of wit, but they struck the gentleman himself as hilarious. The stallkeeper laughed courteously, but the gentleman was in stitches.

"... That's what he said, and of course that bowled me over, then he started singing, 'Apples are so pretty, I know just how you feel...' Ha, ha, ha, ha! He's sharp, that fellow, I'll tell you, he said, 'Tokyo Station is my home.' That killed me, so I said, 'My mistress lives in the Maru Building,' and now it was his turn to be bowled over...."

He just kept rattling off his utterly unfunny jokes, and I found myself feeling more disgusted than ever with the hopeless lack of any concept of what constitutes a sense of humor that you witness wherever Japanese are drinking. However raucously the gentleman and the stallkeeper laughed, I didn't so much as crack a smile, but merely continued drinking and absently eying the year-end crowds that bustled past the stall.

The gentleman turned to see what I was looking at. After watching the flow of people for a while, he suddenly shouted "Ha-ro-o! Me-ri-i ku-ri-su-ma-su!" at an American soldier who was walking down the street.

For some reason I burst out laughing this time.

The soldier scowled and shook his head as if to show how silly he thought the gentleman's jest, then strode off and disappeared.

"Shall we eat this, too?" I said, applying my chopsticks to the plate in the middle.

"Yes."

"Half for you and half for me."

Tokyo is still the same. It hasn't changed a bit.

December 25, 1947, with homeless children in Ueno Park.

Handsome Devils and Cigarettes

美男子と煙草

Bidanshi to tabako

———◆———

*The Setting Sun, published in the fall of 1947, had become a
bestseller, and Dazai was now something of a celebrity.
Particularly popular among young people, he was hailed by
many as the voice of the postwar generation. Fans thronged to
his house, crowds sometimes gathered around him on the
street, and magazines sent reporters to interview him. Dazai
handled his fame with perhaps even less grace than he had his
Akutagawa Prize-era obscurity. His personal life was a
shambles—though he now had three small children at home
and a baby daughter by Ōta Shizuko, he spent most of his
time with his mistress/nurse/secretary, Yamazaki Tomie. He
was in ill health, drinking heavily, and writing at a fairly
furious pace. In spite of his popular acceptance, he was acutely
sensitive to criticism, especially coming from such "venerable"
writers as Shiga Naoya (often referred to in Japan as "the god
of the short story"). Shiga had made a number of snide
remarks about Dazai's work, and in March, 1948—the same
month "Handsome Devils and Cigarettes" was published—
Dazai launched his counterattack in the first of a series of
essays entitled "Thus Have I Heard." These essays were so
vicious (some would say hysterical) that even Ibuse Masuji
began to distance himself from Dazai.*

———◆———

Though I continue to wage my solitary battle, I can now no longer deny that I seem destined to lose, and loneliness and sorrow overwhelm me. But, having come this far, I can hardly turn to those for whom I have until now shown nothing but contempt and beg to be admitted into the flock, telling them I've finally seen the error of my ways. No, I have no choice but to continue drinking my cheap liquor and fighting my losing battle.

My battle. In a word, it has been a battle against the antiquated. A battle against hackneyed style and affectation. Against the transparent pose of respectability. Against smallmindedness, and smallminded people.

I can swear this to Jehovah Himself: for the sake of this battle I have lost everything I ever had. And now, alone, dependent upon alcohol, I appear to be on the brink of defeat.

The antiquated are a spiteful lot. Watching them shamelessly roll out their unspeakably banal little theories of literature, or art, by means of which they trample any fresh new buds that are struggling to survive, and displaying no signs of even being aware of their crime, one can only stand in awe. Push or pull all you like: they will not budge. They know only that life is dear, money is dear, and the greater their worldly success, the happier their wives and children will be, so they create cliques and praise one another to cement their solidarity, the better to persecute those who stand alone.

It looks as if I'm going to lose.

The other day I was in a certain shop drinking cheap liquor when three elderly men of letters came in and, though I'd never met any of them before, proceeded to surround me and to disparage my writing in a disgustingly drunken and thoroughly misinformed manner. I am one who, however much he may drink, hates to lose control of himself, so I merely smiled and let their abuse go in one ear and out the other, but once I'd returned home, as I sat eating a late supper, the vexation became too much for me and I suddenly began to sob. Unable to stop the flow of tears, I lay down my bowl and chopsticks and brokenly unburdened my feelings to my wife.

"Here I am . . . here I am, writing desperately . . . writing for all I'm worth, putting my very life on the line for my writing, and everybody treats me like a laughingstock . . . Those men are my seniors, they're a good twenty years older than I am, but what do they do? They gang up on me . . . Cowardly bastards. It's not fair . . . All right, then, if that's the way they want it, I'm not holding back any more, either. I'm going to come right out in the open and say what I think of *them*. I'm going to fight . . . They've gone too far this time . . ."

I continued rambling on incoherently like this, crying even harder now, until my wife all but rolled her eyes and said, "Goodnight, dear. H'm?"

She led me to my futon, but even after I lay down I couldn't stop sobbing in frustration.

Ah, life is an awful proposition. It's especially hard, and sad, for a man. A man has no choice but to fight. And *he must win*.

It was only a few days later that a young reporter from a certain magazine sat facing me and said the strangest thing.

"Would you like to go to Ueno to see the bums?"

"Bums?"

"We'd like to photograph you with them."

"With the bums?"

"Yes," he said calmly.

Why would they choose me in particular? Perhaps it's a matter of free association: "Dazai." "Bum." "Bums." "Dazai."

"All right," I said.

I seem to have a habit, when I feel like weeping, of confronting the object of my grief. I immediately got to my feet, changed into a suit, and, urging the young reporter to hurry it up, left the house with him trailing behind me.

It was a cold winter morning. Holding a handkerchief to my runny nose, I walked along in rueful silence.

We took the National Railways from Mitaka to Tokyo Station, then switched to a municipal streetcar. The reporter guided me first to his office, where he sat me down in the reception room and produced a bottle of whiskey.

I realized that this was probably the well-intentioned strategy of the editorial staff, who'd undoubtedly decided that Dazai, being the timid fellow he is, would not be able to engage in a decent dialogue with the bums unless he was well liquored up. If I may be frank, however, the whiskey I was served was as singular a substance as I've ever come across. I'm a man who has drunk more than his share of dubious alcoholic concoctions, and by no means am I pretending to have refined tastes, but this was the first time I'd ever come across whiskey that was actually *cloudy*. The bottle itself was genuine enough and bore a fancy label, but the contents were a muddy swirl. Perhaps you could say it was to whiskey what unrefined home brew is to saké.

But I drank it. Guzzled it down, in fact. I kept inviting the reporters who'd gathered in the reception room to join me, but they merely smiled. I had previously heard rumors to the effect that most of the reporters at this magazine were notorious drinkers. But they didn't touch this stuff. Apparently even the average lush drew the line at home-brewed whiskey.

I got drunk all by myself.

"What the hell?" I said, smiling. "Don't you people have any manners? Serving a visitor stuff you won't even drink yourselves."

The reporters, noting my condition and not wanting to miss their chance, thinking, no doubt, that they had to get Dazai together with the bums before his liquid courage wore off, bundled me into a car and whisked me off to Ueno, where they led me to an underpass, a tunnel of sorts, that's well known as a nest for the homeless.

For all the reporters' careful preparation, however, their scheme proved less than a great success. I walked down into the underpass and straight through it without looking at anything until I'd reached the exit, where I spied a group of four children standing in front of a grilled chicken stall, puffing away on cigarettes. Disturbed by this sight, I marched up to them and said, "Stop smoking those things. Tobacco only leaves you feeling even hungrier. Put them out. If you want some of that chicken, it's on me."

The boys obediently threw away the butts. They were all about ten years old, just children.

I turned to the woman tending the stall and said, "One skewer apiece for these kids." I felt strangely wretched.

Was this what you'd call a kind deed? The thought was unbearable. Then I remembered a saying of Valéry's that made it even more so. I would be fair game for the utmost contempt of a man like Valéry if what I had just done were to be judged as kindness by the Philistines of the world. This is what he said:

"When doing a good deed, one must always apologize. Nothing hurts others as much as kindness."

Feeling as if I were catching a cold, I hunched my shoulders and strode out of the underpass.

The reporters—there were four or five of them—chased after me.

"Well?" said one. "It's a regular hell, isn't it?"

"At any rate, it's a completely different world, wouldn't you say?" said another.

"Were you shocked?" asked a third. "What did you think of it?"

I laughed. " 'A regular hell'? Don't be absurd. I wasn't the least bit shocked."

I strode on toward Ueno Park, gradually growing more loquacious as I walked.

"The truth is, I didn't see anything. All I could think about was my own suffering, and I hurried through that underpass with my eyes straight ahead. But I did figure out why you chose to show that place to me in particular. It's obviously because I'm such a handsome devil."

They all laughed uproariously.

"No, I'm not joking. Didn't you notice? Walking through that place, the one thing that struck me was that almost all the bums lying there in the darkness were men with handsome, classical features. Which means that good-looking men run a high risk of ending up living in an underpass. You, for example, with that fair face of yours—you'd better watch your step, pal. I know *I'm* going to be careful."

They burst into laughter again.

A man falls deeper and deeper in love with himself, not listening to what anyone tells him, and the next thing he knows he's lying in an underpass, no longer even human. Though I'd only passed abstractedly through the place, this chilling scenario honestly did occur to me.

"Did you discover anything else," I was asked, "aside from the handsome devil theory?"

"Tobacco. Those fellows down there didn't seem to be drunk, but most of them were smoking. Cigarettes aren't cheap, either. If they've got money to buy cigarettes, they could just as well buy a straw mat or a pair of clogs, couldn't they? They're shoeless, lying on bare concrete, and they're smoking cigarettes. I guess people— at least, people nowadays—can reach rock bottom, end up bare-assed naked, and still need to smoke. It's a warning for us all. I can't say I wouldn't be the same way myself. There, you see? My journey underground has produced some practical results after all."

We reached the plaza that fronts Ueno Park. The four boys from the underpass were there, frolicking merrily in the noontime sun. Without really thinking about it, I walked unsteadily toward them.

"Hold it. Just as you are." One of the reporters pointed a camera in our direction and clicked the shutter. "Now smile!" he shouted again, peering into the viewfinder.

One of the boys looked at my face. "If you stare at someone like this, you can't help but giggle," he said, and I, too, found myself smiling.

Angels dance in the sky, God wills their wings to vanish, and they fall gently, like parachutes, to every corner of the earth. I landed in the snow up north, you in a citrus grove down south, and these boys in Ueno Park. That's the only difference between us. Grow up straight and true, boys, and remember: Don't let your looks concern you, don't smoke cigarettes, don't drink except on special occasions, and find yourself a shy, moderately stylish girl, and fall in love for a long, long time.

Postscript:

Later, one of the reporters brought me two of the photos that were taken that day. One is of the homeless little boy and I smiling at each other, and the other shows me in a truly bizarre pose: squatting down in front of the boys, holding one of them by the foot. Allow me to explain, lest the magazine publish this picture and lead anyone to some mistaken conclusion. ("Dazai's such a poseur. Look at him, imitating Jesus washing the feet of his disciples. Yech!") The truth is, I was simply curious to see what happens to the feet of children who run around without any shoes.

Let me add one more little anecdote. When I received the photos, I called my wife over to take a look.

"These are pictures of the bums in Ueno."

She studied one of the photos and said, "Bums? Is that what a bum looks like?"

I got a shock when I happened to notice which face she was peering at.

"What's the matter with you? That's *me*. It's your husband, for God's sake. The bums are over here."

My wife, whose character is, if anything, excessively serious, is quite incapable of making a joke. She honestly mistook me for a bum.

Dazai at the Tamagawa Canal in early 1948, a few months before he drowned in these very waters. Photo by Tamura Shigeru.

Cherries

桜桃
Ōtō

I lift up my eyes to the hills.
                  —Psalms 121

I like to think that the parent is more important than the child. "For the sake of the children ..." I piously try to remind myself of such time-honored moralistic tenets, but end up thinking, wait a minute—the parents are the weak ones. At least in my household they are. Though God knows it's not for some shameless ulterior motive such as hoping to be aided or cared for by my kids when I'm old and gray, this is one parent who spends every moment of his time at home trying to humor the children. I say "children," but in my home they're scarcely more than infants. The eldest, a girl, is seven, the boy four, and the younger daughter is only one. Notwithstanding which, each of them has the parents securely under his or her thumb. The mother and father seem in effect nothing more than slaves to their own offspring.

Summertime, with the entire family in a single three-mat room for a raucous, disorderly evening meal, the father repeatedly towels his sweaty brow and grumbles to himself.

"There's an old *senryū* poem—'His vulgarity shows/In the way he eats / Sweating like a pig.' Well, I'll tell you, with the kids making a racket like this, even a refined papa like myself is bound to perspire."

The mother, simultaneously nursing the one-year-old, serving the other two children and the father, wiping or picking up what spills or falls, and helping the little ones blow their noses, is as busy as an eight-armed Hindu she-god.

"You seem to perspire most on the bridge of your nose."

The father smiles grimly.

"You don't say. And where do you sweat most? The crotch?"

"Ah. Such a refined papa."

"Wait a minute, we're talking about a medical phenomenon here. It's not a question of refined or vulgar."

"Well, in my case," she says, her expression turning a bit grave, "it's here, between my breasts . . . The valley of tears . . ."

The valley of tears.

The father falls silent and continues eating.

When I'm at home, I'm forever making jokes. Let's say it's a case of needing to wear Dante's "mask of merriment" precisely because there are so many things that trigger the "anguish in the heart." Actually, though, it's not only when I'm home. Whenever I'm with people, no matter how great my mental or physical suffering, I try desperately to create a happy atmosphere. It's only after parting with the company that I stagger away exhausted to think about money and morality and suicide. No, actually it's not only when I'm with people. It's the same when I'm writing. When I'm feeling down, I make an effort to write light, enjoyable stories. My only intention in doing so is to render the greatest possible service to my readers, but there are those who don't understand this. "That Dazai fellow's awfully frivolous these days," they sneer. "He tries to garner readers simply by being amusing; he doesn't put any effort into his writing at all."

Is there something evil about serving people? Is putting on airs, never cracking a smile, such a virtuous thing?

What I'm trying to say is this. Pomposity, pretentiousness, and the art of making others ill at ease: these are things I cannot bear.

In my home, though I'm forever making jokes, I do so in the frame of mind of a man treading thin ice. And, contrary to what some of my readers and critics imagine, the tatami mats in my house are new, the desk is in order, the husband and wife treat each other with kindness and respect and have never engaged in a single reckless argument of the "Get out!" "I'm leaving!" variety, much less physical violence, neither dotes on the children less than the other, and the children, for their part, are cheerful and thoroughly attached to their parents.

But that's merely the surface of things. The mother bares her breast and reveals a valley of tears; the father's night sweats grow steadily worse. Each is well aware of the other's anguish but takes pains not to touch upon it. The father makes a joke and the mother laughs.

When the mother comes out with that crack about the valley of tears, however, the father lapses into silence, unable to think of a clever comeback, as a disagreeable feeling wells up inside him until even he, master clown though he be, grows grim and somber.

"Hire someone to help out," he says finally, timidly, muttering as if to himself so as not to give further offense. "There's no other way."

Three children. The husband is absolutely worthless when it comes to helping out around the house. He won't even fold up his own futon. All he does is make idiotic jokes. Rationing, registration—he knows nothing about things of that sort. It's as if he were merely a lodger in the house. He has visitors. He entertains. He leaves for his "workroom," carrying his lunch, and sometimes he doesn't return for as long as a week. He's forever going on about the work he must get done, yet he seems to produce no more than two or three pages a day. Then there's liquor. He comes home from a binge looking emaciated, crawls into bed, and stays there. And on top of all this, he appears to have young lady friends in various quarters.

The children . . . The oldest, a girl of seven years, and her little

ORTRAITS

sister, who was born this spring, have a tendency to catch cold
rather easily, but are otherwise healthy and normal. The four-year-
old boy, however, is scrawny and still incapable of standing up. He
can't speak or understand a word; his vocabulary consists of sounds
like "Aaa" and "Daa." He crawls around on the floor, impervious
to attempts at toilet training. His hair is sparse, and though he eats
a lot, he never seems to grow or gain any weight.

The mother and father avoid discussing this son of theirs in any
depth. Congenital idiot, deaf mute . . . To give voice to words like
these and nod knowingly at one another would be too pathetic.
From time to time the mother hugs this boy tightly to her breast.
Often the father, in a paroxysm of despair, thinks of clasping the
child in his arms and leaping into the river.

FATHER SLAYS DEAF-MUTE SON

Shortly after noon yesterday, Mr. A (53), a shopkeeper in the X block of
Y Ward, murdered his second son, B (18), in the living room of their
home, by a blow to the head with an axe. Mr. A then stabbed himself in
the throat with a pair of scissors. He survived, but remains in critical condition at a nearby hospital. Mr. A's second daughter, C (23), had recently
married, and her husband, adopted into the bride's family, was prepar-
ing to take over the reins of the family business. The second son, in addition to being a deaf mute, was somewhat retarded, and Mr. A's crime appears to have been motivated by a desire to ease the burden for the
young married couple.

Newspaper articles like this are enough to drive the father to
drown his sorrows in drink.

Ah, if only it would turn out to be merely a matter of slow
development! If only this child were to suddenly shoot up in a
spurt of growth such that he comes to denounce his parents' concern with anger and contempt! The mother and father mention
this secret prayer of theirs to no one, not even relatives or friends,
but assume an air of nonchalance, playfully teasing the boy as if
they weren't worried about him in the least.

Life is a tremendous struggle for the mother, surely, but the father, too, is giving it all he's got. He is not by nature a very prolific writer. He's timorous to a degree. And now he's been dragged out to quaveringly wield his pen in the public eye. It's hard for him to write, and he turns to liquor to drown his sorrows. To drown your sorrows is to drink out of the fretfulness and frustration of not being able to say what you're thinking. Those who can always assert and express themselves clearly don't need to drown their sorrows. (Which is why there are so few female drunks.)

I've never once won an argument. I lose without fail. I'm inevitably overwhelmed by the strength of my opponent's conviction and the awfulness of his or her self-affirmation. I sink into silence. Afterwards, however, thinking it over, I begin to perceive the arbitrariness of the other person's position and become convinced that I was not entirely in the wrong. But, having already lost the argument once, the prospect of stubbornly reopening hostilities is a dreary one, and since arguing with someone leaves me with a feeling of rancor that's every bit as unpleasant and enduring as it would be had we actually come to blows, I merely smile and fall silent even as I tremble with anger, brooding over this and that, and finally end up drowning my sorrows.

Let's come right out and say it. I've been tediously beating around the bush so far, but the truth is that this is the tale of a marital spat.

"The valley of tears."

That was the spark that lit the fuse. As I said before, this married couple have never even shouted vulgarities at one another, let alone lifted a hand in anger. They are an extremely mild pair. It is precisely because of this, however, that they are, in a sense, teetering on the brink of danger. Each silently gathers evidence of the other's wickedness, peeking at one card, then laying it down, peeking at another, then laying it down, and there is always the danger that at some point one or the other will suddenly spread the entire hand out on the table and say, "Gotcha." One might even say that this danger itself is what inspires the deference with which both husband and wife treat each other. The husband, at least, is a man whom the longer you beat, the more the dust would fly.

"The valley of tears."

Hearing those words, the husband took offense. But he is not fond of arguments. He fell silent, thinking: You may have said that to spite me, but you're not the only one who's crying. I worry as much about the children as you do. My home and family are important to me. When one of the children comes out with a peculiar-sounding cough in the middle of the night, I always awake and begin to fret. I'd love nothing better than to please you and the children by moving into a somewhat nicer house, but it's just not within my reach. I'm doing my utmost as it is. I'm not some cold, brutal demon. I don't have the *nerve* to calmly ignore my wife and children and leave them to their fate. It's not that I don't know what rationing and registration are, it's that I don't have *time* to know about such things. . . . So the father grumbled in his heart. But he lacked the confidence it would take to say the words out loud, and, sensing that any retort by the wife would leave him nonplussed and defenseless, he settled for mumbling, as if to himself, "Hire someone to help out."

The mother, too, is an extremely taciturn person. When she does speak, however, it's with a chilling self-confidence. (Not that she alone is that way. Most women are.)

"But I can't find anyone who'd be willing to come."

"You'll find someone if you look hard enough. It's not that they won't come, anyway, is it? It's that they won't *stay*."

"Are you saying I don't know how to manage people?"

"Oh, come on." The father fell silent again. Actually, that was exactly what he thought. But he held his tongue.

Ah, if only she would hire someone. When the mother straps the youngest child on her back and runs out to do errands, the father has to watch over the other two. And each day he has a good ten visitors.

"I want to go to my workroom."

"Now?"

"Yes. There's something I've simply got to finish writing tonight."

This was true. But it's also true that I wanted to flee the gloom pervading the house.

"I was hoping to go to my sister's tonight."

I already knew this. Her sister was seriously ill. But if she went to see her, I'd have to take care of the children.

"That's why I'm telling you to hire . . ."

I stopped in mid-sentence. To touch upon the subject of my wife's family always complicated things terribly.

Life is an awful ordeal. So many chains to bind you. Try to move an inch and the blood comes spurting out.

I stood up silently, went into the six-mat room, and took from the desk drawer an envelope containing payment for a manuscript. I stuffed it in my sleeve, wrapped a dictionary and writing paper in a black kerchief, and breezed outside as if nothing were wrong.

By this point, work was out of the question. I could think of nothing but suicide. I made straight for a drinking spot.

"Well! Hello, stranger."

"Set 'em up. Awfully pretty kimono you're wearing tonight."

"Not bad, is it? I knew you'd like these stripes."

"Had a fight with the wife. I can't stand it, all the pent-up emotion. Set 'em up. I'm here for the night. No two ways about it."

I like to think that the parent is more important than the child. After all, the parents are weaker.

A plate of cherries is served.

At my house, we don't give the children expensive delicacies like this. It's possible they've never even seen cherries. I bet they'd love to eat some. I bet they'd love it if their father came home with cherries for them. If I tied the stems together and hung the cherries around my neck, I bet it would look just like a coral necklace.

The father, however, merely picks away at the pile of cherries on the oversized plate as if they were bitter medicine, eating one and spitting out the pit, eating another and spitting out the pit, eating another while in his heart he blusters and grumbles: The parent is more important than the child.

DISCOVER JAPAN, VOLS. 1 AND 2
Words, Customs, and Concepts

The Japan Culture Institute

Essays and photographs illuminate 200 ideas and customs of Japan.

THE UNFETTERED MIND
Writings of the Zen Master to the Sword Master

Takuan Sōhō / Translated by William Scott Wilson

Philosophy as useful to today's corporate warriors as it was to seventeenth century samurai.

THE JAPANESE THROUGH AMERICAN EYES
Sheila K. Johnson

"Cogent...as skeptical of James Clavell's *Shogun* as it is of William Ouchi's *Theory Z.*"—*Publisher's Weekly*

Available only in Japan.

BEYOND NATIONAL BORDERS
Reflections on Japan and the World

Kenichi Ohmae

"[Ohmae is Japan's] only management guru."—*Financial Times*

Available only in Japan.

THE COMPACT CULTURE
The Japanese Tradition of "Smaller is Better"

O-Young Lee / Translated by Robert N. Huey

A long history of skillfully reducing things and concepts to their essentials reveals the essence of the Japanese character and, in part, accounts for Japan's business success.

THE HIDDEN ORDER
Tokyo through the Twentieth Century

Yoshinobu Ashihara

"Mr. Ashihara shows how, without anybody planning it, Japanese architecture has come to express the vitality of Japanese life"
—*Daniel J. Boorstin*